THE OTHER RAILWAY CHILDREN

A PERSONAL REFLECTION ON THE RAILWAY CHILDREN CHARITY 1995 – 2010

By

DAVID MAIDMENT
Founder

All royalties and profits from this book will be donated to the Railway Children charity, whose website is www.railwaychildren.org.uk. I thank the trustees of 'Railway Children' for permission to publish my personal account of the founding and development of the charity and for their vision in further extending its work since my retirement as Chairman and Trustee in December 2010.

David Maidment
Founder Ambassador
Railway Children
September 2012

Previous titles:

The Child Madonna, Melrose Books, 2009
The Missing Madonna, PublishNation/Lulu, 2012

Published in the United Kingdom by PublishNation

Copyright © David Maidment 2012

The right of David Maidment to be identified as the author of this work had been asserted by him in accordance with the Copyright, Designs and Patents Act 1988.

Cover picture: Streetgirl at Vijayawada Junction, 1998

All rights reserved. No part of this publication may be reproduced or transmitted in any form or by any means, electronic or mechanical, including photocopy, recording or any information storage and retrieval system, without the prior written permission of the publisher, nor by way of trade or otherwise shall it be lent, re-sold, hired out or otherwise circulated without the publisher's prior consent in any form of binding or cover other than that in which it is published and without a similar condition including this condition being imposed on the subsequent purchaser.

ISBN 978-1-291-11437-9

CONTENTS

Preface & Acknowledgements		vi
Dedication		ix
Acronyms used throughout the book		x
Chapter 1	The girl at Churchgate station	1
Chapter 2	Amnesty International	7
Chapter 3	The Consortium for Street Children	11
Chapter 4	The launch	19
Chapter 5	Registered charity No. 1058991	25
Chapter 6	The charity develops	34
Chapter 7	The need to demonstrate UK action	45
Chapter 8	People	52
Chapter 9	The Comic Relief programme	63
Chapter 10	A world vision?	78
Chapter 11	Consolidation in India	90
Chapter 12	On home territory	114
Chapter 13	Fundraising	121
Chapter 14	Professionalism	130
Chapter 15	Networking and advocacy	139
Chapter 16	Increasing awareness and reputation	148
Chapter 17	Last visit to India?	155
Chapter 18	Personal reflections on the past and future	163
Chapter 19	Lessons learned: why has Railway Children been successful?	175
Appendices		186

Appendices

1	Railway Children from 2011
2	Projects funded between 1995 and 2010
2.1	Eastern Europe
2.2	Africa
2.3	Asia
2.4	Latin America
2.5	United Kingdom
3	Railway Children Trustees and Staff
3.1	Present Trustees (to December 2010)
3.2	Previous Trustees
3.3	Present UK Staff
3.4	Present UK Volunteers
3.5	Present India Staff
3.6	Present East Africa Staff
3.7	Previous UK Staff
3.8	Previous UK Volunteers
3.9	Previous India Staff
4	Career of Author/Founder of Railway Children
5	Donations to Railway Children

Preface and Acknowledgements

This book contains my reflections on the charity I founded over fifteen years ago. It therefore has all the bias and opinions of the author and is not an 'authorised' history of the charity, although I am indebted to the charity trustees and staff for allowing me access to papers to remind myself of essential events, names and dates when otherwise my fallible memory would have let me down. I wanted to put on paper my thoughts as I passed over the leadership of the charity to a successor and to leave behind some of the lessons we have learned as I know from my railway career how easy it is to lose the company's corporate memory. Many colleagues and acquaintances in the railway industry and voluntary sector have expressed their opinion that the Railway Children has achieved considerable success especially in recent years and have urged me to write down some of the main reasons for this success and the challenges we faced, for the learning of others. This will have been worthwhile, even if it just helps other organisations avoid errors and build on what we experienced so that their beneficiaries might receive the most effective support and empowerment.

What I describe in this book comes from my own experience and is seen through my eyes, and I owe an enormous debt of gratitude to my fellow trustees and to all the staff of Railway Children who between them have made the Railway Children what it is. The book describes many events, and the ways in which the lives of some of the most vulnerable children in the world have been given new opportunities and the many lives that have been changed for the better. But I did not do these things – they are the results of those dedicated people working day in, day out, at the interface with the children, amid the hardships, thrills and disappointments that are inevitable when you work with traumatised and damaged children, but children who nevertheless deserve, and have the capacity for, a more fulfilling life. The chance to make that difference owes everything to the dedication of staff in the United Kingdom, India and elsewhere who strive year after year to seek out policies and strategies that will benefit the children most, who identify and work with the most effective partner organisations, who toil to raise the money necessary to make it all possible and who sustain and increase that effort every year so that the work is always developing and improving, and not going backwards.

I have some personal thanks I must acknowledge though I am fearful of leaving someone deserving out and causing hurt by that omission. I plead that my memory is not as good as it once was (and I'm not sure that my memory ever was that good). I am pleased to have this opportunity to pay tribute to those colleagues in the early days of the Consortium for Street Children who encouraged me to develop my ideas and who supported me with advice and suggestions - people like Nic Fenton, Trudy Davies, Clare Hanbury and the Consortium's first Director, Anita Schrader, and later Directors like Sadia Mahmud-Marshall and Alex Dressler. I am very grateful for the support and advice I received from my railway colleagues when I first raised the possibility of starting the charity - especially David Rayner, a Board Member and my immediate boss; Geoff Myers, Director of BR's Strategic Planning organisation and a member of the Board of Save the Children at the time; and Sir Christopher Campbell, Railtrack Non-Executive Board Member and Vice Chairman, who took a close interest and helped me obtain the charity's trust grant which enabled the first project to begin.

I am particularly grateful to that small group of railwaymen who formed my first Committee, for shaping some of my ideas, and I pay a very special regard and thank you to Stan Judd, my lifelong friend and railway colleague, whom I dragooned into helping me from 'Day One' and who has assisted me ever since in all the backroom work which is so rarely seen or acknowledged, and even now has played an essential part in reviewing this text and finding for me those names and dates and other omissions and errors I would have made without his conscientious and meticulous attention. I acknowledge the help of a neighbour and friend, Dr Brian Dudley, who has undertaken voluntary work with the charity from time to time, and thank him for the enormous effort he has put into correcting and editing my sometimes clumsy text and persuading me to shorten many of my overlong sentences! I thank the early volunteers from the Methodist and Anglican churches in Nantwich who helped the charity get off the ground before any paid staff were recruited, and then a special word of thanks to

Julia Worthington and Katie Mason, our first two employees who did nearly everything in the Crewe office to establish the Railway Children as a viable charity that would grow and develop and not 'fizzle out'. I must also pay a particular tribute to Terina Keene, the charity's Chief Executive since 2002 whose dedication, vision and skill helped the charity grow into what it is today, to the very able staff she has recruited and supported over the years, and to Mrinalini Rao for fulfilling a similar function in our Mumbai (Bombay) office.

The charity also owes much to its team of trustees, past and present, who have contributed their experience and skills and have always been an active and involved Board, guiding the charity with wisdom and giving of their time and expertise. Again, it is impossible to mention one name without mentioning them all, but I would just say that many of those involved had onerous and responsible jobs and yet were able to make their time available within the hectic pressures and constraints of their professional careers.

On a very personal level, I thank Pat, my wife, for the support she has given me and the tolerance to accept the charity's demands on my own time. When I retired from railway management in 1996 I said that I would devote a third of my working time released to continuing some form of railway consultancy, one third to the charity and one third for our own leisure time. I stuck to the agreed consultancy time, but as for the rest - the charity and the associated work I undertook ...? A little more than the allotted third, I fear.

This then is my reflection on the first fifteen years of my involvement with the Railway Children charity. The views are mine and mine alone and I take full responsibility for them. I believe it is a tale worth telling and I hope the book will inspire many to become more aware of the needs and the potential of these children that we do our best to support; to become their advocates; and to give even more so that the charity can help ever more children.

David Maidment
September, 2012

Dedication

I dedicate the book to the small girl I encountered on Churchgate station, Bombay, back in 1989, who was the stimulus for the idea that grew eventually into the Railway Children charity.

Dead eyes, haunted eyes,
Lonely in the throng.
Tangled hair, bed of lies,
Who has done you wrong?

Filthy skirt, plaited whip
Hidden behind your back,
Surely not to make you skip
Just to earn your snack?

Outstretched arm, begging hand
Pulling at my heart.
Threatened, told just there to stand,
Forced to play a part.

Slave child, bonded girl,
Victim here, for what?
Rupee or two just for a swirl?
Pawn of a conman's plot?

What will become of her?
Will she die or live?
Will she yet my conscience stir?
What can I, will I, give?

Acronyms used throughout the book

AIUK   Amnesty International (UK)
AP   Andhra Pradesh
APPG   All Party Parliamentary Group
BA   British Airways
BR   British Rail
BTP   British Transport Police
CAB   Child Assistance Booth
CEO   Chief Executive Officer
CHRN   Children's Human Rights Network (AIUK)
CRB   Criminal Records Bureau
CRC   UN Convention on the Rights of the Child
CSC   Consortium for Street Children
CSR   Corporate Social Responsibility
CWC   Child Welfare Committee (India)
DFID   Department for International Development (UK Government)
DHR   Darjeeling Himalayan Railway
DMU   Diesel Multiple Unit Train
EMU   Electric Multiple Unit Train
FCO   Foreign & Commonwealth Office (UK Government)
GM   General Manager
GRP   Government Railway Police (of India)
HR   Human Resources
HST   High Speed Train (BR)
JJB   Juvenile Justice Board (India)
KPI   Key Performance Indicator
MD   Managing Director
MRDF   Methodist Relief & Development Fund
NGO   Non government organisation
NRM   National Railway Museum (York)
RCFI   Railway Children Federation of India
RWWO   Railway Women's Welfare Organisation (India)
RPF   Railway Protection Force (of India)
TQM   Total Quality Management
UP   Uttar Pradesh

Some Indian cities changed their names during the period described in this book. I have used the original and best known names throughout, ie
　　Bombay is now Mumbai
　　Bombay Victoria Terminus (VT) station is now Mumbai Chhatrapati Shivaji Terminus (CST)
　　Calcutta is now Kolkata
　　Madras is now Chennai.

Chapter 1
The girl at Churchgate station

It all began because of a small girl in Bombay.

I had been a railway manager for nigh on thirty years. After four years as the Chief Operating Manager of British Rail's largest Region, the London Midland, which stretched from London to Birmingham, Liverpool, Manchester and the Scottish border, I'd been appointed BR's first overall 'Reliability & Quality Manager'. And then, after the Clapham Junction train accident at the end of 1988, the Board Member to whom I reported asked me to chair the small team that was pulling together the evidence for the subsequent judicial inquiry which took place at the Methodist Central Hall in Westminster during the Spring and Summer of 1989. I'd written a number of papers on quality management and, after the Inquiry had finished and before the Inquiry report was published, I was asked to undertake a three week project for Transmark, the BR consultancy company, to advise the Western Railway of Australia in Perth.

When the assignment was finished, I flew home with Singapore Airlines and spent a couple of days sightseeing in the airline's home city, and had arranged a second stop-over in the Indian city then still called Bombay (and since renamed Mumbai, although most of the locals still use its former name). My reason for this, apart from the opportunity of seeing fresh places, was to visit a family with whom my family had corresponded for a number of years. We'd been sponsoring the education of a girl through a scheme run at that time by 'Save the Children' and I'd asked - as my flight was calling at Bombay anyway - if it would be possible to meet her and her family. Arrangements were made and my plane touched down at midnight on a hot, sultry night in September 1989.

I was not feeling well. I was virtually last off the Jumbo Jet and found myself near the back of the huge queue progressing slowly through the immigration procedures in the arrival hall which at that time was not air conditioned. I was nervous at the prospect of meeting the girl's family wondering how I'd be received, whether we would be able to cope with the languages and make ourselves understood. And not only that, I'd made the mistake the night before of taking my once-a-week anti-malaria medication on an empty stomach and was now feeling decidedly queasy. When finally I emerged through customs into the main arrival hall, I found myself caught up in the melée of jostling porters all wanting to drag me to their taxi. I was rescued by someone who kindly pointed me in the direction of the pre-paid taxi queue and, sometime after 2 o'clock in the morning, I huddled in the back of the bumping vehicle as it rushed through the deserted streets into the city centre. I looked out of the taxi window and realised the streets were not deserted as I'd first thought. There were bundles of white rolled up alongside the roadway and it dawned on me that these were people, huddled together and sleeping on the pavements. The swaying of the taxi, the heat, the smell of the city's garbage and my nervousness increased my feeling of nausea, and I was relieved to reach my destination hotel on Marine Drive on the shores of the Arabian Sea at just after three in the morning.

Despite dropping straight into bed, my mind was still in a whirl and the discomfort in my system prevented me falling asleep as I lay there and worried what I had let myself in for. I tossed and turned in the stifling heat for hours and at seven o'clock, with dawn breaking, I could stick it no longer and got up, dressed and went out onto the promenade to take a few deep breaths of sea air and try to calm myself. I certainly was in no mood to face breakfast and wondered how to fill in the time before my appointment with the agency that 'Save the Children' used for running the sponsorship scheme, for that was not until ten o'clock. I consulted my street map and located the area of the city called Colaba where the meeting with the family was to take place. It didn't look too far on the map so I decided on the spur of the moment to use the time by walking across the city rather than waiting and taking a taxi, as everyone had advised me. I went back to my hotel, changed into fresh clothes, unpacked the gifts my family had assembled for the girl and her two brothers, put them into a carrier bag and, with map in hand, set off into the now humming city.

For a while I made my way southwards along the sea wall and then decided it was time to cut into the city centre, for Colaba appeared to be on the other coast of the peninsular on which the city had been built. Immediately I began to get lost as my map did not mark clearly all the road junctions or the myriad small alleyways and criss-crossing back streets I now encountered. After half an hour or so, I stumbled across a large building which turned out to be the terminus of a suburban railway system. As a good railwayman, I thought that I'd at least be able to establish exactly where I was and put my carrier bag down in the crowded concourse of the station and searched to see if I could find it on my map.

I looked up and found myself confronted by a small girl - she couldn't have been more than six or seven years of age. She was filthy dirty and was bare-legged and -chested and she looked at me and held out her hand, obviously begging. Now I'd been warned by a number of people not to give money to the many beggars that I would encounter, for otherwise I'd get swamped by the numbers. In any case I'd no small change – just a wadge of high denomination paper money still stapled together in packs of hundred rupee notes - so I waved her away and intended to make a swift departure. As I hesitated the small girl suddenly produced in her other hand a plaited whip she'd been holding behind her back and began solemnly to lash herself across her bare back and shoulders. I stood rooted to the spot, stunned and shaken. The girl stopped, held out her hand and looked me in the face. Her eyes were dead, her mouth drooped, her hair was a tangled mess. She began to whip herself again and I couldn't take it. I could just not cope emotionally with this girl's actions. I was feeling fragile anyway, and her predicament finished me off. I picked up my bag and fled.

I stopped in the first shop doorway and tried to pull myself together. I realised I was shaking and when, finally, I'd stopped trembling and was breathing more easily, I thought, I can't leave her like that, and went back. I don't know what I thought I was going to do about it, but the girl had disappeared into the rush hour throng. Every minute and a half another twelve coach train disgorged its mass of nearly 6,000 passengers into this five platform terminus and in those few minutes she'd disappeared. I went back to where I thought she'd been, almost being swept off my feet by the urgent flow of humanity pouring out of the station. But there was no sign of the girl. It was as if I'd imagined her. But I know I didn't. If I shut my eyes, I can still, over twenty years later, see the girl's eyes, staring hopelessly at me.

I gave up but as I trudged on past the Flora Fountain and found the teeming Bhagat Singh Marg, walking with increasing urgency down past the entrance to Sassoon Dockyard, my mind was trying to come to terms with what I'd seen. Small children of six years of age do not behave in the way I'd just encountered. Of course, I realised that the girl was under instruction from some unscrupulous or desperate adult who was telling her what to do, in order to elicit a generous donation from a gullible tourist like me. She might have been a child whose father or stepfather had hit upon a profitable ruse. More likely she was a street living child forced to beg by a criminal adult who was exploiting her. If I had given her one of my hundred rupee notes, it would have only demonstrated that such manipulation of a young child works; the girl would have got nothing other than a crust at the end of the day and possibly a beating if she had not extracted enough money from her naïve victims. As this realisation dawned on me, anger took over. I began to notice other children. At every road junction young children dashed out between the hooting cars and red buses to sell trinkets or soiled Indian flags; young women, scarcely more than girls themselves, with a baby at the hip, put their hands to their mouths miming hunger while tapping on the taxi windows.

Later, someone told me that there were an estimated 100,000 street children in the city and environs of Bombay alone - perhaps 90% from the slums, spending the day on the street scavenging, begging, selling whatever they can find, then returning to one of the sprawling slums that infest the city at Daravi or by the stagnant water and concrete pipes of the Mahim Creek.

As I toiled onwards I worried that I would lose myself again or get caught by another scam. With time running out I eventually got pointed in the right direction by some kind soul, and found my destination was a thirty storey concrete block of flats and my appointment was on the 22nd floor, reached by an ancient tiny lift which took an age to reach the appointed level. The flat door was open and I found the family I was to meet assembled there. The sponsorship programme was administered on behalf of 'Save the Children' by an elderly couple, Rusi and Freny Toddywalla, both members of the Theosophical Order of Service, who at that time had over 700 children on their books each receiving a small annual donation towards school fees and medical supplies. My worries and nerves were soon transformed by the engaging activities of the girl's two-year old cousin who broke the ice, and the stiff formality of my greeting was soon dissipated. After introductions, tea and biscuits, and the inevitable garlanding, I found myself taken under the wing of my 'adopted' family. The aunt pressed some notes into the children's hands and they were given the task over the next two days of taking me sightseeing around the city. I tried to protest that I should pay, but I was their guest and the rules of hospitality required that I should accept their generosity with grace.

I saw, of course, their city. We saw the marble monuments, the grand buildings, the Gateway of India where the city had received King George V in 1911, the Taj Hotel where the two year old insisted on going to the toilet amid the gold-plated taps and marble washbasins. We also saw the slums, the dirt. We travelled on an ancient red double-decker bus. We ate - to my trepidation - at a roadside kiosk. They took me to the Hanging Gardens and we drank coconut juice. And I saw the children, dirty, bright-eyed urchins looking longingly at what I was eating and I wasn't hungry. My young guides were cross with me when I gave half of my nan bread sandwich away.

With hindsight I now question many aspects of that visit - the way I was allowed to be taken around the city for two days by those three children is now taboo under all the rules of child protection. 'Save the Children' terminated the sponsorship scheme, concerned lest the selection of some children in a city of the destitute should cause jealousy and rifts between those who received and those who did not. But one result of that visit was that I and my family formed a lifelong friendship with the girl and her family. We still meet up when I'm a visitor to the city for a different reason.

But the anger engendered by that encounter on Churchgate station remained. I saw reminders of that incident everywhere as we roamed around the city. We were constantly followed by young children begging when they saw a white face entering some parts of the city where tourists do not usually go. We saw haphazard cruelty, anger displayed when children were too demanding, children rejected and neglected, children alone in the gutter. All this stayed in my memory. But above all, I could not erase the sight of that child on the station whipping herself, an image even now engraved in my brain. And when I got home, laden with gifts from my enlarged family that I'd felt embarrassed to accept, the little girl on Churchgate station wouldn't go away and my anger grew, it didn't diminish with time. I tried to tell people what I'd seen, but that bit choked me up. After five weeks, I couldn't stand it any longer. I knew I had to do something, but what?

Chapter 2
Amnesty International

I'd always intended to join Amnesty International, the human rights organisation, but I'd never got round to it. During my search for information about charities that might help children like those I'd seen in Bombay, I came across a discarded Amnesty application form and decided that this was the jolt I needed to fill it up and send it in along with an annual subscription fee. On the front page of the form were a series of boxes inviting new members to tick any special interests where they might have some professional or other reason for campaigning on those cases. Because of my encounter in Bombay, I ticked the 'children's rights' box.

Five weeks later I received a phone call from someone in the Amnesty International UK office in Rosebery Avenue, London, advising me of a meeting to be held about children's rights and inviting me to attend. I was impressed that a large bureaucracy like Amnesty was so 'on the ball' in welcoming a new member and noting my interest, and decided, as the meeting was in London, that I could go there after my day's work at the BR office in Euston and before travelling back to my home near Crewe in Cheshire. I was anticipating a public meeting of some sort, and was a little perturbed to find that the meeting was in a small room above the main bar of a public house just opposite the Amnesty office. I entered the room and found about half a dozen people round a table, most looking as bewildered as I felt. A guy called Brian Wood introduced himself as the Amnesty staff member responsible for liaising with a number of specialist networks within Amnesty and then, and only then, did it dawn on me that I had been co-opted - along with three or four other people present - to Amnesty UK's national network for children's rights, the 'Working Group for Children' (WGC) as it was then called.

Amnesty had started in the 1960s from the idea of a British lawyer, Peter Benenson. He'd been angered by a press report of two students in Portugal, who'd toasted 'freedom' in a local café and had been arrested by the Portuguese dictator's police and sentenced to three years' imprisonment for propaganda against the state. From the response to his letter to the newspaper, Amnesty had been formed to campaign for 'prisoners of conscience', people imprisoned or murdered by the authorities for expressing non-violent views that were deemed unacceptable. As membership grew and Amnesty extended its mandate to campaign on a range of human rights abuses, a British man named Alan Grounds had persuaded Amnesty to take up cases of children whose rights had been violated by state agencies and, around 1984, had formed the first 'Working Group for Children' in the British Section. He had gathered around him a committee of like-minded people to identify and publicise cases researched by Amnesty's International Secretariat and this team had regular communications with a number of Amnesty members who had expressed interest in belonging to the 'WGC' network. Unfortunately, Alan had died suddenly in 1989 and being one of those charismatic characters who are full of action, but who rarely write anything down, he'd left a void in the organisation, and the WGC committee had not met for more than a year.

Brian Wood had decided to reinvent the WGC committee and to that end had invited a number of potentially useful members with a professional interest in children to become members of the new committee - a social worker, a teacher, a children's lawyer, the director of a street children charity - and, I gathered, having sought to co-opt a businessman, had come across my recently submitted application form and had invited me. I was a little out of my depth - from new member to national committee for children's rights in five weeks was somewhat daunting - and I wondered whether I could really make any contribution. I was inclined to apologise and suggest that I had insufficient experience of either Amnesty's practices or children's rights to be of any use. However, as they talked about some of the children's cases they were campaigning for, I realised that street children were on their agenda and the plight of the girl in Bombay stopped me leaving the room.

It took me a time to make any contribution. We met monthly and two volunteers would produce a newsletter outlining cases for action by our network members. Amnesty, like most other large organisations - especially my own railway industry - is full of acronyms and it took time for me to follow how Amnesty chose which violations to prioritise and the processes through which activists operated throughout the organisation. One of the highly motivated members of that committee was a British businessman, Fred Shortland, who was also the UK Director of an American charity, Casa Alianza, a branch of 'Covenant House' working with street children in Central American states like Guatemala, Nicaragua, Honduras and Mexico. His organisation had a legal department in one of the states that was regularly challenging the government and justice departments about the abuses that were perpetrated by the police and by vigilante groups condoned by the police, who were beating up, torturing and even murdering the street children, treating them as vermin. I was impressed and moved by one of Casa Alianza's managers based in Central America, Bruce Harris, who spoke about the beating and killing of Nahaman, a 13 year old boy, by four policemen in Guatemala City and the efforts being made by Amnesty to bring the police concerned to justice whilst also protecting Bruce and the three boy witnesses to the murder. I was horrified by evidence produced by Amnesty that 4,611 street children had been found murdered in Brazil around the time of the Rio 1990 'Earth Summit', when the authorities had 'cleansed' the streets of undesirables including street children to avoid criticism of the international media and politicians.

I also met Father Shay Cullen, a Catholic priest, who worked in the Philippines for an organisation called PREDA and who was taking major risks by going under cover and posing as a tourist seeking child prostitutes in the bars of Manila and Olongopo City (near a US naval base), so that he could bring the abusers to justice and rescue the child victims. From these meetings and experiences I began to get a feel for the extent of the problem of street children in many parts of the world and the rejection that they felt. One of the Amnesty WGC's main bases for judgement was the 1989 UN Convention of the Rights of the Child, 54 articles, of which the first 41 outline the protection, provision and participation rights of children and young people under the age of eighteen. I compared these rights with the violations commonly experienced by street children and found that at least 50% of the articles were regularly flouted by governments and individuals in many parts of the world - the right to life, an identity, education, health care, protection from discrimination, forced labour, physical and sexual abuse, humiliating punishment and the right to support and representation when accused of activities against the law. Amnesty was at that time campaigning on a number of child rights abuses occurring in conflict situations, and also on child refugees, children in detention with adults and those suffering violations carried out to put pressure on their parents. However, in the early 1990s most of the cases researched and put through our committee for action by our network were street children from several countries in Central and South America.

Then, in 1992, Amnesty International UK received an invitation from a newly formed organisation called 'Consortium for Street Children' to send a representative to join that group. Without knowing exactly what it involved, I decided to volunteer to be that representative - still guided and motivated by the encounter with the little street child in Bombay.

Chapter 3
The Consortium for Street Children

The Consortium for Street Children is the leading international network dedicated to realising the rights of street children. CSC is continually expanding and currently has over 60 members operating in 130 countries. Network members comprise UK based and international non-government organisations (NGOs), as well as individuals with an interest in street children, but in 1992 there were initially around a dozen potential members, UK based but all supporting street children internationally. The decision to bring street children charities together to share their experiences and good practice and to lobby governments on behalf of these vulnerable children was the idea of Nic Fenton, Director of Childhope and Trudy Davies, Research and Liaison Officer to the All Party Parliamentary Group (APPG) on Population and Development. Baroness Jane Ewart-Biggs, President of UNICEF and widow of the British Ambassador to Ireland who was assassinated by the Provisional IRA in 1976, became the Chair of the Consortium until her death in October 1992, when she was succeeded by Baroness Sheela Flather.

During 1992 this group met at UNICEF's London Fields headquarters or in the House of Commons Tearoom, and after Baroness Flather took over, in a committee room in the House of Lords. It was in the latter part of 1992 that I, as the invited member from Amnesty's Working Group for Children, attended my first meeting of the Consortium, when they were feeling their way and preparing the ground for registration as a UK charity. At one of the first meetings I attended I found that the then Prime Minister, John Major, was taking a personal interest following an encounter he experienced during the 1990 'Earth Summit' in Rio de Janeiro. He had visited a street children project run by Aninha Capaldi, Brazilian wife of Jim Capaldi, the songwriter and founder of 'Traffic'. Aninha and 'Jubilee Action', the UK NGO she was associated with, were founder members of the Consortium, and the Prime Minister had offered to host a reception at 10 Downing Street for the launch of the organisation. During 1993 several meetings were taken up with the arrangements for the launch and registration of the charity and much debate took place about providing a press release to accompany the launch.

In the couple of years since the publication of the Inquiry report by Mr Justice Hidden QC on the Clapham Junction train accident and the earlier report on the London Underground fire at Kings Cross, I had been appointed Head of British Rail's Safety Policy Unit, a new post to oversee the transformation of BR's safety management system from a traditional reactive approach to a more proactive system, taking into cognisance developments in the high tech industries and in academia. Among the systems I introduced as a basis for prioritising investment in safety and in remedial action was the technique of risk assessment, which, in conjunction with management consultants Cooper Lybrand and Tony Taig from the nuclear power industry (later adviser to the parliamentary Select Committee on Railways) I had applied comprehensively to British Rail's engineering and operating activities throughout 1991 and 1992.

It was with this background that I listened to the ongoing debate at the Consortium about how to utilise the opportunities presented by the Downing Street launch and reception. As the discussion meandered on, I started to doodle a risk assessment of being a street child on the back of an old envelope. When the consensus of the discussion around the theme of the causes of children being on the street began to emerge, I produced my scribbled 'Fault Tree' and we began to debate it further. Encouraged by the other members present, I developed a 'Cause and Consequence Tree' using the risk assessment techniques of Fault and Event Tree Analysis.

A Fault Tree seeks to trace back and uncover root causes of the main event - in this case the emergence of children onto the street. The oversimplified analysis that I did along with the other members present identified three immediate causes for children coming to street life - searching for income and work, escaping from destitute families; running away from physical or sexual abuse; and abandonment, neglect or rejection by the family. In nearly all cases this pointed to a breakdown of the traditional family, in some cases through illness and death from AIDS related diseases or from involvement in armed conflict zones; in others because of the stresses caused by economic hardship, with a prevalence of parental drug abuse or alcoholism; sometimes because of the disruption caused by natural catastrophes such as earthquakes, floods and hurricanes.

I then developed an Event Tree which analysed the consequences and their probability, starting with the immediate needs of a child when first confronted with surviving on the street - the obvious need for food, or money with which to buy it; the need for shelter and somewhere safe to sleep; and the need for companionship, usually with other children in the same situation as themselves. The analysis then explored the actions that street children took to meet these needs and the consequent unravelling of their lives as they faced ostracism and rejection by society who often saw their means of survival as anti-social - at best a nuisance, and, all too often, criminal and fear-provoking.

When I had completed this basic risk assessment, I passed it to each of the members present and asked them to insert their own organisation's intervention strategy on the appropriate root or branch of the 'tree' that I had drafted. Some NGOs present were able to do this easily. Large NGOs like UNICEF and Save the Children did little direct work with children already on the street. But in partnership with many other local NGOs, they undertook much prevention work in slum and rural communities, especially in the areas of child health and education and emergency care after natural catastrophes. The organisation that I represented, Amnesty International, worked at the opposite end of the spectrum, in tackling the extreme consequences when the street children faced physical abuse, torture and murder because society condoned the often brutal actions of the authorities to rid themselves of these children and the supposed petty crimes they were thought to have committed. It was harder to pinpoint the focus of some of the other member NGOs. Some ran residential homes for these children, health clinics, drug de-addiction centres. Others ran vocational training schemes for street children to enable them to become self-sufficient, while others again worked in slum areas with children who were not attending school but scavenging or begging, and offered informal education and emergency health care.

When I assembled all the responses and looked at the tree I had drawn and the insertions made, I realised that there was a glaring gap. No-one had identified the first few days - or even hours - when a child first comes to the street as a crucial intervention opportunity. My risk assessment had pinpointed this particular time in a street child's career as one of both high risk and great opportunity. My railway safety management role, involving train, passenger, staff and general public safety, required me on many occasions to work closely with the British Transport Police (BTP). In conversations with senior officers I had mentioned my voluntary work with Amnesty International and my interest in street children, and they told me of their concern for many British children whom they found on our own railway stations.

I was introduced to two Salvation Army captains - a man and his wife - who, in the company of a BTP officer, would patrol a number of London's main line railway termini every evening looking for lone children at risk. These two stalwarts had been doing this for some ten years since the early 1980s, and they told me that they had picked up 3,600 children under the age of 16 during that period, an average of one every night. The youngest was a girl of six from Crewe whom they'd found sleeping on platform 12 at Euston after sneaking out of her home while her parents thought her banished to her bedroom after some family squabble. Even more alarmingly, these Salvation Army officers told me that a lone child or teenager, at any of the main London stations, or Victoria coach station or a West End amusement arcade, had on average around twenty minutes before they'd be targeted by a pimp, paedophile, drug addict or dealer appearing to offer help, but in fact ensnaring them into the world of sexual abuse and drug addiction.

In 1992 I'd attended a railway safety conference organised by Tranzrail, the New Zealand privatised railway company. As my flight back from New Zealand once again came via Singapore and Bombay, I'd taken the opportunity to make a further visit to my sponsored family in India and this time, because of my earlier experience, I was introduced to Father 'Plassy' Fonseca, a Jesuit priest working in that city for a street children charity called 'Snehasadan'. He took me to a small shelter, Amchi Kholi, that the Central Railway of India management had permitted within the huge Victoria Terminus station (now renamed Chhatrapati Shivaji Terminus - CST - where much of 'Slumdog Millionaire' was filmed). While we were talking to a social worker there, a small filthy dirty girl of about eight years of age walked in off a mainline train that had just arrived from Calcutta. The social worker

Victoria Terminus, Bombay

obviously knew her and I was horrified to understand that girls and boys of this age wandered unsupervised around India's vast railway system, surviving as best they could, moving on when the whim took them, always at risk of abusers and traffickers.

I mentioned to Father Fonseca the situation I'd learned of in Britain about the risk to children on London's stations and how short was the time before they'd be approached by undesirables. 'Oh,' said the Father, 'it's minus two hours here!' He explained that the brothel owners employed women to travel a couple of hours outside Bombay on the routes converging from the north, and then board trains headed for the city, scouring through the train looking for unaccompanied and runaway children whose trust they could obtain. Instead of finding them safe havens in Bombay as they'd promise, they'd sell them on commission to the sex industry - boys and girls of eight, nine, ten years of age even. Father Fonseca's organisation had social workers on the station to try to intercept such children and offer real safety and rehabilitation in a series of small children's homes run by foster parents many of whom had been street children themselves.

With this in mind as I assimilated the responses from the Consortium members in the House of Lords Committee room that afternoon, I began to press my colleagues about their focus and the existence of any projects funded by UK charities that targeted early intervention when the children first ran away or were abandoned. We discussed opportunities for such intervention and quickly established that the transport systems were an obvious location. Not only were they the point of entry for many children to the city where their street life began, but they were also places where they could find informal employment or where they could scavenge or beg. They were places of many opportunities and dangers, and many children stayed there initially until they found other street children and moved on. Many would stay at the station and join gangs of other children they found there. In India and the countries of Eastern Europe, the railway station was key for early intervention. In most parts of Latin America and Africa, the bus station was a more likely location.

Not only were these places a danger to new children arriving there because of the easy prey the children were for drug dealers, sex exploiters and other criminal gangs, but they were also the locations where there was a brief opportunity for people of goodwill to offer a child a positive way out before they became traumatised by their experiences and adapted, and often corrupted, to street life. Later I was told that if a child was supported within the first month of living on the street, there was an 80% chance of helping that child find a positive outcome to their predicament – either reconciliation with their family, or moving to an educational or vocational training programme or, as a last resort, to a place in a residential home. After six months living on the street that chance had fallen to 20%, as the child became streetwise, found a new family in the 'gang', and often by that time had become addicted to some form of inhalant or drug.

Now began a period of contemplation. John Major duly hosted the launch of the Consortium on the 18th November 1993. The Consortium was registered with the Charity Commission and more British non-government organisations began to join. I became one of the initial trustees (I did not retire from this until 2008) and I kept talking to colleagues there about the risk assessment I'd undertaken, and the need for a focus on early intervention. No-one disagreed, but no organisation had set this focus as their purpose, and if any such project took place it was not part of any overall strategy. My mind kept coming back to the need for a charity that would seize this opportunity for contacting street children as soon as they came to the street. It was apparent that the railway and bus stations of the world offered a unique opportunity to make this contact, just as the Salvation Army couple had done in England, and Snehasadan was doing at one station in India. I began to talk to colleagues I knew in the railway industry. More and more I felt an inner compunction to do something about it myself. The image of the small girl I'd encountered on Churchgate station in 1989 kept coming back to me. But it seemed a huge step to take and I worried about sharing my vision with colleagues in case they ridiculed my ideas as naïve. I started to talk to other members of the Consortium and they encouraged me. I saw a link between the opportunity to help these children on the stations and the industry in which I worked.

Taking my courage in both hands I began to talk about my ideas to my colleagues at BR's headquarter offices. My own boss, Board Member David Rayner, was interested and didn't dismiss it out of hand. He suggested I discuss it with other members of the British Railways Board. Not all were enthusiastic. One drew attention to the enormous task of starting a new charity amid the competition of so many other charitable organisations. Another put me in touch with a group of railway people in Sheffield who were raising money for children being discovered in deplorable conditions in Romanian orphanages and suggested I meet them and perhaps join my ideas with theirs. I duly met their committee as had been suggested but discovered that their vision did not marry easily with my own and that there was a reluctance to broaden their scope from the Romanian orphans which at that time were receiving a lot of media coverage. Even among people who were keen to help vulnerable children, I found a resistance to the idea of working for street children as they were already stigmatised in many minds as delinquent children. As such they felt their plight would not draw public sympathy nor entice sufficient funds to develop worthwhile projects.

The railway ran its own charity, which for many years had funded two children's orphanages in Derby and Woking. The Woking home had closed and had been converted into a residential home for elderly railway people as the need for residential institutions for children had diminished. The purpose of these two homes had been to make provision for the orphans of railway workers who had either been killed or had died in service. Some 400 men a year were killed in accidents on the system immediately after the First World War, but thankfully by the 1980s this tragic slaughter had been reduced to around twenty fatalities a year - still a bad industrial record. This reduced need and the effect of the 1989 Children's Act meant that after the 1990s a charity running orphanages in the UK was inappropriate. Many employees of the railway industry had given generously to this charity over the years and I felt that there was an opportunity for railway people to widen their interest, and maintain their generosity for vulnerable and destitute children associated with railways internationally as well as on home territory.

Having tested the alternatives suggested and established that I was not conflicting with the railway's own children's charity, I continued serious discussions with members of CSC. One option would have been to merge my ideas with an existing organisation belonging to the Consortium. But there was no obvious partner and I was encouraged to found a new charity, given the potential support from the railway industry that I had uncovered. In any case, it was obvious to me and my colleagues at CSC that I would be reliant on some of them to identify potential project opportunities, where the focus of early intervention could be developed with the financial support that I thought I could generate.

And so, throughout the second half of 1993 and 1994 I was putting my thoughts together, and by the beginning of 1995 I had decided to take the plunge. With the promised backing of CSC and several colleagues in the railway industry, I would form a new charity to offer support to children as they first gravitated to the street. I sought advice from the Charity Commission and began to bring together a small committee of colleagues to help me with some of the practicalities. My boss, David Rayner, was generous in his support, offering the facilities of the railway administration in the first few months. I had a name for the charity - in India I had heard these street children on the stations referred to variously as 'railway' or 'platform' children - so the name of the famous children's novel and film, 'The Railway Children', long out of copyright, seemed to me entirely appropriate for what I had in mind. I had to check that no other organisation had registered this name and I found it was used by just one small pre-school playgroup in Kent whose premises backed onto a railway line. The Charity Commission foresaw no problem in duplicating a national charity name with that of a very local group, but as a courtesy I contacted the playgroup leader and readily got permission to go ahead with the name. So, in the Spring of 1995, the 'Railway Children' charity was born.

Chapter 4
The launch

The launch of the Railway Children charity took place at noon on the 31st May 1995 'under the clock' on Waterloo station concourse. Some 150 relatives, friends, colleagues and potential supporters, and a few members of the travelling public who happened to be passing, gathered before a rostrum that had been set up that morning together with a photography exhibition from the book 'Children of Bombay'. A few months before the launch I had seen some photographs of street children in a Sunday Observer supplement and had found them so appropriate for the charity that I had contacted the photographer, Dario Mitidieri, and the publisher, Dewi Lewis, through the newspaper, and asked if I could use any of them as part of the launch publicity. They both responded enthusiastically and offered a dozen stands of some of the most striking photographs to be exhibited on the concourse for the whole of the following week.

As the crowd gathered I began to realise - perhaps for the first

David Maidment in front of Dario Mitidieri's photo exhibition at the launch of the charity

time - the magnitude of what I was undertaking. I was going public and could not turn back now. My stomach churned with nervous excitement. British Rail was in the transitional phase of privatisation and the Chairmen of Railtrack, Bob Horton, and of the residual British Rail organisation, John Welsby, had both promised to support me by being present and speaking at the launch. In the event, after Bob Horton had spoken, Tony Roche, Deputy Chairman of BR, took John Welsby's place as he had been detained at an urgent meeting at the Ministry of Transport in Marsham Street. Dario Mitidieri spoke briefly about the photographic exhibition and I outlined what had motivated me to found the charity and explained its objectives. Afterwards we had a small reception in the Railtrack offices on the station.

In order to gain some publicity, Bob Horton had twisted the arms of one or two of his press contacts and during the reception I was approached by Christian Wolmar, then transport correspondent of the Independent, who expressed his support for my vision and his willingness to help. His support blossomed - later that summer he visited the charity's first project partner in Romania and brought back photos and a two page story for the Independent. Later still, after registration with the Charity Commission in 1996, he became one of the founding trustees - a role he still holds in 2012.

I remained on the concourse at Waterloo with the exhibition for the rest of the week, assisted by a few friends and colleagues. It was at times a lonely vigil; I found the rush hours to be particularly unrewarding as commuters passed 'heads-down' oblivious to most activity around them. During the middle part of the day, however, some travellers had time to stop and look at the photographs and engage me in conversation. About the third day, I noticed one particular family who must have spent half an hour staring at the pictures before talking to me. The middle-aged married couple were accompanied by two smartly dressed young girls - probably around 8-10 years of age - of seeming Indian appearance. As the mother and girls continued to look at the photographs, the man explained to me that they had read about the launch of the charity and the exhibition in the press, and had brought their adopted daughters up from the Wimbledon area specially. Both girls had been born to street children in Bombay and for their first couple of years had survived with their young mothers on the streets of the city. They had then been taken into an orphanage and had been adopted from there by this English couple. The family had stayed in touch with the orphanage and the girls' school had regular contact with the Indian institution. They had brought the girls to see pictures of the life into which they had been born and from which they'd been rescued.

The Deputy Chairman of Railtrack, Christopher Campbell, advised me to tackle a project as quickly as possible so that I could demonstrate where any donations would be used, with a real example. To this end, he helped the charity acquire our first trust grant of £5,000 from the Dorothy Burns Trust, and this, together with donations made at Waterloo and as a result of the initial media coverage, enabled me to sit down with colleagues at the CSC and discuss the possibility of a first project. Nic Fenton, one of the founding members of the CSC and at that time Director of Childhope UK, advised me of two potential projects in Eastern Europe where street children were living on railway stations - Nic had been one of the colleagues who had encouraged me to develop the 'early intervention' focus. He was keen to support local charities in Bucharest, Romania, and in Sofia in Bulgaria, but Childhope at that time did not have the necessary funding available. The situation at Bucharest main railway station seemed to meet the criteria I had built up - 50 young boys between 10 and 14 years of age were apparently surviving at the station, even descending at night into the sewers there to avoid abuse and violence and also the cold of an Eastern European winter night. A local Romanian charity, ASIS, was trying to help these children and had been offered by the municipality a neglected and empty house on the edge of the city to accommodate them. Through Childhope, Railway Children decided to provide the money to decorate and furnish the house and provide the salary of the ASIS staff to look after the boys. Our ability to do this and continue beyond the first year was greatly helped by the effort of two young men in London Transport's Planning Department who each undertook a 3,500 mile sponsored cycle ride from London to Istanbul that raised several thousand pounds, and by the response to Christian Wolmar's article in the Independent, which brought in donations of over £4,000.

During those first few months I relied for advice and practical assistance on a number of colleagues whom I recruited to form a committee, mainly to publicise the charity within the railway industry, but also to act as a sounding-board when potential projects were identified by me through my contacts at the CSC. These included my boss, BR Board Member David Rayner, Regional BR General Manager, Cyril Bleasdale, Ian Allan of the railway book empire, David Morgan of the Heritage Railway Association, Vidur Dindayal of the London Regional Passenger Consultative Committee, Lew Adams, General Secretary of the trade union, ASLEF, and a number of CSC colleagues including the Director, Anita Schrader. I talked my long-time friend Stan Judd, with whom I'd shared many career partnerships, into acting as Secretary. Stan looked after book-keeping and when our original treasurer retired due to ill health, became de facto Treasurer, a role he retained until the end of 2005. His willingness and skill at dealing with the necessary detail and establishing robust procedures complemented well my more strategic view - and my lack of interest or patience with some of the inevitable but essential practicalities and bureaucracy.

We had always been conscious that there were children, particularly teenagers, in need in the UK. We therefore decided quite early on that Railway Children would devote a minimum of 10% of the donations received on projects for runaway children in this country. Later, in 2003, the Board took a strategic decision to devote a minimum of 20% to such projects. Several people within the industry had experience of the situation in which vulnerable children or young people came to the notice of railway staff on our major stations. There was also concern that some potential donors would want to see their contribution spent in this country rather than all of it overseas, and we debated, quite hotly at times, our motivation for UK initiatives. Initially I was invited to consider a possible project being developed in the crypt of St Pancras parish church – a refuge and drop-in centre for runaway and homeless young people. But it soon became obvious after a number of physical inspections of the premises that any scheme would cost a £1million +, way beyond the means of our fledgling charity.

Another initiative, which surfaced about this time, was a request for some Railtrack London termini to house computer information displays especially for runaways, but the British Transport Police expressed reservations. They felt such facilities would become too obvious a magnet for paedophiles and others looking to exploit vulnerable children whom they would observe using the facility.

This discussion, however, led to another and more successful intervention. I was introduced to Diana Lamplugh, mother of the missing, presumed murdered, estate agent, Suzy Lamplugh. Diana had founded a charity in response to her family tragedy to safeguard vulnerable young people. She was then leading discussions with a number of charities and the BT Police about the need for some form of information system for young people who were ignorant of safe sources of help that might be available to them. She had been motivated particularly by the Gloucester 'Fred and Rosemary West' murders of young girls, some of whom were runaways that they had taken in and then abused.

I was brought in to regular meetings at the BT Police headquarters in Tavistock Place, where I met with Diana and representatives from a number of charities including the Samaritans, Save the Children, the De Paul Trust and the Salvation Army, as well as the Suzy Lamplugh Trust, the Metropolitan Police Vice Squad and the BT Police. As Diana's ideas turned into the reality of a new national phone helpline, using technology which allowed a three-way conversation (a teleconferencing facility) linking a child with the most appropriate help – national or local – I committed Railway Children to assist financially and used my contacts in the industry to obtain the free use of premises in British Rail's Kings Cross East Side offices. We also helped to recruit volunteers to man the phone lines in the early years, and when this new charity was registered, we organised its launch at the Euston Railtrack head office. We also arranged for one of the West Coast Virgin trainsets to be named 'Get Connected' after the charity by Paul Boateng, then a government minister at the Home Office.

I retired from Railtrack in March 1996 when it was transferred from government ownership to a private company, although I retained contact with many of my former colleagues as I had been instrumental in the safety management training of the top 800 managers of British Rail and the newly privatised companies over the previous five years and was thus well known by most of them. I was fortunate in obtaining a generous early retirement package - I had two years to go to the formal retirement age of 60. As a retired railway manager entitled to free travel, I was able to go regularly from my Cheshire home to meetings in London and all over the UK to promote the Railway Children and attend meetings of Amnesty International, the Consortium for Street Children and Get

Connected. I had been offered a part time associate consultancy post with a new small safety management consultancy organisation, International Risk Management Services (IRMS) and agreed with the managing director, Andrew Smith, that I would offer 60 days of consultancy a year with my fees being used in those early years to augment the income of Railway Children. Andrew and his staff became very valuable supporters of the charity and the way he enabled me to operate flexibly was of crucial importance in the initial development of the organisation.

Chapter 5
Registered Charity No.1058991

The 'Railway Children' was registered with the Charity Commission in November 1996 and simultaneously as a company with limited liability. As so often in our experience, we received free or near free advice from companies associated with the railway industry, in this case BR's lawyers, Simmons & Simmons. Although our objective and focus was very clear - making early intervention at railway and bus stations for children running from home, abandoned or neglected - we were advised to be much more general in specifying our aims in our 'Articles of Association' so that there was sufficient flexibility in the future should the need or the priorities change. Thus, as registered, our main purpose was listed as 'the relief of children who are in conditions of need, hardship or distress, anywhere in the world and in particular those who are living on the street'. We have frequently revisited this to consider whether we are working within this stated purpose, but also, as we learn more, to check it is not constraining our ability to do what is best for the children.

At the same time Railway Children had to list its trustees: the seven founding trustees were Stan Judd as Secretary; Gordon Pettitt, former General Manager of BR's Southern Region and Managing Director of Regional Railways; Terry Worrall, Director of Operations, British Railways Board; Christian Wolmar, journalist and author; Chris Jago, Managing Director, Union Railways South (the Channel Tunnel to Waterloo high speed route); Steve McColl, BR's Special Trains Manager'; and myself as Chairman. Within a few months we added Rachel Stephens, Manager of the Methodist Church Relief & Development Fund; and Rick Edmondson, heritage steam locomotive owner (of 'Britannia') and managing director of the maintenance company 'Resco' and special trains operator, 'Merlin'. Several of these colleagues had been assisting me in the committee we had formed to prepare for registration.

The registered address of the new charity was at the offices of Health Shield in Macon Way, Crewe, where the charity was provided with a rent-free room by BR's former health insurance company. They had also provided accommodation for BR's other charity, the Railway Benevolent Fund, which helped active and retired staff who had fallen on hard times. The room was small and windowless, but at the time I was just supported by a few part time local volunteers from churches in Nantwich, with Stan coming up from his home in Northamptonshire each week to maintain our accounts. We were just glad to have a room where we could store our materials, keep our post secure, have a desk and telephone, and have the co-operative staff of Health Shield alongside us to give advice and encouragement. The income received through donations from people in the railway industry and local churches and clubs, together with the income from my IRMS safety consultancy work, soon made it possible to appoint our first paid staff - Julia Worthington as Administrator, and Katie Mason as Fundraiser, both on a part time basis. We also produced our first newsletter, 'Action Stations', with the help of the BR Eastern Region's publicity officer, Bert Porter and our journalist trustee, Christian Wolmar. It was a four page broadsheet in black and white, which we distributed to all the privatised railway companies and the residual parts of British Rail as well as to individuals on our growing database.

The increased income made it possible to start looking for further projects to fund while also maintaining our support for ASIS in Bucharest. My contacts at the Consortium for Street Children were of great value in this, as I wished to avoid the pitfalls of being an amateur in such child protection and development work, with nothing but enthusiasm and a deep concern for the issue. The trustees were nearly all from senior management positions within the railway industry, so the issues of good governance were well covered, and I relied on colleagues at the CSC to bring me up to speed fast on understanding effective means of supporting street children, ably assisted by Rachel Stephens with her vast experience of evaluating project proposals for funding. One of our volunteers was Judith Brinkley, Personal Assistant to Denis Tunnicliffe, Chairman of London Transport, and she became our Meetings Secretary, arranging for our Board meetings to be held in the London Transport Board Room at 55 Broadway, over St James's Park underground station.

One of the members of the CSC, the International Children's Trust, with headquarters at Peterborough, drew my attention to a local partner charity they supported in Mexico called 'Juconi'. This Central American NGO had been founded by Sarah Thomas, a British diplomat who had been employed at the British Embassy in Mexico City and had resigned to start and run a charity for the many street children she'd observed in the city. She had obtained a rehabilitation centre - a halfway house to equip street and runaway children to return home or re-enter a structured lifestyle - at Puebla, about 70 miles south of Mexico City. I discovered through discussions with Sarah and Alison Lane, the Juconi Centre Administrative Director, that Puebla was a key point for identifying children running from the south of Mexico to the capital. Bus routes from the remoter areas terminated in a hub at Puebla, and a regular 10-15 minute frequency bus service plied the dual carriageway between the Puebla bus terminal and Mexico City. Runaway children had to change buses there and try to board the shuttle service buses to the desired destination without being caught by the local inspectors - many drivers conniving with the children and turning a blind eye.

Juconi therefore had begun to place 'outreach' staff at this bus station to form an alliance with the bus authorities and intercept the runaway children, offering them a place in the Juconi halfway house. Whilst not a railway station, the programme named 'Operation Friendship' was totally in accord with the principles on which Railway Children was founded. We therefore undertook to fund this element of Juconi's total programme which also covered much prevention work among market families in Puebla and linked with the local juvenile justice system. I was asked by Transmark, BR's international consultancy company, to undertake some safety management training for the executives of the Mexican Railways - their concerns were the frequent derailments, accidents and thefts of their freight haulage services leading to heavy and costly claims. I took advantage of my presence in Mexico City to visit Puebla, Juconi House and 'Operation Friendship'. By chance, the only opportunity I had coincided with a visit to Juconi by the Duchess of Gloucester and I found myself ushered into the Duchess's limousine to see the various projects run by the charity. I watched a drama and dancing put on by the children for their distinguished visitor and accompanied her as we met both staff and volunteers. I'm still not sure who the children and staff thought I was! 'Operation Friendship' was funded for 12 years and although direct funding ceased in 2009, Railway Children has learned much from the intensive therapy and counselling these children receive and has begun to share their expertise with Railway Children staff and partners in both India and East Africa.

Another CSC colleague, Clare Hanbury, then Programme Officer of the NGO 'Child-to-Child', returned from a conference in India and drew my attention to a project called 'Sarjan', which was part of the overall programme of the Ahmedabad Study Action Group (ASAG) in Gujarat. The founder was a very gentle man called Fulchand Purwar, who believed that vulnerable children could be stimulated and empowered through creative activities. The local charity had been working with the slum communities in Ahmedabad since the catastrophic floods of the Sabarmati River in the early 1970s, and now had intentions of working for street children, having identified six key places in the city where street children congregated. Clare told me that one of those six locations was at Kalupur, Ahmedabad's main railway station, where, apparently, anything up to 50 or 60 children could be found on the station at any one time. Sarjan wished to run a platform school for the children supplemented by food and health care and was quoting the need of only £1,650 per annum to fund two part-time teachers to go daily to the station to run the school for about four hours, providing the necessary simple materials and a midday meal. Some 20-40 children would appear at 10 o'clock each morning for lessons, sitting cross-legged on the station booking hall floor adjacent to platform 1, and would learn to read and write, do role play and drawing through which the teachers would discover the stories and background of the children. They would begin to size up the children's options whilst gaining their trust and confidence.

When I visited the project, I learned that one of the problems the teachers had to cope with was the abrupt disappearance of the children whenever a mainline train arrived in the adjacent platform, as the youngsters would scavenge through the train during its extended halt, searching for left-over food or empty water bottles they could fill and sell. Lessons would resume after twenty minutes or so upon the train's departure - luckily middle of the day expresses were not frequent! The teachers had also taught some of the children first aid, and every week they appointed one of the station children to be 'doctor' for the week to hold the first aid box and render appropriate aid until adults visited for school the next day. In later years two doctors from a local private hospital volunteered to come to the station every week and hold a clinic. A carpet on the concourse floor was the waiting room and each child in turn came forward to be examined and medication prescribed and provided.

Chest infections and skin diseases were rife and more serious diseases such as malaria and tuberculosis could be diagnosed early and treated in hospital, a situation uncommon for street children who often found themselves rejected by hospital staff unless accompanied by an adult willing to guarantee payment of the charges for drugs and food.

In fact, the absence of access to proper health care is one of the major problems street children face. In a survey undertaken by a Bombay charity in 1993 into the lifestyle and decisions of a random 1,000 street children in that city, only 5% reported access to health care provided by adults. 50% said they relied on help from other children and the remainder just put up with whatever ailment they suffered from and rested alone when they were sick.

On my first visit I was shaken by a number of things, not least the story of a young eight year old boy called Razi, who shyly offered me a calendar that he had made as a present. He was unable to speak and one of the Sarjan staff told me that he had run away from home as a result of severe violence he had suffered at the

Sarjan's 'surgery' in Ahmedabad station's booking hall, 2004

hands of his father. His mother was dead and his father was an alcoholic, who removed Razi from school and forced him to beg every day until he had enough money for the man to buy the drink he craved. If he came home at the end of the day with what the man deemed insufficient, as often as not the boy would be beaten. One day he knew he was in trouble and decided to argue with his father. The man, in a drunken rage, snatched up a kitchen knife and cut out the boy's tongue for daring to remonstrate with him. The boy fled and a Sarjan worker found him in a pitiful state on Ahmedabad station and got him to hospital where he was physically patched up, although he lost the power of speech. He was eventually able to describe what had happened through a mixture of role play and drawing. It had been some three months since that brutal incident and when the boy handed me the calendar, he smiled. According to the staff member present, it was the first time they'd seen him smile since he'd been found on the station. I'd like to think that it was at least the beginning of a happier time for Razi, but I was upset to hear a few weeks later that Razi had been unable to cope with his trauma and had run away from the project. Although his is an extreme case of abuse, staff told me that many of the children they came across had heartbreaking stories of violence and abuse they'd suffered before escaping as a last resort.

It was in Ahmedabad that I first tried to use my position as a senior railway manager to influence the railway authorities in India. The Sarjan staff were desperate to have a room on the station that they could use as a drop-in centre during the day and as a safe emergency shelter at night. The station inspector was sympathetic, but advised me to speak to the Area Manager. This I did. He also expressed support but told me that he could not allocate any space without authority from senior management. When later during the same visit I raised the matter in a meeting with the Indian Railways Board Member for Staff (which post had also responsibility for the Railway Protection Force - RPF) I was told that such permission could be given by local staff. This became typical of many of my early encounters with Indian railway managers - support given verbally, but an aversion to commit themselves in writing, and, at local level, a reluctance to act without the requisite piece of paper from someone in higher authority.

During my time as BR's Head of Safety Policy in the early 1990s, I had each year spent a day at the BR Staff College at 'The Grove', Watford, training around twenty senior Indian railway managers in safety management. I vividly remember one particular discussion during which I explained the UK railway management's concern at the number of passengers who fell to their death from moving trains - around twenty a year in the early 1990s. My statement was met with some incredulity by one of the managers present who apparently was responsible for the Bombay suburban service from Churchgate and VT stations - he alleged that they killed twenty a day! I assumed this was an exaggeration until I experienced the crush on virtually every suburban train, with passengers hanging out of the never-closed doors and even clinging to the roof under the overhead live power lines. As a result of contacts made at the Grove, I found I could gain admission to some of the most senior managers at the Indian Railways Headquarters at the Rail Bhavan in New Delhi and I began to lobby them on behalf of the street children living on stations and the organisations trying to help them. In some cases I found that the local NGO staff had been able to develop a good relationship with the area station manager, Divisional Railway Manager or RPF Divisional Superintendent and get some practical support. However, this was very much on a personal basis and often this co-operation did not survive the regular change of personnel as railway officers seemed to be promoted or retire every two years.

Shortly after taking on the Ahmedabad project as our first Indian venture, I received a suggestion from Save the Children, which was also a Consortium for Street Children member. I had approached their representatives earlier, seeking their ideas for a joint project. At first a partner working at Saigon station in Vietnam had been offered, but before we had completed enquiries, the suggested project was funded from a different source. Then we were asked if we would be willing to fund a project they wanted to start in Ulan Bator, capital of Mongolia, where - it was alleged - children were using the heating pipes under the railway station as their main refuge. This again came to nothing, as Save the Children, after we had proffered our willingness to consider this, had to admit that at that time they could find no local organisation through whom we could operate.

We were finally told about a programme in Calcutta that was thought to meet our criteria. That city has two main railway termini - Howrah and Sealdah. Howrah is a vast station, twenty five platforms or more, serving cities to the west, centre and south east of India. Sealdah is split into two - the South station serves stations in West and North Bengal, Assam and stations towards Bangladesh. The North station is purely for suburban stations serving the area known as 24 Parganas and the Sunderbans, where many village slum communities exist. Save the Children India were supporting a project working with 40 youngsters said to be the children of commercial sex workers operating round the Sealdah stations, children very vulnerable to sexual and physical abuse. The local NGO that was operating the programme was CINI Asha, a well-known Calcutta organisation that had a large mother-and-child health programme throughout the rural and urban suburbs, as well as a number of drop-in centres for street and slum children. A first visit to the area identified that most of the children we were supporting were from the 'red light' district of Calcutta named Rambagan rather than from Sealdah station, and I was taken there by CINI Asha's Director of Urban Services, an Irish nurse from Cork called Edith Wilkins.

I remember seeing a large number of children crammed into a couple of small rooms eagerly embracing the informal learning organised by Edith and spent nearly an hour talking to a group of older children who knew sufficient English to make it rewarding. During a question and answer session, one of the 14 or 15 year-old boys asked me why I was helping them - and before I could answer, asked me if it was a 'tax dodge'!

During my first visit to Calcutta, Edith also took me to a number of other projects for street children run by CINI Asha. They had a brand new centre in the city, an office headquarters and the site for many children's activities, which had been opened by Mary Robinson, then President of Ireland, who subsequently became a United Nations Human Rights Commissioner. Edith took me to a tiny drop-in centre and night shelter at Sealdah South station, a former signal cabin at the end of platform 10. A few months later Edith asked me if Railway Children would consider funding the Sealdah North and South station drop-in rooms, as the Irish NGO, GOAL, that had been funding them was having to make cut backs. This started Railway Children's longest running Indian programme. The Eastern Railway trade union, the Eastern Congress, had loaned their meeting room at Sealdah North during the day and the Sealdah South signalbox continued as a drop-in centre until the railway authority decided that its proximity to the track was too dangerous and offered CINI Asha an alternative building in the carriage sidings a couple of hundred yards further away.

By the end of 1997, Railway Children was funding partners in Romania, Mexico, India, Kenya and the UK. The annual income to sustain these programmes had risen rapidly to £75,000 and was over £120,000 in 1998. The charity was registered both with the Charity Commission and Companies House, we had a small office, a group of very professional trustees, two part time salaried staff and a group of willing volunteers from the Crewe and Nantwich areas.

Chapter 6
The charity develops

The charity, of course, was virtually unknown outside the UK railway industry. The fact that we operated in partnership with other NGOs who actually delivered the services both abroad and in the UK made it even less likely that our name would be recognised. Basically, at that time we were a grant-making body acting as a conduit for funds mostly from donors in the railway industry to local NGOs, albeit encouraging them to focus on my vision of early intervention to protect and offer options to new children on the street before they could be exploited, abused, corrupted and traumatised by their experiences. Then in 1998 a train of events occurred that would change our role and add even greater value to our intervention, so that the Railway Children became a true child development agency.

It began with an audacious and, in hindsight, a very optimistic application for a grant from the UK national lottery. Although we were only three years old, the trustees endorsed my suggestion that we should apply to the National Lottery Charities Board for support for work in India. I drafted and submitted an application for almost a quarter of a million pounds (over 3 years) to develop our partnerships, encompassing the running costs of our joint programmes with CINI Asha in Sealdah, Calcutta, Sarjan at Ahmedabad and three new potential partners. Two of these were developed through my association with Edith Wilkins, an Assistant Director of CINI Asha and in charge of some 23 individual projects in their urban street children programme. She took me to Howrah station (Calcutta) the far side of the Hooghly River where the Indian railway network branched from the sprawling station to points west and south to the rest of the Indian sub-continent. The 25-platform station hosted its own city of street living people, and many children - perhaps as many as 300-400 at any one time. Many would be coming in daily from the slums to earn money through informal trade, scavenging and begging. Others were children who had drifted to the station years earlier and found opportunities to survive, carving out territories for their commercial - often illegal - activities and maintaining a tenuous relationship with the railway authorities and police, often through corrupt means. Then there were the newly arriving runaways from the hinterlands, children running from physical and sexual abuse, or attracted to the city to try to earn more than they could ever dream about in their rural villages. Estimates have been made that major stations like Howrah, New Delhi and Victoria Terminus in Bombay were then each receiving as many as 20 or 30 new children every day.

Edith introduced me to one local Indian NGO working at Howrah, named SEED, led by a devout Moslem, Sadre Alam, which was opening up a project for a group of 30 young girls who'd been discovered sleeping rough on Howrah's platforms. The youngest of these girls was four, the oldest thirteen. They'd all been raped or sexually molested on the station, as a result of which several were HIV+. They were working in the local slum community during the day – an area made famous by the book and film 'City of Joy' (Anandnagar). SEED had managed to obtain the loan of a classroom of a small private school five minutes' walk from Howrah station and every night at 6pm two social workers employed by SEED would open up the emergency shelter, greeting the young girls with water for a wash, clean clothes and a hot meal. Afterwards, they would provide health care and advice, some basic education and an opportunity for these young girls to play and dance. After sleeping safely there, the girls would go back onto the streets in the morning as the school needed its classroom back.

Railway Children had begun to fund this project early in 1998 and I was invited to the opening. A group of elderly white-robed males was seated at the top table with the girls sitting cross-legged on the floor and a few local adults sitting, full of curiosity, at the back. After a number of speeches, which I could not understand as they were in Bengali, I was invited to say a few words which Edith translated for me. My efforts were greeted with guffaws of laughter from the children and I was a little taken aback as I was unaware that I had cracked any jokes! Edith told me afterwards that the children were laughing at her execrable Bengali! During the further speeches one young girl crawled out, plonked herself on my lap and promptly fell asleep. This was seven-year-old 'Babli'. Edith told me that she had survived by fetching water for the slum community from the nearest standpipe a kilometre away, eight hours a day, seven days a week, fifty two weeks a year for the princely sum of one rupee a day on which she was expected to survive. Now, when I make school visits to talk about street children, I often call for a seven year old girl to try to lift and carry a bucket of water across the hall or classroom, and rarely do they manage more than a few paces before we have to stop in case I'm in trouble with the teachers for flooding their school floor! In later years SEED was able to lease a building nearby to house the girls that wanted to leave the street and go to school, and many years later the Railway Children office received an e-mail from Babli thanking us for 'giving me my childhood back'.

The other Indian charity Edith commended to me was in far-away Andhra Pradesh in a city called Vijayawada, an important railway junction on the eastern coastal mainline route from Howrah to Chennai (Madras) and the far south, and the junction to the joint cities of Hyderabad and Secunderabad, and to the Deccan plain. The NGO 'SKCV' ('Street Kids Community Village', but in reality an Indian language acronym) was founded by an Englishman, Matthew Norton, son of a Cheshire GP, who was educated until aged 13 at St. Ambrose College in Hale Barns. He had a varied and colourful youth, was a nightmare teenager twice expelled from subsequent schools and finally left home to become

Matthew Norton, aka 'Manihara', at SKCV, 2001

a hippy, living on the streets for a year. At eighteen he married and in 1971 had a son, Marc, later known as Madhava. He and his wife joined the Hare Krishna Movement in 1974 leading a meaningful life after so much seeking. Later they sadly divorced, Madhava remaining with his father. Matthew travelled widely in the States and Europe but whilst working for them in India in his late 'twenties' he became worried about the plight of the thousands of children living on the streets and trains.

One night he was visited by two young boys one of whom was desperately ill, he got them treated in hospital and opened his home to other children from the street. The following night he had six children asking for help; by the end of the week twenty children were trying to share his flat! He took in nine of them but the Hare Krishna organisation was not interested in helping so he left. He decided to move to Pune, about 120 miles east of Bombay, to lease an old colonial house. He was discovered by other street children and eventually he set up a project there with a local secretary called Bhakti, whom he later married. SKCV Children's Trust was registered in 1984. Three years later he was approached at a conference by the mayor of far-off Vijayawada who explained the plight of street children in that city, especially at the station, and offered a house to Matthew if he would set up a project there.

After my visits to CINI Asha and SEED, I visited Matthew, though the journey was an experience in itself. I'd been booked on a train from Howrah through to Vijayawada, a 24 hour journey, but when I arrived at Howrah station I found chaos as the Bengali state railway staff were on strike and no trains were running within the state of West Bengal. I took a taxi to the airport and managed to find a flight to Visakhapatnam, a naval city on the Indian Ocean coast an eight-hour train journey away from Vijayawada. I got to the station about 3 o'clock in the afternoon and to my dismay found that there were only two trains a day southbound, one leaving in five minutes' time. I had no ticket, no reservation for this train, and saw long queues at the ticket office (I had still not fathomed the mysteries of Indian train booking hall procedures). It seemed hopeless until some guy saw my obvious confusion and (for an appropriate tip) got me a ticket ahead of the queue and bungled me and my luggage onto the slowly departing train, putting my documentation into the hands of a travelling ticket inspector, shouting at him to find me a berth. I duly arrived at Vijayawada at eleven o'clock at night, eight hours before I was expected!

Matthew (he styled himself 'Manihara' in India) met me the following morning and showed me round his headquarters in the city – a night shelter for street children, a sick bay, a vocational training centre (with computer training as key) and small admin office. He then took me to the Boys' Village on the banks of the River Krishna, rented for a peppercorn rent from the local small mosque. Up to 150 boys were housed there – after three months' regular attendance at the night shelter, boys were offered a place in the village if they wanted to leave street life and gain an education. The situation was idyllic and the day-to-day management, under Matthew's overall supervision, was in the hands of fourteen senior boys, known as the 'Future Group'.

Bhakti was headmistress of the school. Matthew had good relations with the city authorities, the local Divisional Railway Manager and Railway Protection Force Superintendent, and with our help set up a 'Child Assistance Booth' on the station jointly with Childline India and about three other NGOs in Vijayawada with whom Matthew collaborated closely in a city 'Children's Rights Forum'. On the station I saw many young girls as well as boys and Matthew expressed concern about their risk of being trafficked into domestic or sexual slavery – girls from the slum communities out of school faced the same risk, and Matthew asked

SKCV's 'Future Group' in session, 2001

if the Railway Children could find funding to set up an emergency shelter for such girls as he had previously done for the boys. We therefore included an application for this and for the SEED girls' shelter in our lottery application.

The final project we included in this lottery application was a small programme in Tamil Nadu in southern India called 'WORD'. I'd received out of the blue an application from a man called K.B.Samuel for support for shelters for children on stations on the metre gauge railway line between Katpadi Junction (Vellore) and Villupuram on the main Madras to Madurai route. The project plan seemed to fit exactly what I was trying to achieve in the charity and I had included it therefore in the grant application to the lottery. I duly travelled overnight by train and was met at Madras Egmont station by a very bewildered group who seemed very unsure of the purpose of my visit. En route to WORD's headquarters in the village of Polur, I discovered that the man who had applied to me for the grant for his programme had died suddenly the previous week and mystifyingly had said very little to his colleagues about his plans. However we continued. I showed the dead man's brother and widow the correspondence and project plans, and they committed themselves to take the project forward in his memory. Perhaps I was naïve in allowing this to go forward but their sincerity seemed so great and the widow – a senior grade nurse – and her brother - the local schoolteacher - were obviously highly committed, so I took the risk. I advised the lottery board of the changed circumstances and agreed to reduce the size of the grant for this aspect of my application to some initial pilot work including the purchase of a suitable building as a shelter for the children.

To my immense surprise and pleasure, I found that my application for £225,657 had been approved and was available for starting the programme from June 1998. A couple of years later, a member of the lottery grants programme team visited WORD. The report was mixed – the children were being looked after with care and were happy and all was in order financially, but the assessment indicated that the NGO was complacent and had little forward vision to change the situation for such children on a wider scale. We were reminded that we had other more mature and innovative programmes and that we should use our position as partners of several of them to add real value and not just be a means of providing needed financial resources to projects. In essence, we should become a development agency, using our experience and knowledge to strengthen our partners, facilitate networking and stimulate forward planning to identify the most effective ways of positively changing these children's lives.

Our Board of trustees took this implied criticism very seriously and debated our future strategy at length, realising that in the three or four years of our existence we had gained considerable insight into the lives of such vulnerable children both directly and through our involvement with other NGOs at the Consortium for Street Children. This lottery feedback report was important and was the catalyst for a major development of the charity.

We had not relied completely on the lottery grant. We had been active in developing our fundraising in other ways. In 1997 I had been invited to take part as one element of the new TV Channel 5's charity telethon 'Give 5' in the autumn. I worked closely with Zerbanoo Gifford, an Asian woman who was prominent in her society in Harrow and north west London. Zerbanoo was filmed in Bombay watching and talking to young street children and the presentation on one night of the telethon week was very effective and might have made a major funding contribution except for two facts. Channel 5 was still in its infancy and few households could yet receive it, and during the week it was broadcast the media was overwhelmed with the sudden death of Princess Diana and the telethon froze in its tracks. We had organised collections at the same time on a number of Railtrack stations and raised about £2,400 from that, but the telethon itself failed to raise more than £1,400 though that was twice the amount that any of the other telethon charities managed to raise that week.

A much more effective fundraising initiative around the same time was an approach I made to the Britt Allcroft company who had taken on the 'Thomas the Tank Engine' franchise from the Rev Awdry's family. I was invited to a lunch at their Southampton headquarters with their Marketing Director who explained their reluctance to partner any charity specifically but liked the possible link with the Railway Children and promised to see what they could do. Over lunch we had chatted about some of my railway experiences when I was a 'Fat Controller' in my own right (as a stationmaster and later as Chief Operating Manager of the BR London Midland Region where I was also 'Officer in Charge' of the

Royal Train). The following day I received a request to outline the plots of a few of my experiences which the Britt Allcroft scriptwriter could use in a new series of stories for the next video, 'Thomas and Friends'. A couple of days after I'd submitted my morning's scribbling on the typewriter, I received a call offering me a £10,000 donation for the charity and a two year contract to review the scripts of the videos to help them avoid complaints from adult 'children' who would write in to say that the stories had the signals back to front or the engines had the wrong number of wheels or rivets! I even got to attend a filming at the Shepperton studios of 'Gordon' ploughing through the station bufferstops and falling into the road outside – a scenario based on a famous poster of a French Crampton engine plunging through a station wall into the street, with an appropriate epithet stemming from the lips of the unfortunate engine driver! I often wonder if the Queen ever sat down to watch a 'Thomas' video with any of her grandchildren and if so, whether she recognised that one story, when the Fat Controller's mother on a VIP special complained of her bath water hitting the ceiling, was actually based on a real incident on the Royal Train! When the video was in the shops I noticed that I was named as the Associate Railway Consultant and I've even signed autographs on the video cover for two year olds as a result.

A further visit to India, in the company of Stan Judd, now the charity's official Treasurer, took place in the April of the following year, 1999. With a rapid increase in income, greatly helped by the lottery grant, we were able to look hard at possible further partners there. The number of children around India's railway stations was staggering and Edith Wilkins took us to visit a number of small NGOs working in the Calcutta slum suburbs around the railway tracks. Edith herself had been moved on from CINI Asha by GOAL, the Irish NGO that had sent her to India in the first place, asking her to use her experience to develop a number of smaller NGOs working with street and working children.

As a result of her recommendations we started to partner a number of local NGOs working beside the suburban lines out of both Sealdah and Howrah. One was OFFER, an NGO working at Dum Dum Junction north of Calcutta, where we funded the purchase of a residence to act as an emergency shelter for children arriving at the station. Another was Sabuj Sangha, which wanted to build a home for street girls in a suburb where there was a Hindu shrine which was the focus of red light activities, putting the girls at great risk. Cosmos and VSS were another two NGOs that set up informal schools in the illegal settlements on railway land adjacent to the running railway lines.

A visit was made to one of seven informal schools on the line from Sealdah to Budge Budge, run by Cosmos. The school was a bamboo structure beside the line opposite Lakeside station (a misnomer if it referred to the stinking stagnant pool that one could sense if not see from the station) in an area of Calcutta known as Tollygunge. It served a community of some 300 men, women and children, with somewhere between 75 and 100 children aged between 5 and 12 crammed into its tiny confines to be taught by one teacher. After the usual welcome (garlands, concert of party pieces) we looked at the children's work and mingled, before being invited to join one of the parents for a cup of chai under the one long platform that serve the 12 coach electric suburban trains. 106 homes were quite literally hollowed out under the platform, the only access being from the railway line, which hosted a train approximately every ten minutes on this busy commuter line. I crawled in with some trepidation, and found a spotless earth home and a brightly 'sari-ed' lady serving the brew from burnished implements.

The Tollygunge slum, just before its destruction by fire, 1999

Early the following morning I was awakened with the news from Edith that the whole slum had burned down during the night as a result of an upturned open stove. Stan and I quickly agreed that I should return to the site to give what help I could, while he would fulfil our commitment to meet the Railway Divisional Manager that morning. I hurried out to find a smouldering acre of land with no remaining building of any sort except for the bamboo school. Apparently the local population valued this so much that they'd given it priority for saving over their own homes. Many people from the community had been badly burned and one child – one who had been in the welcoming party the day before – had died. No fire engines or ambulances had attended the slum and we found a pitiful group of people standing helplessly around surveying the wreckage.

Edith took charge. Two of her own charity's trustees were present, one of whom, like her, was a nurse. A local doctor came, who attended the community occasionally to offer free treatment to the children. We all pooled whatever cash we had immediately available and the doctor and I walked a mile to the nearest chemist and bought up his stocks of medical supplies that we thought would be most useful. Meanwhile Edith and her trustees gathered the injured into some sort of priority queue. It was over an hour before we returned and found the long and silent queue except for the sound of an occasional whimper from one of the injured children. We cleaned up an area on the floor of the school as best we could and set up an emergency treatment centre. The doctor diagnosed the treatment required while Edith and her colleague applied burns ointment, cleansed and bandaged, and I acted as medical orderly, cutting bandages, finding the right painkilling pills, bottles of disinfectant etc., trying all the time to interpret correctly the cacophony of Hindi, Bengali, Irish and English voices. After more than five hours in the debilitating heat and having just reached the last patient in the diminishing queue, a politician turned up with a TV camera crew and tried to take credit for what Edith and her helpers had achieved. He received short shrift from the adults present, who forced him off their land while two of the children took Edith gently by the arms and guided her between the burnt out tarpaulins to the safety of the main road. We all followed her, embarrassed at the profuse and excessive expressions of thanks that were coming from many members of that impoverished community.

When we were back at Edith's office, we began to think of the next things the community would need and made contact with our organisations and donors back in the UK to seek – and were given – funds for bamboo poles and tarpaulins to provide shelter to the community. The problem was the temporary nature of these slums and the ever-present threat of eviction by the city or railway authorities. In fact, several years later, this slum was demolished by bulldozers sent in by the authorities and the people were scattered, most without any compensating alternative housing. As well as the distress caused to each of the families, it disrupted the education of the children in the informal schools and brought to nothing some of the investment made. This was not the only reason why Railway Children began to question the effectiveness of such informal slum schools. We found many parents reluctant to allow their children to attend such schools as they needed them to earn money to augment family income; sometimes the children were the only breadwinners! Frankly, these communities needed government or large agency investment in adequate housing, sanitation, health care and income generation as well as education, and Railway Children did not have the resources for such a holistic approach.

I had also assumed that the children in these slums were genuine 'railway children', at risk of drifting from their communities beside the track to the main city stations. However, I began to discover that this was not often the case. Certainly some of the older children would travel into the city centres to earn money, but most would return at night to their families. The children in the main stations with little or no family contact tended to be from distant rural villages. Therefore, over the next few years, Railway Children gradually withdrew from such projects, leaving them to be partnered by agencies such as UNICEF and Save the Children, while we concentrated on the newly arrived lone children who had lost contact with their families or had been abandoned by them.

Chapter 7
The need to demonstrate UK action

The Railway Children Board decided early on to devote a percentage of its charitable expenditure to projects for runaway children in the UK. Since 1997 we had been seeking an opportunity to do more to help runaway children in London. So when the St Pancras parish church crypt scheme was deemed impracticable, and the British Transport Police discouraged the provision of information computers at London rail terminals, we developed the partnership with the Suzy Lamplugh Trust as described earlier in chapter 4. I used my influence to persuade Railtrack to provide a base and communication facilities at Kings Cross station East Side offices for the Trust's new 'Get Connected' subsidiary organisation and found myself acting as Chair of the trustees of this newly registered charity when Diana Lamplugh, having launched the free phone referral scheme for children, stepped down to encourage it to develop independently of the Suzy Lamplugh Trust, although she retained a close and inspiring interest for many years.

The early trustee meetings of 'Get Connected' were exciting affairs as we recruited and trained volunteer operators to receive the children's calls, offer support and make suggestions to our increasing number of callers. We appointed an excellent Chief Executive, Di Stubbs, and Fredwyn Hosier, our trustee from the Samaritans, undertook – with Diana Lamplugh - much of the early training. We wrestled with the necessary legalities in separating the charity from its founding partner and drawing up our new Articles of Association and Rules & Guidelines, developing the charity's membership to include both organisations and individuals, and ensuring a balance in the Board of Trustees of skills from the original committee of participating charities, individuals and volunteers. Much of this detail is now forgotten, but I do remember the generous supply of Jaffa Cakes with which those early meetings were so copiously supplied.

This charity's national scope and media publicity among children and young people soon ensured a recognition rate of around 20-25% from those thought to be the target beneficiaries and annual call rates of 12-15,000 – excluding hoaxes and children who rang off before speaking. After running on a shoestring for two or three years, a new Chief Executive, Justin Irwin, managed to develop a very beneficial partnership with the Carphone Warehouse who saw the synergy with their own business activities. They provided new premises and equipment jointly with their own, enabling many staff of the company to become volunteer shift operators. Charles Dunstone, founder and Chairman of the Carphone Warehouse, took over as the non-executive Chair of 'Get Connected', whilst Andrew McNaughtan of Save the Children replaced me as Executive Chair. Railway Children provided substantial funding during the early years but was able to scale this down as the Carphone Warehouse increased their involvement with the helpline, ultimately retaining contact and interest through membership of the English Coalition on Runaways.

Other Railway Children partnered UK projects followed. Another helpline we supported was the 'Runaways Helpline' (part of the Missing Persons NGO) where we funded the permanent non-volunteer staff on the night shift, a critical time for young runaways. We questioned the need for three national helplines for children but concluded that each did have a specific role and there

Volunteers manning the 'Get Connected' UK helpline, 2004

was little if any duplication – Childline was a phone service for youngsters to report abuse and bullying and receive phone counselling and advice; the 'Runaway Helpline' was focused very much on child runaways and finding them emergency accommodation; 'Get Connected' was a 'catch-all' for a wide variety of children's and young person's issues and was basically a signposting and referral service.

Railway Children also worked in partnership with the Scottish NGO, the Aberlour Trust, to fund a drop-in and counselling centre – 'Running Other Choices' ('ROC') - in Glasgow working closely with the Strathclyde police. This led to the Scottish Executive funding an emergency 3-bedded short term refuge for children for whom other social services and fostering placements were not working. We funded a family worker in Cheltenham - of all places - to work with children at risk through an NGO called 'ASTRA' which worked closely with the local authority there. One of our early young advocates in our brochures was a young woman, Sarah, who had lived on the streets of Cheltenham and Gloucester from the age of 12 and had been helped by ASTRA and now

Sally Thomsett names the HST Power Car 43098, 1998

wanted to give something back, having the ambition to become a social worker.

We were aware that few children were being found on our railway stations compared with the previous decade – stricter barrier controls, CCTV and police presence were inhibiting factors – but encountered children begging on London Underground stations. We therefore commissioned and funded the Children's Society to research the plight of Roma children found on the streets and platforms of London – a piece of work deemed innovative and courageous by our chosen partners in the light of society's frequent stigmatisation and condemnation of such children. During this project we became aware of other research into running away in the UK (*Rees G & Lee J, 2005, 'Still Running 2: Findings from the Second National Survey of Young Runaways.' London: The Children's Society*) and the large numbers of estimated annual runaways – 100,000 under the age of 16 – including large numbers of children who drop off the edge, as their families for a number of worrying reasons fail to report them missing.

In May 1998, Railway Children decided to fundraise jointly with Centrepoint, the London based project for homeless youth, through a Dinner and Ball held at the National Railway Museum in York. One of our trustees, Steve McColl, and his wife Helen, knew that Centrepoint had experience in running such events and they promised to combine with us pooling their knowledge with our enthusiasm and contacts within the railway industry. Steve also negotiated sponsorship of a special High Speed Diesel Train (HST) with Virgin to carry our guests from London to York via Birmingham – GNER at that time were not yet 'on board' with the charity. I knew he'd fixed something special before departure from Euston and found I was to be part of a naming ceremony. An ex-works HST in Virgin livery awaited us by a rostrum on the platform near the rear power car, No. 43098, and the 1970 'Railway Children' film star, Sally Thomsett did the honours with the Deputy Chairman of Virgin Trains, revealing a splendid 'Railway Children' nameplate with the charity's logo, a brief description of what the charity did and its telephone number. A year or so later, the charity office received a phone call from a group of 'Rotarians' from Bakewell in Derbyshire who regularly took day trips by train and were nicknamed 'The Railway Children' by their colleagues. They'd been photographed by the HST at Chesterfield during one

The Railway Ball reception in the National Railway Museum's Great Hall, York, 1998

of their outings, noticed the phone number when the photo was printed and rang to find out who we were. They have been regular and generous donors ever since!

The Dinner and Ball at York was a great success – a school orchestra performed on the turntable in the main exhibition hall and dinner was served alongside the royal train exhibits. Guests danced amid the burnished steam engines and £60,000 profit was made which we split with Centrepoint, some of the funding going to a small refuge opposite Kings Cross station in property owned by the Peabody Trust. At the end of the evening the Chairman of English, Welsh and Scottish Railways, Ed Burkhardt, presented the charity with a nameplate from a withdrawn EWS diesel, 47712 'Lady Diana Spencer' to be auctioned to raise funds. The following day I staggered home in a cramped diesel multiple unit with the 8' long nameplate occupying the seat next to me which caused a certain amount of wry comment from the other passengers. We arranged initially for a well-known auction company to put the nameplate on its next auction list, thinking that it might raise some interest from the USA as well as the UK, but it failed to reach the reserve. So we tried again through Ian Wright of Sheffield Railway Memorabilia Auctions who managed to get a most useful £10,200 for us.

A couple of years later we felt we could use the experience we'd gained by running our own event for people within the industry. One of our trustees, Chris Jago, had, as Director, Railtrack Southern Zone, attended an Airports Authority charity dinner and ball as a guest of Gatwick Express, when the beneficiary charity had received around £180,000. Chris and another of our trustees, former General Manager of BR's Southern Region, Gordon Pettitt, got together a committee of senior managers from the industry to plan the outline, and Railtrack generously provided £20,000 risk capital enabling us to hire a professional events company to run the whole evening. Our first 'solo' Railway Ball was held at the Intercontinental Hotel near Hyde Park in London and raised £110,000 profit for us. The success of this event and the fact that this was the only social event of the privatised railway encouraged us to seek a larger venue the following year, and every year since we have held the Railway Ball on the last Friday evening of November in the Great Room at the Grosvenor House Hotel.

The event is organised for us by the Railway Ball Committee and the Conference Line Events Company and has averaged a return of around a quarter of a million pounds annually. By 2010 it had brought in more than £2 million for the charity, in valuable 'unrestricted' funds. Such undesignated income on this scale is of huge importance and it is unusual and increasingly welcomed as it is not tied to specific projects, but leaves us free to use it as needs and priorities dictate. Each year we manage around 1,000 dinner guests – often oversubscribed and have run up a waiting list! In the earlier years of the event it brought in some third of our annual income and caused me a few anxious moments as we relied so heavily on it. The problem was the risk of having to make a late cancellation should some catastrophe happen days before. Indeed, the train crash at Hatfield nearly caused just such an eventuality and we

Nameplate of diesel locomotive 47.712

debated with our journalist trustee whether we ought to cancel, with not just the consequential loss of revenue but with heavy costs to bear as well. He advised that few would begrudge an event raising money for some of the most vulnerable children in the world, but Railtrack managers had taken a lot of 'flak' over the accident and felt they could not be seen to be joining a social event at that time although they generously donated the costs of the tables they had already booked.

As a result of this narrow escape from a damaging financial blow, we set up the Railway Ball as a separate company that would donate all profits to Railway Children. This safeguarded the charity's funds should a disaster occur causing the Ball's cancellation. I'm pleased to say that this has not yet been the case. While the core income comes from the sales of over eighty tables, other fundraising opportunities take place at the event including both a table and silent auction and various games. The railway industry has supported the event magnificently by sponsorship, the donation of prizes and fundraising on the night.

The Ball Committee continues to have representatives of many train operating and infrastructure companies as well as of suppliers of equipment and providers of financial and legal services. During the Ball, I have been able to say a few words about the charity's work when I've talked about our partners in the UK as well as in India and elsewhere and have shown excerpts from videos shot in India that have had television coverage. The Railway Ball is still an annual fundraising fixture, raising 10% of our annual income. This remains an important event, but we are not now quite so dependent on it as we were at first, having progressively diversified our fundraising since in many directions.

Chapter 8
People

I was never quite on my own. Very quickly I recruited Stan Judd, my former 'best man' and friend since the early 1960s, to help me with the admin and book-keeping. I asked other railway colleagues to join a committee I formed to advise me while we got the charity off the ground and several of them became trustees once the charity was registered, as recounted in chapter 5. Initially I also had some help on the necessary admin work from volunteers from local churches. Within a couple of years I'd been joined by part-timers Julia Worthington and Katie Mason and not long after by Helen Collison as a part time administrator, but by the end of the century it was becoming very apparent that I needed some full time help. It was recognised that apart from increasing management capacity to meet the needs of the growing size and workload, it was necessary to reduce the vulnerability of the charity as so much information, know-how and effort was in my hands and those of Stan Judd. We were well aware that this kind of vulnerability had been the downfall of many a small but valuable charity in the past.

In particular, as our range of partner projects increased in India, I was finding it difficult to spend sufficient time with our partners there, which now ranged from Delhi in the north west, and Calcutta in the north east, to Bombay on the west coast, and Vellore and Villupuram in Tamil Nadu in the far south, all more than 24 hours away from each other even by the fastest trains. I made it my policy to travel by train in India, partly to see and experience the reality of street children on the railways and partly because it was so much cheaper than flying. I was pointed in the direction of a fount of knowledge on Indian rail travel, a former Indian Railways officer, who ran a travel agency in Wembley. I would purchase an 'All-India Rail Pass' for two or three weeks and he would arrange the reservations essential on all main line trains. I was never once let down by bookings made there – every coach I travelled in duly had my typewritten name correctly assigned to my berth on the side of the coach. For my visits in the late 90s and early the next century I would typically be alternating between a night on a train and one at a hotel, many of a quite satisfactory standard costing less than £10 a night. This, in the heat of the country, could be a little wearing, especially as a couple of years I'd delayed my visits until April, when the land was heating up towards its maximum before the onset of the monsoon.

With the developments stimulated by the lottery grant and through Edith Wilkins' recommendations, the sheer number of projects I needed to visit each time was becoming impracticable. At first I asked Matthew Norton at Vijayawada to act on my behalf to keep an eye on our partners and become a conduit for our funds to the individual projects. He had his own heavy workload to supervise and he was not a fit man, so it was essential to find some more permanent assistance within India. In other countries we were working with UK NGOs who themselves were supervising their partners abroad, so the problem was not so acute elsewhere. In Ahmedabad in the western state of Gujarat I had been introduced by the management of our partner, Sarjan, to a well known architect, Kirtee Shah, one of their patrons, who in turn commended a friend of his to me, Gopal Dutia, who lived in Bombay and was a retired senior manager of UNICEF. I met Gopal in his flat close to VT station and discussed the possibility of him helping me find some assistance in India. We discussed the types of people needed to fulfil the roles we envisaged, and Gopal persuaded a friend of his who was a 'head-hunter' to put his skills

Mrinalini Rao playing cricket with streetboys at Sealdah station, Calcutta, 2002

at our disposal. The result was a short list of people that Gopal and I interviewed to cover our projects in the west of the country and we quickly determined the most suitable of these to be a young woman graduate from a good Bombay university who had experience of working with some of the most difficult street youth through a local NGO called Saathi. Mrinalini Rao was a godsend and ten years later was our Indian Country Director based in Bombay, and was later appointed to the vital role of being one of the three-person Juvenile Justice Board for that mega-city.

Matthew Norton in Vijayawada and colleagues at New Hope, a programme of emergency night shelters all down the east coast railway, brought a number of names to me, but commended a young man, Mohan Rao, who had been brought up in New Hope and who, with his brother, had been running a small charity for street boys at Guntur station about 25miles from Vijayawada in the state of Andhra Pradesh. Both appointees had a number of language qualifications – in particular, Mrinalini had Hindi, Kanada, Marathi and a smattering of Bengali as well as English at her command, a very useful skill in a country where so many languages were spoken. We arranged for these two Programme Officers as we called them to work from their homes and each had the supervisory responsibility for four or five partner programmes, spending a week or so at each every six months or so as well as time with us and Matthew. A further idea we pursued with some enthusiasm was the forming of our network of partner programmes into a Federation – the Railway Children Federation of India (RCFI) – and to my surprise, in a country that I thought was the prime exponent of bureaucracy, I found that Matthew and his colleagues, with some appropriate signatures, were able to set it up legally almost overnight. This was done during the visit I'd made to appoint Mrinalini and Mohan and we even appointed officers of the new Federation from those we had gathered at Vijayawada. These RCFI appointments were temporary in order to get the organisation registered and we added other officers from partners in the north and west when we got the Federation partners altogether for the first time a few months later. The purpose of the RCFI was primarily to enable our partners to meet with each other and network, sharing their experiences of what worked – and what didn't.

Initially under the Chairmanship of Matthew, the RCFI operated enthusiastically and shared ideas well and brought our partners together for useful exchanges of experience. Later personalities changed and, like many networks in India, became less effective when some individuals sought their own interests first and eventually we found it more effective to co-ordinate and share experiences with the Railway Children office in Mumbai taking the initiative.

We continued to work closely with Matthew, however, who was known throughout SKCV as 'Pitaji' (father). 25 years of caring for children was life's blood for Matthew but it took its toll on him. He also suffered from severe osteoporosis sustaining many broken bones and requiring two new hips, and finally severe pain from a nerve trapped in a healed broken back. He was given the prestigious Annual Award from the All-India Rotary International for his outstanding services to children. A year later, greatly incapacitated, he died suddenly and quite unexpectedly on 1 June 2009 aged fifty six, a loss to both SKCV and Railway Children.

It was on this earlier trip, I think, that I experienced one of my more exotic Indian rail journeys. Mohan or Matthew – I can't remember which – had booked me a reservation on a train to Anantapur, in the south of Andhra Pradesh, and assumed that I'd rather go all the way via a through slow train that did not require any changes rather than on two expresses involving a four hour wait at Guntakal, a large railway junction. This meant a hair-raising taxi trip in the dark on the 25 miles of dangerous roads to Guntur before joining the slow passenger train, which was booked to call at all stations and take 14 hours. At Guntur a porter took my case onto his head and resolutely refused to believe that I was really travelling on this particular train! There was no such thing as a sleeping car, second or third or any class, and I found a corner seat on the wooden bench in a compartment whose windows were open to the balmy air with only three bars across them to prevent large objects entering or leaving the train. Once the train was in motion, I found I was the object of much friendly curiosity, being visited by a large percentage of the train's passengers come to marvel at this white man travelling on an all stations slow train. I can't remember how many times I was asked if I knew someone's relative in Bradford or Southall! About halfway as dawn was breaking we spent nearly 45 minutes manoeuvring an extra coach full of Indian army soldiers onto the front of the train and then, later as the sun was really hotting up, stood for two hours in the baking heat outside Guntakal station, where, I was reliably informed, they were still changing the gauge from metre to Indian Railway's standard 'broad' gauge to allow us into the platform!

I eventually staggered out of the train in mid afternoon, some three hours late, to be met by a very patient Charles, Director of the YMCA project for street children in Anantapur, with whom Railway Children had linked through Y-Care International, one of the CSC members in London. I was made welcome in his home by his wife and two daughters and visited the project which had a residential home for street boys which included some interesting vocational training elements including an Emu farm and a plantation of trees for eventual felling as timber – both businesses being used to teach some of the children a trade and to help the project become financially self-sustaining.

During the course of my travels on Indian Railways I became highly conscious of my former work as a senior safety manager in British Rail. On one occasion I was led by my NGO host and a woman from the Railway Women's Welfare Organisation (RWWO - mainly made up of the wives of railway senior officers) from the end of platform 1 at Howrah station where we'd been looking for potential accommodation for a night shelter, right across the tracks at the throat of the station to platform 15 where there was said to

A typically overcrowded Bombay suburban train, 2002

be a vacant small building. It was dusk, and electric trains were constantly on the move in and out of the station as we picked our way over the tracks with what looked like half of the rest of Calcutta's poor population, and I was petrified. Later, in Bombay, I joined a suburban EMU at its originating station - I'd visited a small nature park near Borivli with our family's sponsored girl and her family - but after scrums at the next three stations I found myself pushed out of the open door on the opposite side to the platforms and hung on grimly to the waist of the man who'd shoved himself in front of me, now well outside the carriage door. Both times I was reciting incredulously to myself 'you are a safety manager - what are you doing here?' On two other occasions I joined Bombay suburban trains that were so packed that I travelled well beyond the station where I wished to alight.

Gordon Pettitt, who had supported Railway Children from its inception, became Deputy Chairman and accompanied me on another hectic visit to India late in 1999. I think he was a little startled by how much I was trying to squeeze into the torrid days and suggested we took the Sunday off and do some sightseeing. I had to admit that I'd been so busy with projects on the stations or in the slums that I'd seen little of the fantastic sights India has to offer. We went to the tourist railway booking office at Delhi and

Gordon Pettitt outside an informal school for street and working children, Calcutta 1999

despite my scepticism, managed to obtain two tickets for us to visit Agra for the following day, out on the Shatabdi Express and returning on the Taj Express. We duly allowed ourselves to be chaperoned by a taxi driver for the day for the not unreasonable sum of 1,300 rupees - about £15 - and got to see the Moghul Emperor Akbar's deserted vast palace complex at Fatehpur Sikri as well as the Taj Mahal itself. However, we missed out on the Agra Fort as our taxi driver - clearly in cahoots with one of the very many tourist traps - insisted on taking us to a carpet and marble gift shop instead. When we arrived back at Agra station, we found there had been a major power failure and all the station lights and signals were affected. We struggled in the darkness to discover our train, as all were running around four hours late and most only had Hindi script destination boards. Eventually we found our seats on the right train and got back to Delhi at midnight in one piece.

I had another palace visit on my next visit in 1999, although this time in the line of duty. I'd been introduced to the Chief of Staff of an Indian Maharajah in a Delhi club by one of the British ex-pats working in the city, who took an interest in my activities and had introduced me to a small NGO run by a former street boy in Delhi Cantt station (the former British army cantonment). On my way from Delhi to Ahmedabad I was persuaded to alight at Jaipur and invited to tour the Maharajah's palace and then brief the Maharajah himself on street children work, as there was to be a Millennium banquet there and someone had suggested that any profits from the event should go to a street children charity. After my tour of the palace I was introduced to the Maharajah, a gentle elderly man of some 70 years, but whose first question threw me: he wanted to know what a 'street child' was! I was amazed that such an apparently kindly man did not know, and I felt like taking him to his palace gates and saying 'Look! There!' pointing to the myriad scruffy children playing and scavenging outside. Then I realised that he'd been insulated from such sights for years - he only left the palace in a darkened limousine en route to his 5 star hotel or golf club and was genuinely unaware of the ragged children within a stone's throw of his palace. We discussed the plight of these children and as a result I went in search of a local Jaipur NGO working for street children in the city, but in the event the costs of the spectacular banquet were very high and I'm not sure if any profit was made.

I had another experience of the attitude of some high profile Indian celebrities on the same visit - but this time in my view with much less excuse. I'd been invited to give a paper at a 1999 child rights conference organised by Calcutta University at the Science Park conference centre - I think Edith Wilkins had suggested me. That went well enough and aroused some interest from the 500+ delegates and simultaneously, apparently, there was a youth conference going on. At the last session three young girls - I would guess 14-15 year olds - were invited to present their conclusions from the youth conference which they did very eloquently before a panel of three academics chaired by a male TV personality (who reminds me now very much of the quizmaster in the film 'Slumdog Millionaire'). After polite and supportive comments by the academics, the celebrity Chairman weighed in with a scathing attack on the presence of these girls and their presentation, implying patronisingly that such inexperienced youth had nothing of value to give. The conference was appalled and gave the girls a standing ovation. Afterwards I was interviewed by two of these pupils of St Xavier's school in Calcutta, as they wanted to put something about the Railway Children in the school magazine they were writing. I congratulated them and assured them that the conference totally rejected the reaction of the panel Chairman and had appreciated what they had said. Ten years later I was contacted by e-mail by one of these girls who was now doing work with vulnerable children in the voluntary sector, was a journalist and clearly highly qualified and motivated.

Having appointed two India Programme Officers - Mrinalini Rao and Mohan Rao (no relations) - I now turned to the needs of the British organisation. Our income was now reaching nearly half a million pounds annually with the Railway Ball, lottery grant and increasing recognition and support from a number of railway companies. We had also become a partner with three other CSC members of a payroll giving scheme, opening this up to our industry company network as well as the databases of the other charities – ChildHope (our joint partner in Romania), International Children's Trust (with whom we worked in Mexico) and the UK children's helpline 'Get Connected'. We celebrated this in the summer of 2000 by taking part in the weekend open days at Old Oak Common diesel depot where we had a stand in the former train crew office where I'd worked during college holidays some 40 years previously. There we named another locomotive after the 'Railway Children Partnership', this time a newly painted English Welsh & Scottish Railway class 90 electric locomotive, No. 90031, the ceremony being conducted again by Sally Thomsett but this time jointly with Clare Thomas, an 11 year old girl who had played the same role of 'Phyllis' in the Carlton TV remake of 'The Railway Children' film the previous year.

We therefore advertised for a Chief Executive and got four applicants whom I, and a couple of my colleague trustees, interviewed. One applicant, Terina Keene, withdrew as she'd been appointed to a good IT post – she'd just returned from a 2-year spell with her husband in Houston, USA – but she advised us that if we found none of the other applicants suitable, she'd reconsider as she was drawn to our post for personal reasons even though it did not pay as well as the other. We took Terina up on this and appointed her in January 2002, our first full time employee. Before her spell in the States Terina had been Financial Director – and for a short time Acting Director – of another locally based charity, CLIMB, which undertook research and supported families of children who had rare metabolic diseases. The founders of that charity, incidentally, also lived in the same road as me in Nantwich and their daughter, who suffered from one of those diseases, attended the same school as my children – small world!

Terina soon realised the inadequacies of our Breeden House office and negotiated with the Borough Council for an office at Scope House, just ten minutes walk from Crewe station (eight minutes if you're accompanying Stan Judd!). We started with just one small office there but Terina had mentioned that we were an expanding organisation and therefore qualified for, and got, a larger room in a block earmarked for developing companies as Crewe was trying to diversify employment from both the motor (Rolls Royce) and railway industries. Terina and I realised we needed a full time administrator as Helen had resigned and Julia was increasingly occupied with helping Katie on fundraising opportunities, so we decided to regularise this and appointed Pete Kent, a young man with an MSc in Development Studies and with overseas experience in the voluntary sector that looked more than adequate for the work we required him to do. In fact, he'd lived for a couple of years teaching at a village school in Tanzania run by a charity, which he and his mother had started. Clearly Pete had career development opportunities in this field and we were lucky to get him – but he wanted to stay in the Crewe area for family reasons and there were not too many opportunities for voluntary sector employment there, most being in London or the South East.

We'd been holding our Board meetings at the headquarters of London Transport, 55 Broadway, over St James's Park tube station. We'd formed that contact during an earlier reception the charity had hosted at the London Transport Museum in Covent Garden. Judith Brinkley, our Meetings Secretary, commended to me Rosemary Day, a London Transport Board Member with many other Board and charity sector interests, and she joined us becoming in due course our Treasurer in succession to Stan Judd, and later still, Deputy Chair of the charity when Gordon Pettitt retired. In 2000 we celebrated our five year anniversary with a reception at the London Transport Museum in Covent Garden and had the presence - and the support - of three towering figures from the railway industry, namely Sir Alistair Morton, then Chairman of the Strategic Rail Authority, Sir Philip Beck, Chairman of the Railtrack Board, and Denis, later Lord, Tunnicliffe. Judith also introduced us to the Catholic Building Society and we held a number of our Board and Committee meetings later at their offices in Victoria.

UK Railway Children staff on a canal outing, 2004 – left to right: Julia Worthington, Stan Judd, Pete Kent, Frank Gillies, Terina Keene, Katie Mason, Lindsay Gardner

We'd applied in 2002 to Comic Relief for a major grant, especially as our three-year lottery grant was coming to a close, and I'd prepared the application with Terina to cover five years' costs of a number of our Indian partners, as Comic Relief had opened up a new category of funding – international grants for street and working children from twenty specified countries outside Africa, their longstanding overseas priority. These new countries included India and I was pleased when we passed the first stage and had a five-hour assessment in our new Scope House Board Room with one of Comic Relief's experienced assessors. The strong focus of our work backed by professional methodologies and the robust systems we had in place for management which reflected the Charity Commission's eight 'hallmarks of an effective charity', meant that we were recommended for a grant and were delighted at our first effort to receive news of a five-year grant of nearly £600,000 to support six of our Indian NGO partners and the Railway Children Federation of India itself.

Chapter 9
The Comic Relief programme

The Comic Relief grant enabled Railway Children to make a sustained deepening of its work in India, assured now of a five-year rolling programme underpinning between a third and half of our work there. We were developing a common pattern of early intervention by supporting Indian NGOs that had outreach through street educators and social workers on railway platforms and meeting key trains; obtaining rooms on stations or nearby to act as drop-in centres for street children and emergency night shelters; providing immediate child welfare needs - protection, food, health care; providing opportunities for child development through education - informal, mainstreaming to state schools or boarding schools; giving opportunities for vocational training for older children; and providing counselling and rehabilitation if a child was prepared to go back to a suitable home.

A number of key partners were included in this grant. Three were in the city of Calcutta where at one stage we'd had seven partners, although we had ceased to partner a couple of these that were in slum settlements beside the suburban railway lines. CINI Asha was our longest standing Indian partner - a major player in the city in health care for women and children in particular and with a large urban programme including street children shelters and drop-in centres. We'd started with the children in the red light areas, but had concentrated on the two shelters at the Sealdah stations. At the end of platform 10 at Sealdah South was an old signalbox which had been a street children shelter for many years, originally supported by the Irish NGO GOAL, but taken on by Railway Children in 1997. Anything up to 50 children could be found there daily, squashed into the small space having informal school lessons or receiving food and general help. From time to time the railway authorities would try to close the centre, citing safety of the children as a reason. It was not the safest location, it must be admitted, with trains going in and out of the station just yards away, but it could equally be argued that without the shelter the children would be even less safe. More than once we had to call on help to save the shelter, on one occasion from a local powerful politician, Mamata Banerjee, later Minister of Railways in the Congress coalition government. Eventually the railways decided they would not allow the centre to operate there any more - the lengthening of the platforms was on their agenda - and they found us another and better building a few hundred yards away beside the carriage sidings. It was certainly more self-contained and safer, but a bit too far from the station to be a natural drop-in for the children and became more of a temporary residential centre for children who had become detached from their families.

The other drop-in centre at Sealdah was at the North station, a further dozen or so platforms and separated from the South by a cart track – 'road' would be too grandiose a word - alongside which was a room belonging to the Eastern Congress, the railway trade union. They had loaned the room to CINI Asha as a further drop-in centre for some of the boys who hung round the main line station. The role was similar though and CINI's staff visited both, and teaching at the informal schools there as well as proving food and health care. CINI Asha had a number of other drop-in centres in the city for girls as well as boys, but they received funds from a number of sources, so Railway Children concentrated on the two station shelters and their running costs and gradually weaned their funding off the other locations such as the informal education of children in the red light areas, for though it was useful it was not really within the particular remit of Railway Children.

SEED was the second Calcutta NGO to be funded by the Comic Relief grant. I have described earlier (chapter 6) the girls' shelter that had rescued the thirty girls found sleeping rough on Howrah station, but SEED also had a boys' drop-in centre and with the grant we were able to help them develop a residential centre for boys undergoing education or vocational training before moving on home or into the community. I had watched one of the BBC TV series on 'great railway journeys of the world' and seen Ian Hislop taking the train from Howrah to one of the Maharajah's palaces in Rajasthan and travelling on the 'Palace on Wheels' special opulent train. Before he boarded the train in Howrah, a boy crippled by polio scooted by on a skateboard, begging. Ian made a sympathetic remark about the boy's plight and I wrote telling him about our work at the station. I was pleasantly surprised to receive a few hand scribbled words from Ian a few days later and a very

Boy begging at Howrah station, Calcutta, 1999

generous cheque 'for the street children of Calcutta'. He has since supported us every year and we used the money to retain the drop-in centre while using the Comic Relief grant for the girls' shelter and boys' 'half-way house'.

The third Calcutta NGO to receive funds from Comic Relief via us was an NGO called 'OFFER' at a large junction to the north east of the city called 'Dum Dum' where presumably the bullets of that name were invented. This station had a great many platform children and we'd helped fund a residential centre for children there who had no family contact. The Comic Relief grant helped cover the salary costs of the staff at the home and the outreach work on the station which included training the two different railway police forces there, the Railway Protection Force (RPF) and the Government Railway Police (GRP). I attended one of the training sessions with 50 police officers although I could understand little as it was conducted in Bengali.

I had met Gerry Pinto, the UNICEF Child Rights Officer in Delhi on one of my visits and his wife, Rita Panicker, who had founded one of the better known Indian NGOs in the capital, 'Butterflies'. It ran a number of programmes for street children, which strongly supported their safety and livelihoods on the street. Rita did not believe in institutional care except for the youngest and most vulnerable, and provided the means for children to survive on the streets with resilience and a degree of panache. She had helped them form a street children's trade union to protect themselves from exploitation and was later to develop a children's bank. Railway Children got involved in supporting her 'health co-operative', which paid for a mobile clinic vehicle to visit roughly 1,000 street children weekly in their known locations, including New Delhi and Delhi Junction stations. Those children who wished could join the 'Health Co-operative' by paying one rupee a month which entitled them to come to meetings to get health education and advice, and use their power to request medical staff to tell them about health issues of particular concern.

Elsewhere, in the state of Andhra Pradesh we drew SKCV(described earlier in chapter 6) further into the long-term partnership and in particular used the Comic Relief money to fund the outreach work on Vijayawada station and the night shelter two minutes' walk away in addition to the girls' shelter which we had funded from the lottery grant. Several of our partners including SKCV had become the agents of Childline India, partly modelled on the example of the

Child Assistance Booth at Vijayawada Junction, 2004

British 'Childline' organisation but with some important differences. The Indian 'Childline' would not only receive free phone calls but, because they were run by local charity agencies

66

instead of being just a centralised phone line, they could and did respond to calls by picking a child up and taking him or her to safety - a child possibly sick or injured, or beaten up or robbed or just lost. We funded SKCV to have a 'Child Assistance Booth' (CAB) at Vijayawada Junction station and five NGOs in the city, including SKCV, manned it on a shift basis daily. Currently Childline India is operating in over 60 cities with several of them run by Railway Children's partners.

The other major beneficiary of the Comic Relief grant was an NGO called 'New Hope' which had small emergency shelters on or near railway platforms in a number of locations up and down the East Coast main line from Kharagpur and Bhubaneswar in the north through to Hyderabad in the centre and Visakhapatnam in the south. Each of these shelters housed up to 25 boys and the aim was to manage their reliance on wandering on the railway and to rehabilitate them and get them home. When Comic Relief and the BBC wanted to film one of our projects for the Sport Relief BBC TV telethon, they chose New Hope and visited one of the shelters near Visakhapatnam and the 'half-way house' where children who wanted to go home were prepared. The BBC filmed one of the boys - Vijay - who had run away from home at eight years of age because when he came home from school one day he found his

New Hope's platform school in the Goods Shed at Rayagada, 2004

mother crying as she had no food for the large family. As the oldest, Vijay felt he must be a burden to her, so he ran away and survived for two years living on the railway until he was picked up by one of New Hope's platform workers and persuaded to come into a shelter. There he was found to be suitable for home reintegration, his family was traced and his parents were keen to have him back, so he spent some time at the half-way house being prepared for his homegoing which coincided with the BBC visit. The comedian, Patrick Kielty, fronted the process and accompanied him home, with a new outfit and money to ensure he returned to school and viewers saw the emotional reunion with his family.

Two years later Comic Relief and Patrick Kielty revisited India and wanted to find out what had happened to Vijay. They eventually found him on Villupuram station in Tamil Nadu and were concerned that he'd run away again - but no. He wore a little badge saying 'social worker' because, after spending the mornings at school, he returned to the station in the afternoon looking for children to bring to the emergency shelter there. One of the distressing events the BBC filmed during their first visit concerned an accident to a young six year old boy called Subu. He was with a group of older boys on an express train while they were being interviewed for the programme when the train lurched and Subu fell through the open door (no locked doors on Indian trains!) at around 50 mph. The train was stopped and the film crew ran back expecting to find a corpse, but Subu was still alive though badly injured. They called an ambulance and paid for his medical care and in a few weeks he made a miraculous and complete recovery. He featured in the telethon film and as a direct result Comic Relief made an extra £30,000 available to Railway Children for medical expenses of its NGO partners' children who sustained accidents on the roads or railways.

One of the consultants working with New Hope's Director had a real concern about the risks of street children becoming infected with HIV/AIDS and persuaded us to seek funding from the Elton John AIDS Foundation to build a hospice for many of the infected street children who would otherwise be abandoned to die, stigmatised, in the gutter. We'd organised a small conference in Calcutta with our partners and a few expert speakers to discuss the risks to street children from their exposure to the infection and possible systems to support such children and, in the words of one

Subu with David, 2004

of the key speakers, hoped this was not yet another conference without resulting action. We discussed the difficulties of testing street children without parental or guardian permission and the limited capacity of special hospitals or hospices for children who were HIV+. We came forward with the idea of a number of treatment centres-cum-hospices which could test and diagnose children, provide medication for those infected, provide temporary beds for those suffering from an AIDS related illness and, finally, a caring hospice for those children whose illness was terminal.

We had talked to the Methodist Relief & Development Fund who provided us with some funding for such a pilot development and were pleased to receive a grant from the Elton John AIDS Foundation of £100,000 spread over two years which was in two parts. The first was to fund Project Concern International (PCI), one of our Delhi partners, who had experience of AIDS programmes for adults, to train all of our Indian NGO partners in incorporating education about AIDS into the outreach to platform children, and specifically to mount an HIV/AIDS protection programme around the Delhi station at Nizamuddin where PCI operated. The grant also enabled New Hope at Visakhapatnam to be fully funded to develop the hospice 'hub' concept. They had land in a rural village,

Kottavalasa, about a dozen miles from the city, and I carried out (under instruction) the ritual of digging the first sod – involving cracking open a coconut and pouring the juice and oil into the foundations before the site was blessed. In addition to the building of a twenty-bed hospice and treatment centre, a boys' home was built nearby to try to integrate the children and avoid the separation and stigma being attached to those who were HIV+ children. The children wore small ribbons of different colours to allow staff to be aware of the identity of the infected children so that due precautions could be made for their own safety and that of the other children, without the children realising the meaning of the colours which they thought were to do with the teams or houses they belonged to.

One of the early inhabitants of the hospice was a young boy

Sreenu with New Hope's Director, Eliazar Rose (right) and Railway Children Programme Officer, Mohan Rao, 2004

called Sreenu. He had obviously developed the HIV infection when still very young, if not from birth, and had been found by a member of New Hope, abandoned in a gutter in the city. Unable to find any organisation to take him in, initially the man had taken him into his own home, then found an old people's home - the only residential centre that would accept him. Sreenu subsequently spent very happy years at the New Hope hospice with many other children, but died suddenly from a related illness a couple of years later. He was just eight years old. At least during the last two years he had been cared for and loved. I visited the hospice just a few weeks after its opening, met and played cricket with Sreenu and the other boys and spent time with the nurses in the hospice with those children who were too ill to play outside. The hospice had 20 beds, but 26 children had been admitted already, with the overflow accommodated in a building that was being developed so that children from the city slums could spend a few days in the country working in the community's fields and playing in the fresh air. Some of the children admitted had the disease from birth from

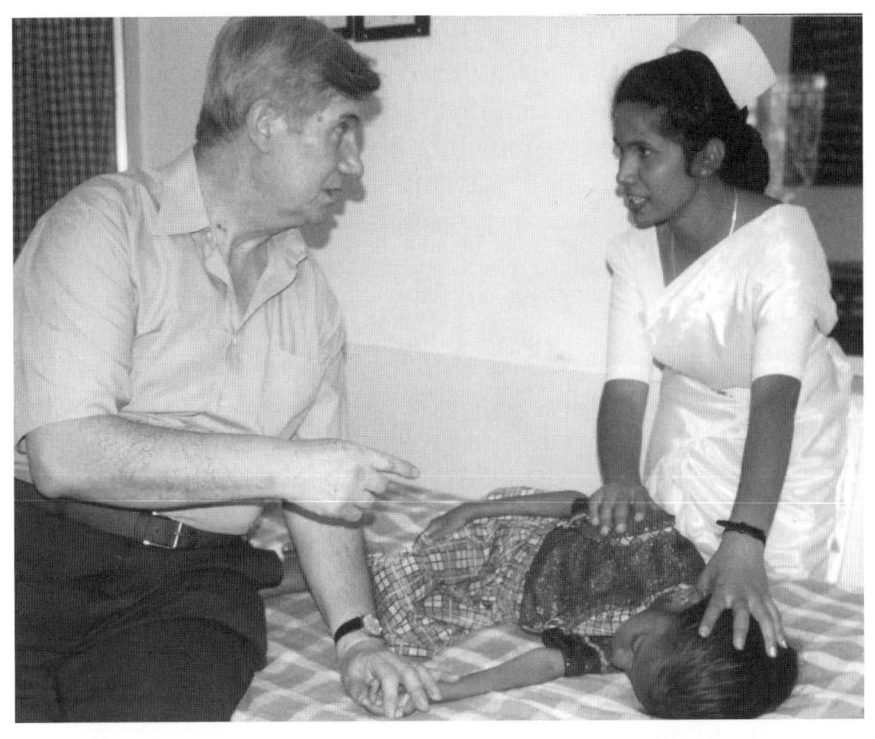

At the New Hope hospice for HIV/AIDS infected children, 2004

their mothers. I spent some time with a rather bewildered little boy who was not much more than a year old, and was upset when holding the hands of an eight year old girl, all skin and bone, who looked no more than four or five, while the nurse tenderly examined her. I looked into her huge brown eyes staring from the sunken face and just hoped that her suffering would not last long. It was just too painful to look at her.

Back in the north, I talked to Henry Alderfer, the American Director of PCI, and to Rajesh Singh, the Indian Assistant Director there. The direct work they were undertaking in the community was going well, although only one boy out of 100 tested was found to be HIV positive. The aim was to prevent the infection spreading through those most at risk. The government had prioritised truckers and sex workers, and the education of children through schools, but of course street children missed this, almost by definition, and were highly vulnerable through drug use and sexual abuse and activity. PCI had discovered that using 14-15 year old boys as peer educators was the most effective way of raising awareness of the dangers and risks among the community, and they gained respect not just from other street children, but also from adults in their locality. We had asked PCI to use their trained staff to educate the front line street educators and social workers in our other partners but we ran into some difficulty on this. For some reason there was a strange reluctance on the part of some NGOs to be 'trained' by a peer organisation rather than by Railway Children, even though they had more experience. A couple of NGOs opted out, implying that they knew the risks and didn't need further training, so after the first year we hired a couple of trainers for the Indian-based Railway Children organisation and got PCI to train them to deliver the AIDS element as part of an integrated outreach training programme. In hindsight, this worked much better without the sexual element being pulled out as something special. A lot of the platform workers had been reluctant to focus on sexual behaviour with the children as they found it difficult to discuss – a taboo area in their culture. This is where the PCI approach in Delhi worked, using peer educators as the children seemed to have no such inhibitions.

The Indian organisation was now getting into its stride and we were benefiting from our two Indian Programme Officers' knowledge of the local cultures and languages. They were able to get closer to our partner NGOs' staff and children and establish better than I ever could the effectiveness of what we were doing and the integrity of our programmes. We had always been aware of the risks associated with working for such vulnerable children and ensuring our partners had the right motivation. We worked hard with our India based staff to ensure that we put measures in place that would protect the charity against misuse of our funds - and even more importantly, ensure that there were proper safeguards to protect the children, as such programmes can too easily become the targets for individuals whose interest in such vulnerable children can be unhealthy or even criminal. We worked closely with a trusted Indian accountant and auditor who trained our partner organisations - where necessary - in financial management good practice, and we began to test within the Indian context the child protection systems being developed by the Consortium for Street Children with its members.

During one of my visits to India, the Methodist Relief & Development Fund (MRDF), of which I was a trustee until 2000, asked me to pay visits to two of the projects they funded - one in the far north in the Himalayan foothills, and the other at the opposite end of the country in the extreme south, near Madurai. I took the train from Delhi to Kathgodam in the state of Himachal

Hill people working in the forests in the foothills of the Himalayas, Nainital, 1999

Pradesh, close to the Nepalese border and was then taken by jeep up the steep forest-clad hills to the Bhimtal and Nainital Valleys where the MRDF partner, CHIRAG, was engaged in a 500 acre reforestation project. The hill tribal people had cleared many trees over the years for agriculture and firewood and the steep hillsides now had little protection from the monsoon rains so landslips were common causing damming of rivers and flash floods in the valleys.

The local people were being taught to replant and manage the forests - in particular the women and children. I accompanied the local project director as he visited a number of women's groups and schools and saw the children being given tree shoots to plant and nurture on the hillsides.

I was agreeably surprised by the fact that all the children I saw went to school (invariably on the top of 8,000 foot-high hills as I breathlessly chased after my 6' 6" long-legged host on our all-day marches!) and I was told that the vast majority went on to secondary school and 4% to university. I only saw one child labourer - a 10 year old girl looking after her family's cow.

On the last day of my 'inspection' visit I was to be treated to a visit to a viewing site from which the high Himalayas could be seen. Unfortunately, the night before there had been a torrential thunderstorm and I awoke to find ourselves shrouded in thick mist. We went by jeep to the site just in case, but it was even worse

School children planting tree shoots, MRDF project, Nainital, 1999

there - the mist swirling about our faces and visibility down to a few feet only. I was to return to Kathgodam station by jeep immediately after lunch to catch the overnight train back to Delhi, but my driver took me back to the viewing point in case the mist had lifted - we could just spot a tiny patch of blue sky directly overhead. We arrived at the hill summit to find it still very misty. Then, even as we watched, the mist miraculously lifted and there was the panoply of the vast snow-capped Himalayan range in front of me, with the 26,000 feet Nanga Parbat to the fore and the mountains of Nepal towards the Annapurna range far off to the right. After feasting my eyes for over 30 minutes, we turned to get back into the jeep, and as suddenly as the mist had lifted, it came down again until we could see nothing! When I collected my bags from where I'd lodged overnight, a British volunteer, who was teaching weaving to the local women, said she'd been in that area for over two months and had yet to see the high mountains as they'd been lost in the heat haze.

At the other end of the country, after visiting the WORD projects in Vellore and Villupuram, I stayed in the Methodist college grounds in Madurai and was taken by the resident missionary, Margaret Addicott, who'd been there for many years, to a refuge, 'Arugulam', for rejected and battered women - many rescued from the sex trade with their children. Afterwards we travelled to Dindigul, 40 miles or so further north, to see progress on the building of an AIDS hospice funded by MRDF - initially a 20-bed facility with the possibility of adding two further floors to give 60 beds. The building was about 60% complete and seemed to be progressing well after earlier difficulties. While I was staying at the college - my abode a small chalet in the forest in the grounds - I was awoken one night to be taken in my pyjamas to the main building to answer a desperate phone call from the administrator of the railway safety consultancy organisation for which I worked part time. Apparently the Irish government wanted our small company to make a presentation in Dublin to officials from the government's safety regulatory authority just one week after my return to the UK and our administrator wanted my assurance that I could attend. It clashed with the AGM of the Railway Children in London and to cut a long story short, as soon as the AGM was over, I was whisked by taxi to London City airport where a private light plane had been hired to fly me to Dublin and another car took me straight to the government building where I arrived breathless - and desperate for the loo - about three minutes before we were 'on'! I'm pleased to say we got the contract.

I had by now amassed sufficient experience to be able to respond to the increasing number of requests I was getting to give talks about the Railway Children. I was also still a member of the Amnesty Children's Human Rights Network and was listed as a schools speaker on children's rights, so I found myself increasingly doing assemblies, classroom talks, Amnesty Group talks and visits to churches, clubs, Mothers Unions and Women's Institutes, Rotary, Probus, Inner Wheel and Soroptimists. I'd assembled sets of 35mm slides most of which I'd taken myself in India and used these very flexibly to talk about how I'd got involved with Amnesty, the Consortium for Street Children and Railway Children and illustrated the violations of children's rights and what I felt could be done to support vulnerable children through my experience of working for street children in all three organisations. I carted my old 35mm slide projector around, despite the Railway Children office staff pressing me to use powerpoint technology, for I have too many experiences of technology not working at the crucial moment and preferred anyway just to talk from pictures without any screened text. Several organisations appreciated the quality of the old slides and the absence of text messages detracting from the talk and the fact that I could respond more easily to the audience, interrupting my presentation to answer questions, and omitting or adding slides at the last minute when I gauged how things were going.

Mind you, even my simple technology had its moments. At one Soroptimists' meeting in Cumbria, to which I'd travelled by train, the local secretary had borrowed a sophisticated computer-driven projector. Although it worked, we found we couldn't control the focus and the slides went in and out of focus in such a way that we were all soon feeling seasick! Unfortunately, because the projector was borrowed, no-one had a clue how to correct this fault and frantic calls to husbands were in vain. On another occasion, I'd slipped on an icy footpath and dropped my own projector and had borrowed a very old one that hadn't been used for years from a neighbour. I set it up in a school hall before 180 nine to eleven year olds, the lights went out and I tried to adjust the cartridge to show the first slide. I pressed the wrong button and all the slides fell out onto the floor as I'd not realised that this cartridge was side- rather than top-loading. Great embarrassment all round! And sometimes, despite assurances that the classroom or hall in which I was to speak had curtains or blinds, I would arrive to find the classroom had been switched or the blinds were broken, so I have learned to bring a standby USB stick for powerpoint if necessary - all schools are equipped these days with that facility. However, as I feared, some school laptops are encoded to reject imported equipment to prevent virus contamination, so it's not all plain sailing!

Normally I introduce my talks with a brief description of my encounter with the young street girl on Churchgate station in Bombay leading to my involvement with Amnesty and the Consortium for Street Children, and go on to explain the risk assessment that was the catalyst for the founding of the Railway Children. After talking about a couple of cases of street child torture and murder from Amnesty files, I move to the more positive aspects of work with street children, depicting some scenes that illustrate the need - children working and scavenging on the stations, being arrested, hungry and sick - followed by slides taken of our projects showing platform schools, vocational training, sickbays, leisure opportunities, our work in East Africa and the UK as well as India and finish with the stories of some of the children in our care and the positive changes brought about. Often I speak to quite small groups - perhaps a dozen elderly ladies - and just receive a donation of £15 or £20 for the charity. Early on it was suggested to me that speaking to such small groups with so little return was a poor use of my time and that I should look for a minimum of £80 to justify my going. We put this debate to bed after a cheque for £20,000 was received one day from a man at a London address who had not been on our database. We contacted him to find out how he knew us and he said he'd had an unexpected windfall in the city he'd not budgeted for and had asked his mother if she knew of any deserving cause. She'd apparently been one of my audience in the village Women's Institute the previous week! On another occasion the group I'd visited apologised for the small donation as they were not well off, but they'd all remember us in their wills!

Chapter 10
A world vision?

Our very first project at the end of 1995 was at Bucharest in Romania and our second was in Puebla, Mexico. It was only subsequently that we began to focus on India with a few projects in the UK. However, more by chance than design, we had picked up a number of small projects mainly through contacts I'd made at the Consortium for Street Children. Anita Schrader, the CSC Director, was very keen to help projects in South America and persuaded Railway Children to fund an NGO called Aidenica in Lima, Peru, for boys found living in the railway station and down by the river nearby. She knew one of the Aidenica patrons, and we provided funding to buy and renovate a home for them, and some of the staff salary costs. Rachel Stephens, one of our trustees, had known through MRDF an NGO, 'IMPACT', in Johannesburg, South Africa and persuaded us to fund this organisation, which was developing volunteering of South African young people with street children projects. Then we funded an NGO in Nepal for a couple of years to cover a gap in its finances until it got a more secure source of funds.

A slightly longer-term project was a partnership with an organisation called CSKS in Dacca, Bangladesh, that was founded by a Bangladeshi lawyer, Lutfur Rahman. It had a shelter and school aboard one of the ferries on the Ganges that was moored-up undergoing routine repairs. Their home changed every time repairs were finished and a new vessel came in for attention. This was genuinely early intervention as the ferry system was as common a means of transport in that country, as rail in India, and bus in Africa. This project was overseen by Mrinalini Rao for a time, then MRDF got a Comic Relief grant to develop CSKS and entered into an agreement with us that we would undertake staff training there and do an evaluation near the end of the grant period.

Katya, our interpreter, showing photos to Alex Cooke and girls at the emergency shelter, Shelkovo near Moscow, 2003

We still had Juconi in Mexico and ASIS in Romania and then I met Alex Cooke from a small Isle of Wight based NGO called 'Love Russia' which supplemented the state budget in a number of children's institutions in the 200 mile triangle south of Moscow down to Ryazan. Alex took me to Moscow and we visited a couple of emergency shelters for runaway and abandoned children in an area about 20 miles west of the city, near a Russian space research station.

Alex had developed a sound relationship with officials from the Russian Department of Education and there was an agreement that 'Love Russia's' funds would be added to the basic budget for several centres to provide an improved diet, better facilities, health and dental medication and equipment and games and toys. We funded two of these shelters and while in Moscow I was introduced to a senior pastor of the Russian Pentecostal church who had been in Siberia and had supported the growth of a Pentecostal church in Chita, (which is the railway junction where the Trans-Siberian Railway splits, one line going to China, and the other on to Khabarovsk and Vladivostok). This rapidly growing congregation (some 800 strong as I understood it) had found about 50 young boys on Chita station sheltering underground by the warm heating pipes to stave off the winter temperatures of minus 40 degrees centigrade. They had started working for these children, providing an old bus to operate as a food and soup kitchen and providing warm clothes and other support. Their bus was collapsing and needing renewal so we funded a replacement bus through the NGO's UK partner, ARC. Apparently the Russian Orthodox authorities in Chita had complained to the secular government that the 'Helping Hands' NGO as the church organisation was called, was making conversions and competing with the state church as a result of this humanitarian work and called on them to put a stop to it. Interestingly, the state authority said they'd think about it if and when the Russian Orthodox Church locally got round to doing something similar!

Our first foot in Africa was made through the CSC via my relationship with Geoff Cordell, the new Director of ChildHope who had succeeded Nic Fenton. He drew my attention to the dangerous situation for young girls round Nairobi city centre in Kenya, many of whom were at risk of indulging in casual prostitution to survive, often because they and their mothers had been displaced from their tribal lands by relatives following divorce or death of the husband. A British ex-pat, Martin Swinchatt, who ran an organisation called Pendekezo Letu supporting such girls, met me when I was visiting my daughter Catherine, who was working with street children in the notorious Kibera slum. We began to fund part of Pendekezo Letu's programme which involved offering girls a few months' placement

Girls at the Pendekezo Letu farm, Kenya 2000

at a farm near Thika about 40 miles to the north of Nairobi, where they were rehabilitated while social workers belonging to the NGO assisted the mothers in finding legal income generation work so that the girls could continue their schooling on return from Thika.

The contact point to find such girls was not really the railway station - after all, one train a day each way to Mombasa hardly constituted a hive of activity to sustain such families - they were more likely to be found hanging round the bus station and the bulging matatu (minivan) transports and taxi ranks, looking for business. Initially, the NGO was working with 13-15 year olds but experienced resistance as the girls found they could earn too much and were loath to give up such income. Pendekezo Letu therefore started working with girls between 6 and 12 years of age, many being younger sisters of those they found in the city. They also extended the training time at Thika to ten months to ensure the success of the rehabilitation process and give time for the family situation back in Nairobi to be improved so the girls had a chance when coming back.

These various scattered initiatives - they could hardly be called a programme - nevertheless required attention and supervision and because of Pete Kent's experience in Tanzania and his development qualifications, we promoted him to be our Programme Officer for the 'Rest of the World', a rather grandiose title for picking up and supervising such a disparate group of projects. So far, most of these projects had been acquired in a reactive way - we had responded to requests for help and had provided funding. However, our trustees had learned from the Lottery Fund visit to WORD in India and were determined to be more than just a funding agency. This meant that we had to consider what our role could be outside of India and the UK, and in early 2004 we held an Away Day at the Carphone Warehouse Head Office in London through our partnership with 'Get Connected'.

We looked at relationships in the supply chain from UK funders (the large trusts, corporates, individual donors and their needs) through to other UK partners - such as CSC members - to the local NGO partners we were funding and finally, to the street children themselves. We decided that we were in business to add value to the local partners by making their interventions with street children more effective and recognised that the provision of funds was only one - though an important one - of the resources needed.

We needed to be able to train, advise, stimulate, help develop plans and programmes, obtain feedback, learn, and finally document and share our learning. We could not satisfactorily achieve this with such a scattered programme and needed to replicate the type of organisation and portfolio of partners that we had in India.

We had a full debate about the pros and cons of working in particular countries and felt that in the short term we should concentrate our resources to be more effective and go deeper in a few specific areas rather than spread our resources too thinly. So far, we'd supported partners in ten countries overall - India, Bangladesh, Nepal, Kenya, South Africa, Mexico, Peru, Romania, Russia (including Siberia) and the UK - but we took a decision that for a couple of years we'd seek just two or three partners in each of Eastern Europe, Central America and East Africa as pilot projects and evaluate our experiences of these in depth before deciding which major area to concentrate on in addition to India and the UK. Pete had the job of developing these pilot projects and we homed in on one in Moscow, an additional one in Guatemala (while retaining our Mexico Juconi project) and three new partners in Kenya and Tanzania.

Through the CSC I'd become a member of the BEARR Trust, an organisation supporting UK and local NGOs working in the former Soviet Union, and I attended their annual conference in November when a few key representatives from Russian NGOs talked about their experiences and concerns to an audience of 50 or so people particularly interested in work in Eastern Europe. I'd also visited a fast-growing NGO called 'Hope and Homes for Children' which had a base near Salisbury to learn from their founder, a British Army officer who'd led the UK contingent of the peacekeeping force in Kosovo. His organisation started to support projects for children in war-affected areas but had taken a major initiative to try to persuade the Romanians to replace their dreadful orphanages, whose condition had scandalised the Western media when the country was opened up after the fall of the Ceauşescus, with a policy of fostering, adoption and small residential family-sized homes. However, they had not tackled Russia itself where the many children's orphanages were poorly run and funded, although not as notoriously bad as the ones in Romania. During the maternity leave of the then Director of the CSC, Sadia Mahmud-Marshall, a temporary appointment had been made of

Nikhil Roy, previously with the Anti-Slavery International organisation, and he became a trustee of Railway Children when Sadia returned. He had knowledge of Russia and the Asian republics of the former USSR and introduced me to Mary Murphy, a Russian speaker who was with Penal Reform International and who promised to accompany me to Moscow to look for an effective partner.

While visiting Russia earlier with Alex Cooke, I'd met the Railway Police Chief covering six of the most important Moscow train termini (including Kurski, Kazanski, Yaroslavl and Leningradski) and been appalled at the run-down state of the police accommodation, where children found on the station were taken and interrogated. We had made some modest funding available to improve the environment for both children and police and had tried - not very successfully - to influence the railway police to be more sensitive to the plight of runaway children. Apparently some 500 children every month were passing through police hands at these six stations though we suspected many were duplications for often the child would merely be returned home on the next train without any solution to their problems. The police engaged in this activity were severely underfunded - we were told, for instance, that phone calls outside the Moscow area were barred from the police office and children were only brought to emergency accommodation in Moscow if they were from the immediate local authority area. A lot of the children were said to be arriving at the Kurski station from the South East - the areas neighbouring the Caspian Sea, the Caucasus, and from some of the Islamic republics and Kursk itself - and Mary Murphy knew of a reputed Russian NGO that might have the political strength to make an impression on the issue.

Mary accompanied and introduced me to, and had meetings with, Oleg Zykov, the President of the NGO, NAN (No to Alcohol and Narcotics in English) who had been a member of President Putin's Human Rights Commission covering youth issues, and also to a journalist and to a member of the Russian Duma (parliament) who were both concerned about the growth of the street children and gang problems in Moscow. The upshot was that we developed a proposal to carry out an 18-month action research project in 2005/6 in partnership with NAN at the six Moscow stations we had contacted before together with three or four of the busiest metro stations. The project was linked with the Belgian Medecins Sans Frontières staff, who would carry out some of the social welfare work with the children and refer them to the NAN shelter, the only shelter in Moscow authorised to be run by a voluntary organisation outside the State system. Children would be intercepted at the stations, interviewed by the researchers rather than the police who would endeavour to establish the reasons for their running and offer help at the shelter and/or home reconciliation and repatriation.

I visited Moscow again towards the end of the research project, to gain an insight into the emerging conclusions and as Mary was unavailable to act as guide and interpreter she commended to me an excellent interpreter - a young Russian Orthodox priest and a postgraduate in mathematics at Hull University who knew Ian Hill, the Methodist chaplain at the university who had been our local minister in Nantwich. Such is the small world! A further highlight of this visit was an audience with the Vice President of Russian Railways in her palatial Baroque board room, this having been fixed for me by the Russian cellist and conductor, Mstislav Rostropovich and thereby hangs yet another set of coincidences. Gordon Pettitt, Deputy Chairman of Railway Children, had been chatting to a woman sitting opposite him in the train during a journey from Lancaster where he'd been visiting family. When, during the conversation, she heard about the Railway Children and its work she revealed that she was a friend of Rostropovich, living next door to a flat he used when giving concerts in London. She said that Gordon and I must meet him and frankly we thought we'd hear no more of it.

Suddenly, out of the blue, Gordon received an invitation to a short meeting at her flat and I accompanied him. We'd expected perhaps twenty minutes at most with the great man, but found we were to be guests at a small dinner party. Unfortunately, Gordon had to leave as he had another engagement, but I stayed on and when Rostropovich arrived, somewhat late, I was introduced and prevailed upon to eat his steak as he had given up meat for Lent, a fact not known to our hostess. Having demolished two steaks - and a glass of wine - I was privileged to listen to nearly an hour's advice on voluntary work in Russia from the man who was highly esteemed in that country because of his heroic stand with Yeltsin at the Russian parliament building when the Communists threatened to take control again. He had been exiled in America during the later Communist years, returning at Gorbachev's liberalisation, having been friendly with four American presidents - Carter, Reagan, George Bush senior and Clinton - all of whom had been guests at his 75th birthday party. I say this, revelling in the saying that everyone has only six degrees of separation from every other human being, for I can now claim only one intermediary link exists between me and four American presidents, not to mention Gorbachev, Yeltsin, Putin et al! Rostropovich and his wife Galina, a great Diva, had several charities in Russia that covered both music and health and he explained that he could therefore offer me no financial support, but I could use his contacts, one of whom was this Russian Railways Vice-President.

Perhaps we used the opportunity too soon for she swept into the room and got down to business straight away requiring to know what assistance we wanted. We explained the purpose of the research we were engaged with and she left us contacts to take up when the research was finished. I subsequently met Rostropovich once more at the Barbican when he conducted Shostakovich's 10th Symphony, a favourite of mine, but he was already a sick man and died of cancer shortly afterwards. We could have done with his influence later for the research report recommended the intervention of social workers at Moscow's stations, funded by the State but trained by NAN – which, although agreed in principle as part of a national child protection system developed under Putin, got bogged down in the bureaucracy between the Transport and Interior Ministries, and stalled. Railway Children still has some funds earmarked to follow this through should the situation ease but later developments in Russia concerning NGOs and the suspicion of foreign organisations has meant that this is an infertile ground for development at present.

We had been partners with the Juconi programme in Puebla, Mexico, since 1996 and continued to support the outreach work of 'Operation Friendship' at the bus station while also taking great interest in the concentrated therapeutic work being undertaken to rehabilitate the children at the Juconi 'half-way house'. Each child received into the rehabilitation programme was assigned a particular staff mentor and both child and mentor had regular objectives to achieve around the child's development and these were carefully monitored and reworked if necessary. The programme covered the child's physical, cognitive and emotional development and was intensive. Although it could be applied to only a relatively small number of children because of the staff-child ratio required to deliver such a programme, the result was assessed and the methods used deemed to be very effective for the vast majority of children, who were able to go back to their families and communities successfully after 'graduation'.

As a second pilot in Latin America we joined forces with another NGO met through the CSC, 'Casa Alianza'. Although it was a part of a well-known USA NGO, 'Covenant House', it had a Central American programme part financed by Casa Alianza UK, whose Director was Fred Shortland whom I'd known for many years - he was another member of the Children's Human Rights Network Committee that I joined at Amnesty back in 1990. Casa Alianza had been well to the fore in defending street children's rights through legal processes, identifying and accusing the police authorities in countries such as Guatemala, Nicaragua and Honduras when street children were found abused, tortured or even on occasions murdered by the police or such violations perpetrated by others with their knowledge. Casa Alianza had been generous to Railway Children in sharing information about funding sources and we had reciprocated. We therefore chose Casa Alianza as a potential partner and agreed to fund their outreach work on the street in Guatemala City for three years. As part of our sharing and learning programme, Mrinalini Rao from India and Andy McCullough, our UK Policy & Strategy Officer, spent time in Guatemala City looking at the programme. They were horrified to find that one of the weekly duties of the Programme Officer there was to visit the mortuary to identify any bodies of street children who had died during the previous week - most murdered or shot in the regular battles and conflict between the police and street gangs. Not all the children were innocent of gang involvement - often the gangs were the only people who showed them respect and acted as family for them - but many younger street children would get caught just being in the wrong place at the wrong time. Andy McCullough was warned to cover up his numerous tattoos for fear of being mistaken by the police for a gang member and shot first before questions were asked - and this was perhaps not an idle threat!

Our third pilot area was East Africa. We had ceased funding Pendekezo Letu when another of their partners, ChildHope UK, had obtained a substantial two year EU grant for the programme which included everything we had been previously funding, and we looked elsewhere. I visited Nairobi regularly for family reasons and was pointed in the direction of the Undugu Society in the city as that organisation had been the key link when the CSC had funded an East African conference of NGOs working for street children several years earlier. The Undugu Society had been founded by a Dutch priest in 1973 and had grown to be one of the largest NGOs for children in Kenya - it also had other activities including being a major conduit for 'fair trade' produce. I met Aloys Opiyo, the Chief Executive, and Josephine Mulu who was in charge of their children's programme. Josephine explained the size of the street children problem in the city, with many lone children arriving from the remote rural areas for various reasons, including extreme poverty, famine, and violence, while the huge slums of Kibera and the like within the city spawned children who spent their lives scavenging and surviving in the alleyways of the slums or begging in the city centre.

The Undugu Society had three residential centres for street children holding at best around 200 children, and they were well aware how inadequate this was when the city authorities estimated

The elected committee of a Nairobi street 'Association' with the Undugu Society's Children's Programme Officer, Josephine Mulu

60,000 street children in the city and 250,000 in the country. They therefore put a revolutionary plan to Railway Children which involved the closure of two of the three residential centres, one being turned into a training centre. The other one, at Kitengela about 90 minutes' road journey out of the city, would act as a short term rehabilitation centre for younger street children prior to home/community repatriation. The main thrust of their proposals was to support the formation of thirty 'associations' of street youth who would be formally recognised; would choose their leaders who would receive training in their roles by Undugu; would meet regularly and formulate their own rules; would have an association bank account and who would have Undugu to help them find legitimate work and protect them from police harassment. In return, the association members would look out for new lone children arriving in the city and bring them to Undugu at Kitengela for rehabilitation and family reintegration.

Pete Kent developed this concept with the Undugu Society and also linked with the International Childcare Trust, another CSC member, to part fund an NGO, KYPT in Kitale, in northern Kenya which received many street children from the surrounding rural area and further north, an area which was subject to frequent drought and famine. The operation of this NGO, the only one working for street children in Kitale, was often difficult, but Railway Children decided to persevere when the other CSC member pulled out.

Pete Kent had contacts from his pre-Railway Children life in Tanzania and he researched possible partners in that country. The scale of the street children phenomenon in Tanzania was not as great as in Kenya - such children were numbered in thousands rather than hundreds of thousands - but the problem was growing and there was the opportunity to try to stem the flow before it increased to unmanageable proportions. One of the biggest NGOs for street children in Tanzania, Mkombozi, worked in the cities of Moshi and Arusha, and was run by a British woman, Kate McAlpine, who had engaged with the Tanzanian government to protest about the periodic round-up of street children undertaken by the police under ancient colonial laws about loitering and vagrancy. Railway Children agreed to fund some advocacy work by Mkombozi around this law and the resultant police actions.

We also took an interest in a joint CSC project with some of its East African members that undertook action-research in a slum community notorious as a source of street living children, funded by the Baring Trust. As a result, a minister in the Tanzanian government asked the CSC to undertake some survey work in eight Tanzanian cities to gauge the size of the problem, and to organise a conference on the issue and potential solutions as a prelude to forming a national strategy on street children. Railway Children conducted the survey in the city of Mwanza in conjunction with a local street working NGO there, 'Adilisha', and subsequently formed a partnership with that NGO to fund their street operations and become heavily involved in the CSC initiative with the Tanzanian government.

Pete Kent, as Programme Officer for the 'Rest of the World', would monitor carefully the outcomes from the programmes in Russia, Central America and East Africa and, with Terina, produce recommendations after twelve months on which continent we should develop a major expansion, to join the substantial body of work we were continuing to strengthen in India and the UK.

Chapter 11
Consolidation in India

Britt Angel, a British Airways air hostess, had inspired an initiative called the 'BA Runners' to respond to the outcry in the media about the state of Romanian orphanages that came to light when that country opened up to the West after the collapse of Communism there. Many flights to that country took goods for the children and 'BA Runners' had linked with ChildHope to extend that help to street children organisations in Eastern Europe. Britt had visited the Consortium for Street Children in 1998 and offered to support other members' overseas work where the project was within two hours' road journey of an international airport that BA used. Railway Children was one of three CSC members who responded, and BA agreed to visit our projects in Calcutta.

When the scheme started operating Railway Children had seven partners in that city and I approached Tim Grandage, founder and Director of Future Hope (which Railway Children did not fund), whom I had met through the CSC. Tim had been the HSBC's Bank Manager in Calcutta and had already started work with street children when his employer wanted to promote him to a senior post in the bank's headquarters in Hong Kong. Tim had resigned in order to maintain and develop his street children work and was a person I knew could help me with the import regulations necessary for BA to be able to bring in goods for the street children. Even better, the father of one of Tim's senior project staff was in charge of customs arrangements at Calcutta's international airport and smoothed the way for BA's regular cargoes of toys, clothes, sports equipment and educational books and materials that BA collected - a full load of boxes of up to 720 kilograms on occasions. Tim and his staff would help distribute the goods fairly and appropriately between our partners.

BA had a warehouse at Heathrow in which donations of the goods were received from BA staff, local schools and communities in the Hounslow area, making them up into flight-loads responding to the priority needs that our partners advised. Volunteers sorted and made up the boxed loads and each visit to

Calcutta involved three or four 'Runners' - flight deck or cabin crew - who would spend a few days of their own leave entitlement visiting our projects, playing with the children and taking them on outings - picnics, visits to museums - even on one occasion, a quick flight round the city. 'BA Runners' eventually grew to involve some 130+ volunteer staff involved in this activity and was reconstituted as 'BA Action for Street Children'.

One by-product of this was the offer of a number of free flights for the partner NGO's own staff to visit the projects overseas. Railway Children have had eight free flights allocated annually until 2010, when it was raised to eleven, which is a substantial cost saving for the charity. We have used the flights from Heathrow to both India and East Africa for Railway Children staff making visits to supervise and develop our programmes, to bring Bombay staff to the UK for key staff and Board meetings and to take both trustees and staff to India, Russia and Africa to see and be motivated by the work. The flights are, of course, standby tickets, paying customers having priority if the plane is full.

The availability of this flight facility meant that I was able to make frequent visits to India to understand and promote the work, and often took fellow trustees out as a way of increasing their knowledge, interest and motivation. No matter how much one prepares, it is always a culture shock to go to India, especially to the mega cities of Bombay and Calcutta. On one occasion I'd taken Chris Jago and Michael Holden and we'd been booked into a hotel at Juhu Beach some ten miles north of Bombay city centre, but not too far from the Railway Children office in Andheri. Because of the uncertainty about flight accommodation on our standby tickets, we'd allowed a day to acclimatise before the programme began in earnest, and as the journey went smoothly we had a spare day in which to indulge in some sightseeing. We hired a car to take us to the south of Bombay to see the Gateway of India, the Taj Hotel and other well-known buildings in the tourist area, but we got caught in the usual road traffic gridlock and took two and a half hours of fume-filled air to get to our objective. I determined not to endure a similar journey on the return so we paid off our driver and returned by rail in a suburban train from Churchgate station - at a cost of 7 rupees each if I remember rightly compared with the (not unreasonable) 500 rupees we'd paid for the car. The only problem was that we were in the rush hour (a term that seemed to cover most of the day in Bombay) and the crush in our coach was so great that we were unable to alight at our destination station and only just managed to get out at the next. One learned to wriggle one's way towards the gaping exit door some two to three stations before one wished to alight - a big problem if you didn't know which side the platform would be! I remember Michael - who was Managing Director of South East Trains at the time - managed just to squeeze a camera above the standing throng and take a quick snap which he vowed to send to any passenger who dared to complain of overcrowding on his trains to Charing Cross or Cannon Street!

The road systems of Calcutta were another source of frustration and some amusement – unless you were already late for an appointment. There were a number of one-way streets in the city, narrow but busy roads. This sensible arrangement was ruined by the decision to change the one-way direction of these roads at 2pm every day, which meant that between 1.30pm and 2.30pm nothing moved, the two streams of traffic facing each other, neither side giving way. The efforts of police to sort out the chaos usually only contributed to the mess and further increased the shouting and tempers of the marooned car passengers. When I first visited India I had attempted far too ambitious a schedule based on the expectation that trains would run (roughly) to time and people would turn up to meetings on time. I soon learned that this expectation was profoundly mistaken and had to insert copious 'recovery time' in my plans and not to get tense if no-one had appeared three quarters of an hour after the time I'd agreed to meet them. I learned to relax and let things flow, putting my fate in the hands of others. I ceased to worry if my train was running a couple of hours late - after all it had probably been on the move for 36 hours already. My hosts meeting me would have allowed for that. If by chance a train I was on ran to time, I knew I'd need to wait until some breathless individual would turn up half an hour later full of excuses about the traffic. I found perversely that it was only trains that were scheduled to arrive around five o'clock in the morning that ever ran on time - or even early – just when another couple of hours sleep would have been welcome.

After the first filming of our partner's work in India by the BBC for the Sport Relief 2004 programme, and the viewers' response to the excerpts shown of a six year old lad called Subu and his recovery from the train fall, and of Vijay at Villupuram, Comic Relief called me and wanted to discuss a possible expansion of our programme in India. We were encouraged to go for a full £1 million grant - the maximum allowed - over a four rather than five year period and in particular build on one of our learning experiences. We had conducted situational analyses at three or four stations - including Howrah, New Delhi and Ahmedabad - to learn something about the children on the stations there, and had found that many of those without family contact had run from the northern states of West Bengal, Bihar, Uttar Pradesh and Rajasthan. Many of the arriving children at the mega city stations had already been travelling around the railway system for several months and were already beyond the point of the 'early intervention' that we had tried to focus on. If we were to hold true to our objective of reaching the children in the first few days after they'd left home, we realised we needed to have a presence on stations nearer to the towns and villages from which they were running. We therefore supplemented our further application to Comic Relief with a proposal to look in the northern states for two new partners each year of the grant.

We had been working with an NGO in Delhi called Prayas, an organisation that had taken over a state-run observation home for runaway and delinquent children after a series of bad experiences there that had been poorly managed by the state authorities. Prayas had been founded by a senior Delhi police officer, Amod Kanth, and had briefed our partners at an RCFI meeting on the requirements and opportunities under the new 2000 Juvenile Justice Act. Using his police knowledge and contacts, Amod Kanth had been able to persuade the RPF to set up a 'Child Assistance Booth' on New Delhi station, and a shelter for boys nearby. Many children who needed a longer term residence and educational opportunities were found a place in the Prayas home at Tughlakabad, a Delhi suburb. Prayas was prepared to open up new work in Bihar and we therefore funded them under this second Comic Relief grant to start work in a large railway junction at Samastipur.

When discussing our work with the railway authorities or police, one of the issues often referred to was the need for NGOs working at the bigger stations to work together and approach the railway management with a co-ordinated plan of working. At stations like

New Delhi, Bombay VT and Howrah several city NGOs were already working on or near the platforms and Railway Children tried, because of our contacts and relationships at senior level in the railways, to get them to co-operate with each other. At Howrah we called a meeting of around six of the charities who were working with street children on the station and undertook a situational analysis there, identifying the various categories of vulnerable children - the long term residents, the newcomer runaways, the local children whose families were around the station, and the children commuting daily to find income from activities around the station. We surveyed the hours when most children were on the platform, which trains were used most by arriving street children and which NGOs had a presence, when and where. It was clear that benefit could arise if the organisations agreed to cover different platforms and hours to give a more comprehensive support to the children, especially at night, and that as the children's needs were different and the NGOs were strong in different activities, a cooperative system could work well with children being referred to the NGO best placed to serve the individual need as appropriate. I'd seen such cooperation in Vijayawada through the partnership of that city's NGOs in their Child Rights Forum.

However, it proved more difficult to achieve in the larger cities. Not all the NGOs we invited at Howrah came to the meeting and although those present found the discussion useful and said the right things, I can't feel confident that as much progress was made as I had thought possible. At New Delhi there were at least nine NGOs at work around the station and it was even more difficult there. I managed to get all nine of these to attend a meeting together, but the different approaches and philosophy of intervention of several was very apparent. All had strengths and there would have been much to gain - especially for the children - by the NGOs agreeing to share the 'child assistance booth' on the station and referring children to the most appropriate organisation, but two or three of the stronger organisations would not recognise the appropriateness of different approaches and again, despite a paper commitment they made to share and work together, the attempt was abortive.

There was much to learn here. We had conducted a situational analysis at New Delhi and found that despite the NGO 'crowded' presence, only 35% of the children interviewed on the station were in contact with these NGOs and only 15% actually used their shelter facilities. Many of the children, especially the older ones, could earn more money on the platforms than the NGOs' street outreach workers who were trying to help them! The feedback from the children was that they badly needed protection from the violence they experienced there, and help to escape from their addiction to intoxicants, both needs that the NGOs seemed unable to address effectively, although one of our partners, 'Butterflies', was perhaps the organisation trying hardest in this direction.

We have continued to work at both Howrah and New Delhi - we cannot ignore those important places - and continue to try to get NGOs to work together but it is a difficult task for a number of reasons, some practical, some cultural and some because of different philosophies and values underlying their programmes. At another major station, Bombay VT, we have had more success. Partly this was because the difficulty of working in that

Lucknow station Child Assistance Booth, 2011

environment was so great - the attitude of the police there and the amount of crime on the station - that the NGOs found working together for mutual protection had its own benefits. A major NGO, Don Bosco, led a programme of co-ordination at the station – the project was called Bal Prafulta. This was stimulated and funded by us and is working towards the joint benefit of all the stakeholders and children at that station, and I found on a recent visit that much progress is being made with the railway staff and police there.

Uttar Pradesh (UP) is the most populous state in India and also scores low on human development indices. From a study undertaken by Railway Children in 2005, it was established that, 44% of the total number of children interacted with at Delhi were from the State of Uttar Pradesh. We therefore looked for a local organisation to partner there. 'Ehsaas', in UP, was a relatively young, non-profit organisation, registered in the year 2002 with the distinct goal to work towards integrating street children into mainstream society so that they can lead a respectable life with no stigma attached. In fact, Ehsaas was the first organisation in the State capital city, Lucknow, to establish a home for the street and working children there. They identified nearly 4000 children in a first ever city level survey of street and working children. Photo identity cards of 2000 children were prepared and mapping of areas where most vulnerable children were found had been undertaken. Therefore, after undertaking a needs assessment in 2007 at the UP cities of Lucknow, Kanpur and Varanasi, Railway Children decided to work at Lucknow, and possibly Kanpur, by partnering with Ehsaas.

With the financial support of Railway Children, Ehsaas started to work at the Lucknow station (Northern and North Eastern Railways) from October 2007. In this short span of time, our partner established an excellent stakeholder network in the city. The organisation was also successful in gaining permission to have a child assistance booth at the railway station. Strong lobbying by the railway surveillance and protection cell has resulted in the formation of the 'Railway Task Force' (formed by the Northern Railway authorities of Lucknow). The special task force has formally announced that by 2011 Lucknow station would be made India's first 'child-friendly' station. This is a major step towards protecting and rehabilitating all those children who live alone and are in need of care and protection in and around Lucknow railway station. From June 2008 to May 2009, 485 children came in contact with Ehsaas and accessed various services like outreach, nutrition, health and other referral services. Of these, 93 children were reunified with their families.

Another major partner we established in response to the commitment we gave to Comic Relief was an organisation founded by Sanat Sinha, a social worker, in Bihar's capital city and large railway junction, Patna. The organisation, called Bal Sakha, has been working in the area of child rights protection since 1993. It aims at promoting community-based, non-institutional care systems for the children to ensure child protection. The partnership was initiated in 2004. The relationship between Bal Sakha and Railway Children has been a learning and evolving partnership. Being a process-oriented organisation, Bal Sakha slowly but steadily strengthened its intervention efforts and strategies. Railway Children's constructive and continuous feedback and input played a vital role. The organisation has addressed the issues of children at risk, comprehensively and effectively, at Patna railway station. It has also been able to make bold and innovative intervention efforts, such as a drug de-addiction treatment for children in conjunction with a local specialist organisation. Approximately 200 children can be found at Patna station on any

Lucknow's Railway Task Force, 2011

given day. Bal Sakha runs a day care centre and night shelter for the platform and street children. Between June 2008 and May 2009, it contacted 398 children in and around Patna station of whom 78 children were reunified with their families and 74 were referred to other appropriate organizations, others remaining in their own drop-in and overnight centres.

I visited Patna in July 2009 and saw the work at the station at first hand. I travelled with Bal Sakha's Director to meet the Eastern Railway's Acting General Manager, whom I discovered had spent a few months in the UK undertaking senior management training at BR's staff college. He promised co-operation and indicated that the RPF in particular might be able to authorise accommodation on the platforms for the outreach work to the street children. My initial introduction to Patna, however, was at a meeting Sanat Sinha had called of people appointed to the Child Welfare Committees (CWCs) and Juvenile Justice Boards to form a 'federation' of such officials in the state of Bihar. Many were new appointments, some of them political appointees, others recommended to the state authorities by Sanat Sinha with his long experience of social work in the state. Although such CWCs and JJ

The Bihar village school where the child rights awareness session took place, 2009

Boards are required throughout India, under the Integrated Child Protection System developed nationally, their implementation is very erratic with many states still needing to make appointments. It was good to see the enthusiasm of over 70 members present at the Patna meeting, for the state of Bihar needs a comprehensive child protection system probably more urgently than any other Indian state.

A new venture we piloted with Bal Sakha was to identify some of the rural villages from which many of the runaway and trafficked children migrated and fund a Child Rights Worker to tour these villages on a regular basis, making both the children and local community aware of the dangers and try to pre-empt the children falling prey to trafficking or running to the cities without the knowledge of the pitfalls ahead – a sort of 'early, early intervention'. I visited one such village and saw at first hand a session after school with some seventy children aged between five and the early teens. They listened to stories warning of the dangers, enacted little dramas, sang and played games that drove the lesson home, watched by the local women who would continue to work with the children when the Child Rights Worker moved on to another village. Whilst in the school, the heavens opened – it was the Monsoon season – and our jeep had the utmost difficulty in manoevring its way out of the village and staying on the muddy cart track.

The village in the Monsoon rains after the school visit, 2009

A third partner NGO we engaged, because of their engagement with the government system and their work in children's homes as well as stations, was an organisation called Praajak. Established in 1997 as a social development agency, Praajak works with marginalised children and adolescents in the state of West Bengal. Their ultimate aim is to create a gender-just environment of care and protection around these children, so that they grow up as more responsible, productive and law-abiding citizens. Most of its programmes are on education, health and social rehabilitation. Praajak works mainly with boys and the youth, because it sees crime, violence, sexual abuse, gambling and substance abuse as determined by the social construction of masculinity. Using a range of awareness-raising methods, like art and theatre workshops, Praajak seeks to restore self-esteem, social responsibility and creativity in children in order to empower them. The focus is on the active participation of the children as well as the various institutions that make up their surroundings. Children on railway platforms, children in institutions, children in conflict with the law, children (boys) in prostitution and the entertainment industry and other working children are their main target group.

Praajak in association with the Railway Protection Force (RPF) had already established a successful model called 'Muktangan' (which means 'open courtyard') at Malda station in West Bengal. Railway Children started supporting the Muktangan project in 2004 which is also part supported by Groupe Development (France) and is based on active collaboration with RPF. The Muktangan model is unique since it is an NGO - RPF collaboration in totality. All the Muktangan shelters are operational in spaces provided by the RPF. In most of the locations RPF is also involved in the daily functioning of the shelters in terms of referring children, following up on the referred cases, participating in activities and supporting the team during family reunification. Praajak has a special training initiative with RPF recruits at the Kharagpur RPF training institute which substantiates their networking efforts.

The Muktangan shelters provide nutrition, clothing and recreational activities. Praajak in addition focuses on livelihood training and empowering young boys through the concept of group homes and cooperatives though this component of the project is supported by other funding agencies. Currently Praajak works at 3 base locations – Malda, Kharagpur and Asansol and extends outreach to 2 extension locations of Bardhaman and Rampurhat. These shelters are based around the railway route that extends northwards from Calcutta and project into North Bengal where another of Railway Children's partners has been established for several years - at New Jalpaiguri, twin town with Siliguri at the southern end of the Darjeeling Himalayan Railway. New Jalpaiguri is a strategic location because it is the exit point which connects Darjeeling to neighbouring countries like Nepal, Sikkim and Bhutan and the extreme north east of the country, Assam and beyond.

This started as another police initiative, the idea of a local police chief and his wife, who were concerned at the number of children they saw destitute and desperate on New Jalpaiguri station. They sought space for a drop-in centre on the station and readily obtained the support of the railway police when - only four months after starting the project - the police reported a 75% drop in reported petty crime. And the children, when questioned, also no longer saw the police as enemy, and the relationship between police and railway children became positive. The NGO, CONC'RN, in its initial days provided minimum basic services like food, shelter and medical support to children. The mode of intervention was charity based and children would be provided with these resources in order to lead healthy lives. Over the years the organisation has developed into a professionally run charity and focuses on providing a holistic model of intervention and services based on an ideology of empowerment and child rights.

Railway Children had entered into a full partnership with CONC'RN in 2004. The project has an emergency shelter outside New Jalpaiguri (known as NJP) station which provides 24 hour shelter facilities, nutrition, clothing, non-formal education and recreational facilities for the children. Currently the project also includes two short stay homes for boys and girls which support the mainstreaming and family reunification activities of the project. Most of the children in the short stay homes go to formal schools and vocational training institutes. CONC'RN's girls' home is not only an important component for the project but is important for the entire field of NJP since there are very few residential options available for destitute girls.

Family reunification is an important component of the project and the team acquired effective support from various stakeholders like the Government Railway Police Force and coolies' union during reunification of children. The follow-up systems are also extremely innovative, where children are given creative tools like drawing books, pencils etc and these books are checked when the outreach worker visits the child as a follow-up schedule in order to understand the mental and social adaptability of the child within his family environment.

Railway Children's interest in the area began after Edith Wilkins had moved to the Siliguri and Darjeeling area and through her and the railway contacts I had, I was invited to a joint UNESCO/Indian Railways conference in 2002 which was to discuss the 1999 announcement that the Darjeeling Himalayan Railway (DHR) had been designated a 'World Heritage Site'. The conference was held in January in Ghum, the highest point of the DHR where it reached 7,400' before dropping down to Darjeeling which lay at 6,800' above sea level. The hotel had been specially opened up for the

Children scavenging for unburnt coal beside the DHR locomotive, 2002

conference as resorts in the hills were closed in the non-tourist season and was freezing cold. I remember that four of us - Mrinalini Rao, our India Programme Director, a consultant who worked with us on issues in the Siliguri/Darjeeling area and a representative from an Indian charity working at Siliguri - used to meet in one of the small bedrooms for pre-session briefing. We huddled round a one-bar electric fire in what we named 'penguin order', supposedly in a reference to the TV pictures one sees of King Penguins huddled together against the Antarctic storms. We managed to persuade Mrinalini to get up at 6 o'clock one morning to see the sunrise over Kanchenjunga opposite - a splendid sight bathed in the early pink rays of the sun - and realised that it was the first time she had ever seen frost which crunched under our feet as we strode to the best viewpoint.

The purpose of our presence at the conference was to respond to UNESCO's expectation that local people should benefit from the 'World Heritage Site' status of the 'toy railway' as it was known locally and that we should put forward ideas in the sessions on how to involve children in the area, especially the poorest, so that there was a developing ownership of the railway and its income generating potential for those most in need of it. The Indian Railway officers present were talking of investment in the line to improve its tourism potential, including renewing its ancient locomotive fleet and possibly building new engines to the 1880s design. We visited stations at Kurseong and Darjeeling to look at the potential for station improvements and their possible adoption and decoration by local school children. In fact, the daily school train from Kurseong to Darjeeling and return was still hauled by one of the ancient British built steam engines and after one of our Darjeeling station inspection tours I travelled back the five uphill miles to Ghum in the school train behind a leaking and wheezing No. 791 designed by Sharp Stewart & Co of Glasgow and built by the North British Loco Company, also of Glasgow, in 1914. We progressed so slowly that the school children kept hopping off the train and racing ahead of it, then jumping back on. We managed to drop a quarter of an hour on our one-hour 5mph schedule, thereby demonstrating the urgent need of attention from the Indian railway authorities. Edith Wilkins made us aware of the vulnerability of children in the area - the disease in the poorly maintained slums during the monsoon and winter seasons and the trafficking of children over the borders nearby - with Nepal, Sikkim, Bhutan, and Bangladesh through Assam.

When the conference was over, I visited some informal schools at Sukna and Siliguri Town stations at the lower end of the route and Edith took me to see the Truck Stand community in the old DHR Siliguri Goods Shed which was probably the worst slum I have ever encountered. The conditions were truly dreadful, unhygienic and overpowering, but Edith mingled with the drug addicts, the women with AIDS, the naked toddlers, hugging everyone and picking up and cradling the children. Everyone swarmed round her, treating her as a visiting angel. The issue was how could the development of the DHR really be made to help such people as these. The more likely scenario was that their homes - awful as they were - would be removed as part of any clean-up to improve its attractiveness for tourists. UNESCO officials had been adamant at the conference that one of the main purposes of granting 'World Heritage' status to the DHR was to improve the lot of the local people who lived on and round it, as well as the preservation of the line.

Later, back in Delhi, and as a follow up to the DHR conference, I was invited by the Heritage Director, Mr A.K.Agarwal, who organized the Ghum conference, to an event at the National Railway Museum, a splendid open site with a treasury of locomotives and coaches from the British Raj and later. The day was attended by the Chairman of Indian Railways and his wife to

Delhi's 'Open Air' National Railway Museum

formally cut the tape for the first run in steam since preservation of India's first steam locomotive, the 1853-built 'Faery Queen' which the Chairman's wife, Mrs Mahotra, drove up and down a hundred yard stretch of track with the footplate full of notables. I managed to have a word with the Chairman about my agenda for co-operation with Indian railway officials and he promised support - but as so often happens in the Indian civil service, he had retired within weeks and before any concrete action promised had taken place. Later on I had a meeting with his successor, Mr R.J.Singh, which I thought might be more fruitful. Increased co-operation from the RPF in particular did become apparent in the following months, but whether anything was a result of our meeting I shall never know. I did get an Indian Railway Museum tie for my pains which I now wear frequently to suitable events. A further connection is now support from the Darjeeling Himalayan Railway Society in the UK, which has included original water colour paintings for our Christmas cards by the DHR Society Chairman, David Charlesworth. These always include at least one DHR scene - with children - which are very popular, and not only with DHR Society members.

In 2004, following a major international jamboree and campaign in Bombay on the world development goals and debt cancellation, the Asian World Council of Churches met at a peaceful centre near Vihar at the northern end of the Bombay rail suburban service. The hierarchy of the churches had raised concerns about street children and the need for the churches to do more to support this group of vulnerable children and I was asked, as one of half a dozen NGOs, to join the church leaders from South and South East Asia to make presentations and take part in the subsequent debate with the church leaders. One of the contacts I made there was Brother James, a Christian NGO Director from Madurai in Tamil Nadu. He was very interested in Railway Children's early intervention approach and in due course we partnered his organisation, 'Nanban', to work with both boys and girls found living on the streets of that city.

We had, through our contacts in the south, opened up partnerships with other NGOs there. We had sought out other NGOs around Vellore (Katpadi Junction) and further down the main line to the far south, at key stations like Jolarpet Junction, Salem and Erode, where our partner's outreach staff on the platforms were initially competing with the railway police to reach runaway children first, trying to encourage the children to come to our drop-in and shelter accommodation before they were detained by the police and taken to one of the unpopular children's 'Observation Homes'. This was because, try as we might, we'd been unable to persuade WORD, one of our early project partners, that our main objective was the support of new children coming to the street and their rehabilitation and return home if possible, rather than WORD's programme which had developed into a residential home and support for schooling for the poorest children in the village. We partnered another NGO, SAVE, which supported street and working children around the temple town of Tirupur and were continuing to expand New Hope's emergency shelter network throughout eastern and southern India.

At the end of the year, on Boxing Day 2004, South East Asia was hit by the massive tsunami triggered by an underwater volcano off the Sumatra coast, 9.3 on the Richter scale. Whilst the worst of the damage and the highest number of fatalities occurred in Indonesia and Sri Lanka, the Indian coast of Tamil Nadu and parts of Andhra Pradesh and the Andaman & Nicobar Islands were badly hit too. Fatalities ran into tens of thousands, with many coastal fishing villages being wiped out and families disrupted leading to a risk of orphaned and frightened children taking to the street. Several of our partner organisations reacted to try to help - street children in Delhi at Butterflies made a collection for the children affected by the tsunami and raised 2,000 rupees from their own efforts. Half a dozen of our partners offered to go to the stricken areas and give initial help to retain vulnerable children at risk of becoming lost or even trafficked in the subsequent confusion. Advice from our Railway Children office in Bombay was that much initial international aid would go in the emergency, but that there would be ongoing work needed to address the trauma and loss that many children would have experienced over a much longer timescale. We approached Comic Relief with the advice and informed them that, given funding, three of our partners could make a significant difference over a 2-3 year timescale.

A grant of £250,000 was awarded by Comic Relief for New Hope in Andhra Pradesh, one of our Tamil Nadu partners, TNTDS (Tamil Nadu Tribal Development Society), and Prayas from Delhi who offered to work in the swamped Andaman Islands. In fact we found that the fishing villages affected were close-knit communities and as long as they could get support to rebuild their villages and boats and nets, they were very protective of their children and the emergence of large numbers of street children that followed disasters like Hurricane Mitch in Central America did not happen in India. The two NGOs working in Tamil Nadu were each given ten village communities to support and work continued for several months. Railway Children involved 'Dreamcatchers', a small Bombay consultancy working with traumatised children and we wanted to use their therapeutic skills in dealing with the biggest need - conquering the children's fears and traumatic experiences of loss that had suddenly hit their whole communities. 'BBC Sport Relief 2006' had filmed a visit by the English Test cricket team in Bombay - with Andrew Flintoff playing alley cricket with some of the boys at our partner Saathi's project - and a celebrity cricket team visited the tsunami affected areas and played cricket with the kids on the beach - part of the therapy to persuade children back to play by the sea.

One of the major thrusts of our Comic Relief 2 programme was a drive towards reintegration of runaway children with their families and wider communities. We had always believed that a child's best place was in its own family provided that family was not abusive and was willing to receive the child back - and, of course, that the child was willing to go. Success was erratic and often families were long distances away or were difficult to trace and follow-up, even if a child was chaperoned home, was often non-existent. Sometimes there were spectacular successes. I remember one lad I met during a visit to the Sarjan programme in Ahmedabad. The boy's name was Pintesh and he was eleven years old and living in a slum home on the outskirts of the city when I was taken to greet him and his family. Apparently when he was nine, his unemployed father, an alcoholic with terminal TB, removed him from school and sent him to work for a local tea stallholder to earn money to buy his drink. One day Pintesh dropped and broke something and his boss grabbed the nearest thing lying on the red hot stove and burned the boy badly as a punishment. The lad ran away and was found by a Sarjan social worker at the main railway station. After a couple of days getting to know the boy and obtaining his trust, Pintesh admitted to the Sarjan worker that he missed his mum, but was scared to go back home for fear of what his father would do.

The social worker found his family living in a lean-to in the slum and arranged visits to the mother when the father was out or too drunk to notice. After a couple of months the social worker negotiated with the father for the boy's permanent return, schooling in the morning and work with a reliable stallholder in the afternoon. This worked so well that the father was impressed and gave up alcohol! Later, after the earthquake disaster that was epi-centred on Bhuj but had affected Ahmedabad badly too, Pintesh's mother, although nearly destitute, spent over ten weeks working as a volunteer at the relief camp for those who lost their homes as a thanksgiving for her son's return and her husband's restoration. Unfortunately not all homecomings are as successful as this one.

One of our partners, Sathi, which had outreach workers on the platforms of a number of stations - mainly on the Bombay VT to Bangalore route - had developed a particular type of intervention to reunite children with their families and claimed an 80% success rate. The first priority was to contact runaway children within hours of their arrival and often home repatriation would be achieved fairly simply once parents were contacted and the cause of running away was addressed. However, for children who had been gone from home for months or even years it was harder. Sathi developed a model intervention for these boys, which involved taking a group to a 4-week camp in the countryside away from the temptations of railway and city. The first week would be spent in acclimatisation and games, fun. In the second week the leaders explored with the children their experiences on the street, the hardships and privations, the dangers and risks, disease and rejection. In the third week they began to talk to the children about the families they'd left, the positives and gradually remind the children of what they'd lost. In the final week they identified those children who had elected to return home and began to explore with them what needed to be put right for them to remain at home. Each child going home would be accompanied and negotiations with the family and the wider community would take place to try to overcome the reasons for the child running away in the first place. A public ceremony would take place in front of the village community so that all felt a responsibility to watch over and care for the child. Their follow-up checks revealed that a high proportion of these children were still living with their families a year later.

Railway Children asked Sathi's founder and Director, Pramod Kulkarni, to present his methodology to the Railway Children partners and many of them, some with Pramod's involvement, took up the process. In the last couple of years around a quarter of the children contacted by Railway Children's partners in India have been reunited successfully with their families - that is around 4,000 a year. It is still difficult to follow up all the children as often as we would like, because of the distance that so many live away from the locations where they were found. This is an issue that needs strengthening in future work, linking where possible with NGOs working in the communities that the children come from, or with the increasing number of state appointed Child Welfare Committees.

We had known that the majority of street children around India's railway were boys. However, there were girls, even if sometimes they were harder to find. We knew that some girls cut their hair and disguised themselves as boys to protect themselves from assault and rape. Other girls sought protection in the gangs of street boys but had to submit to sexual advances from the youths in return for their protection. One partner told us that the sight of

David playing 'Carrom Board' with former street girls at an emergency shelter, 2004

girls up to the age of about ten was common on stations but after that they seemed to disappear - and feared that part of the explanation was the trafficking of such vulnerable girls into the sex trade or domestic slavery. Matthew Norton, down in Vijayawada, had recognised this many years previously and had persuaded us to support an emergency shelter for girls in his programme. Saathi had catered specially for older girls in their Mumbai programmes after the findings that resulted from the research that we had funded. Partner NGOs, SEED and CINI Asha in Calcutta, had both set up shelters for street girls - in fact a state census of street children had estimated that 47% of Calcutta's street children were girls, a much higher proportion than anywhere else we'd found. Probably the majority of these were young children in the slums on the streets only during the day, but for any that had left home life was particularly tough and risky.

One partner that approached us about that particular vulnerability was Jeevodaya, a programme at Itarsi, a large railway junction in the centre of India, where the main trunk routes from Delhi to Madras and from Calcutta to Bombay crossed, the centre of a continental 'X'. Around 140 mainline trains a day used Itarsi station and it was a railway town - the Crewe of India - with large electric and diesel engine maintenance depots, and not much else. A diminutive nun, Sister Clara, from a local Catholic order, had noticed the street children on the station and had led the nuns to set up a drop-in centre for children from the platform in a small railway building she'd persuaded the local Divisional Railway Manager to loan to her. She'd been discovered by a British couple, Ashley and Jane Butterfield, who ran railtours round India and who had helped her build a residential home for the street boys. Railway Children had been supporting her with the running costs for a number of years and one day she drew our attention to the girls from the platform that she could take into the drop-in centre during the day but for whom she had no night shelter provision. She was extremely concerned for these girls, many of whom were vulnerable to trafficking, and had an ambition to set up a girls' home on land adjacent to the boys' home which happened to be for sale. However, the owner wanted nearly £30,000 and gave Sister Clara only two months to find the money as he alleged he had other purchasers waiting.

Although Railway Children rarely funded capital projects, we could see the urgency for Itarsi's young girls, and sought a source for buying the land. The Butterfields put up £10,000 and I mentioned the need on a visit to the Waterside Headquarters of British Airways and a cheque for £10,000 was produced within 30 seconds of me completing my presentation of the case. The last £10,000 was a little harder to achieve and a loan was made to try to obtain the land before it was too late, but then the owner increased the ask and was making things difficult, so Jeevodaya found a much larger plot of land about two kilometres away and purchased that. In the meantime the HSBC Bank had elected to fund street children programmes as their corporate social responsibility (CSR) project and the Indian branch made £10,000 available to complete the purchase and enable the loan to turn into a donation for the running costs. Sister Clara persuaded the Japanese Embassy in India to finance the construction of a large residential home on the purchased land and Railway Children, with part of the Comic Relief 2 money, entered an agreement to fund the running costs. Sister Clara decided to move the boys to the new home and use the boys' home which was right by the

Sister Clara with David during the visit to Jeevodaya, 2009

station to house the young girls. This was because most of the boys no longer had contact with their families whereas many of the girls were from street-dwelling families around the station, but at risk of trafficking and sexual abuse and rape. In that way the girls could be protected at night, be funded to go to school during the day, and still retain contact with their families.

I have visited Jeevodaya a couple of times and one of the Railway Children trustees, Rebecca Klug, who worked for BA in India several years ago and became the Customer Services Director of Virgin Trains, took Jeevodaya to heart and makes regular visits there. Sister Clara is a remarkable woman - all 4' 6" of her! She has persuaded her bishop - initially against his wishes - that she should remain in charge of the street children programme as her vocation and although she has the help of a couple of nuns, most of her staff are Hindus or Moslems and there is no pressure on the children to convert to Christianity, although her motivation and care is very much built on Christian principles. She is widely respected by the railway authorities and police, despite the fact that Christians are sometimes viewed with great suspicion especially in that state and when I visited the Divisional Railway Manager in Bhopal nearby, I received a glowing testimonial about her work. Because of the visits I've made, I interested children at the churches in Nantwich and at a Roman Catholic Primary School in Leek in twinning with the children in Jeevodaya and from time to time there is an exchange of greetings, Christmas and Divali cards and photographs.

By 2007 the Railway Children programme in India had reached its maximum outreach through some 21 partners at over 50 railway station locations contacting between 20,000 and 25,000 children each year. However, we were beginning to ask more questions about the depth and sustainability of our outcomes, about the long term changes in the children and how we could demonstrate - and assure ourselves and our donors - that the children we contacted had made a positive change to their lives. We had decided a couple of years earlier to disengage slowly from the slum community children's educational work and concentrate on the most vulnerable children - those whose family contact had been lost or was negligible. In a couple of cases changes to the leadership in our partners led to changes in direction or we came to the end of our funding agreement and decided that either the partner had sufficient resources from elsewhere to continue or that we did not feel that the interventions were strong enough to renew the partnership.

The work undertaken by the vast majority of our partners was carried out by devoted humble people, determined to put the interests of these children first and do their very best for them with scarce resources, often in extremely trying conditions. Most of our partners appreciated the fact that we sought genuine partnerships where we shared ideas, opportunities and problems, carried out joint training and advocacy and were not just grant-makers wanting nothing but feedback to furnish our fundraisers with motivating stories.

The Comic Relief 2 funded programme ended in 2009 and Railway Children submitted, and received approval for, a further four year grant, Comic Relief 3, for £1 million, which was to be concentrated on a few of our most effective partners, particularly those in the north of India from where so many of the street children were running. We, the charity, had learned much from our two previous funded programmes and Mrinalini Rao and her team had spent time in 2009 reviewing the Railway Children's strategy in India, looking at ways in which our learning could be shared with our partners and those various stakeholders in India who could influence the lives of these children for the better. The Railway Children Federation of India, whilst admirable in concept, had struggled to be an effective forum as it lacked resource back-up, and some of the elected officers were reluctant to commit resources to it that would enable it to flourish separately from their own NGOs. So Railway Children staff trainers and programme officers, led by the India Country Director, took over most of its roles of documenting change and impact; exchanging ideas and best practice; and undertaking advocacy with the railway authorities, railway police and those national groups appointed by government to progress the integrated child protection policies that the national government has developed. Some 50% of Railway Children's continuing work in India is currently supported by the Comic Relief 3 grant, with the remainder, particularly in the south of the country, being funded by independent trusts or by Railway Children's unrestricted income.

Chapter 12
On home territory

We had not ignored the situation in our own country. Interestingly, Railway Children was the only member of the Consortium for Street Children that partnered projects in the UK as well as overseas, excluding the large NGOs like Save the Children. We had committed ourselves to spend at least 20% of our income to support runaway children in the United Kingdom, indeed our charitable expenditure on our British programme by 2003 was almost 30%. Whilst we had worked closely with Centrepoint in the beginning, their focus was on the support of young people over 16 years of age, and we were aware from discussions with our partners that many child runaways under that age had few organisations to whom they could turn. In addition, my own association with 'Get Connected' had highlighted for me the needs of the under 16-year olds when we analysed the number and types of calls our volunteers were receiving. Most of the 15,000 calls per annum were from 13-15 year olds and there was a significant number from even younger children. Family conflict and domestic violence came high on the list of reasons that children gave for seeking help.

We had analysed the referrals 'Get Connected' made and found disturbingly that over 20% of the calls in one year were referred to the Samaritans, an alarming statistic demonstrating the severe magnitude of the distress of some of our callers. The Samaritans was also the organisation which we were most reliably able to contact when we made a call on behalf of a child caller. We often tried to connect a child with 'Childline' but frustratingly their lines were heavily engaged, and one year I remember only 20% of our attempted calls to them were successfully connected, another indication of the need of such facilities to listen to children's concerns.

We had maintained our support of ASTRA, an NGO working closely with the statutory authority in Gloucestershire, and with the ROC project in Glasgow. There, as a result of our funding, the Scottish Executive had made a substantial grant to purchase and renovate a building to act as a 3-bedded refuge - at that time three of only twelve beds authorised for under 16 year olds in the UK outside the provisions made by Social Services through their children's homes, fostering or emergency overnight accommodation. However, many children in this situation need time to reflect and discuss their options with an independent counsellor as some children have ongoing problems with their Social Services contact or have even run away from problems at the children's home or emergency fostering arrangement in which they'd been placed. Since then, the refuges in Torquay and London have closed through lack of funding and in 2011 only five beds for under 16-year olds independent of Social Services remained available in the whole of the UK - the three in Glasgow and two in the Sheffield NGO, 'Safe@Last', which we also support.

The results of some research on Roma children in London which we'd funded through the Children's Society were published (specifically about the needs of children found begging on London Underground stations) and in the course of this partnership we had come across Andy McCullough, who was leading some of the Children's Society work on runaway children, closely associated with the research they had carried out on the scale of the problem in the UK (*Rees G & Lee J, 2005, 'Still Running 2: Findings from the Second National Survey of Young Runaways.' London: The Children's Society*). Andy was clearly keen to take this work further and the Railway Children trustees had decided that, with the growth of our UK partnerships, we needed a full-time resource to develop our involvement. We therefore advertised the post and were not unduly surprised, though pleased, when we saw Andy's name on the list of applicants. He was keen to maintain priority on the issue of UK runaways, as he had personal experience of living on the streets, understood many of such children's issues and really wanted to see things through to make a real difference. This corresponded exactly with our aims too, so we brought Andy on board in the summer of 2005 and realised very quickly how great an asset it was to have someone who could speak with such authority on the issue.

With Andy in post, and with his connections to other UK NGOs and with government resources, we increased our UK portfolio of projects. We joined in partnership with a couple of NGOs in the North West - firstly with 'Safe in the City' in Manchester who worked for runaway and at risk children and child asylum seekers.

We funded a programme aimed particularly at children from different ethnic backgrounds. Secondly, we linked with 'Talk Don't Walk' in Warrington, a counselling centre working in a hub of charities in Warrington town centre right next to the local authority's youth service, so that constant contact was maintained with its youth workers there. This project had a seconded senior police woman working with the NGO staff seeking to defuse problems in families that had arisen before the child actually left home. Their methodology was of great interest and the local police were enthusiastic as the results of their preventative work had substantially reduced the number of child runaways - including children running for a second and even third time - and the number of petty crimes committed by children in the area. As a result, the police calculated that they had saved at least £1 million a year in the costs of dealing with crime - the court appearances and the costs of home visits taking back runaway children and dealing with the consequences. Railway Children was keen to document the process and produce a 'toolkit' for replication elsewhere. The local MP, Helen Southworth, took a great interest and with Andy, founded the 'All Party Parliamentary Group (APPG) for Children who Runaway or Go Missing' and she invited Andy and Railway Children to act as the APPG's secretariat at meetings in the House of Commons.

Andy felt strongly that many of the smaller UK charities who were working directly with children on the streets or in other extremely vulnerable circumstances rarely got their voices heard by government. He started talking about the value of creating a coalition of such charities for they had first-hand experience at grass-roots level, and within a couple of years had formed the English Coalition for Runaway Children and was voted its Chair by the membership. Being Chair of the Coalition and also Secretary to the APPG gave him and Railway Children access to government ministers and Andy was appointed to a Working Group considering guidelines to local authorities on child runaways by Ed Balls, then Secretary of State for Children, Schools and Families. This Group published their guidelines, called 'Young Runaways Action Plan' in 2008, identifying that recent reports had recommended the delivery of coordinated, multi-agency responses to vulnerable young people, especially integrated front-line service delivery. It set out a number of actions for government and local authorities and stated that progress would be monitored by one of the 'National Indicator Sets' for Local Government - NI 71. Andy remained part of a cross-Departmental working group for young runaways.

One of the concerns raised in that Action Plan for Runaways was the need for emergency accommodation for such children, supported by counselling and advice from a number of services. I have already mentioned the lack of specialist independent refuge places available and Andy came to the Railway Children Board with a proposition to help the Sheffield NGO 'Safe@Last' to buy and provide just such a refuge and work in close consultation with agencies in the Sheffield area. This was done and a two-bedded refuge was eventually given authorisation under the 1989 Children's Act to house children under 16 years of age for up to 14 days while their problems and issues were addressed and the children counselled on the options available to them.

With our first hand evidence from the Railway Children UK partners, Andy's experience, and the data available from research undertaken by the Children's Society on the numbers of young runaways, Terina, the Chief Executive, and Andy proposed that the Railway Children acquired its own researcher to undertake a deeper investigation into the life of children living on the streets of the UK. The Children's Society research was numerate but our team felt that we needed evidence from the lives of such children to make any real impact and bring about change for the most vulnerable group of children - those 'detached' from families and support agencies, who had fallen through the safety net and were existing, in great danger, on the streets of this country 24 hours a day.

The research that had provided the available knowledge about British runaway children had involved Emilie Smeaton, a Principal Consultant of the Children's Society based at York University, and Andy had worked with her and respected her work. We advertised the 'Researcher' post, were pleased to see that Emilie had applied and appointed her to carry out this important piece of research. She was enthusiastic to have the scope and funding to carry through an in-depth qualitative body of research that, by exploring the stories of children living on the street, would produce real evidence behind the figures on which some policy was being based. Both Andy and Emilie were aware that many of the 100,000 children quoted in the Children's Society's research ran from home to friends or relatives for relatively short periods, but within this figure there were some children who were genuinely 'detached' from home and society and who spent time living on the street at great risk of harm. Andy knew from his contacts with the police that there were many children within the quoted number who were 'off the radar' in that no-one had reported them missing. These children were at even greater risk without any agency intervention or supervision and it was Railway Children's objective to get some robust evidence about them, their lives, their reasons for leaving home and their experiences on the street.

We realised that such research might be difficult to undertake, for it required finding such children and getting them to talk frankly about their lives. We were also aware that we would probably be highlighting a problem that would not be popular with either the public or the politicians, as many such children were already likely to be stigmatised in the media as 'hoodies' or even worse, 'feral children'. But both Andy and Emilie knew such children were there, even though the term 'street children' was not one that the British public would associate with children in their own country.

We spent some time planning the research, and working with Emilie on her own safety in carrying out such a remit. She had worked earlier in a hostel for homeless young people so she was aware of some of the issues and risks. She recommended to us that she should interview a relatively small number of children in depth rather than try to get a larger number and cover the issue too superficially and we also needed to give her time to find the most appropriate children and gain their trust and that of the community in which they existed. We therefore agreed with her that the children to be interviewed would be those that had lived on the street 24 hours a day for more than a month while still under the age of 16. We also agreed that Emilie would cover children in all parts of the UK and would seek children in a number of towns – not just the 'assumed' hotspots of London, Glasgow or Manchester. In the end she arranged interviews with children in market and tourist towns and cities throughout the UK. It included a set of children detained in a Young Offenders' Secure Unit.

103 children eventually took part in the research, giving Emilie interviews varying in length from two to five hours. Although our

researcher used one or two of our partner agencies to identify some appropriate children, Emilie found that the most apposite method was to hang around the street, often with the advice of the adult homeless who seemed to be the people most aware of the youngsters living there. Emilie would establish the validity of the interviewee according to the criteria we had set – she often found several children wanting to tell their stories although some, because of age or time on the street had to be disappointed – and most often would invite the child for a coffee and something to eat while they answered her questions and she gained their trust. Some of the interviews then became remarkably frank and sometimes it was as if a floodgate had been opened. At the end of each interview Emilie would seek the opportunity to suggest some positive action that the young person could take, offering to refer them to a suitable agency if they were willing. 75% of the children she interviewed had never had an intervention from any agency whatsoever, they were truly 'off the radar' - which became the title of her research report. One young girl had been so damaged by her experiences and was now in such a state that Emile could think of no suitable course of action that the girl was likely to find acceptable, and she apologised profusely at the end of the interview that she could not help her. The girl shook her head and said, 'You've helped me already. You're the first person in my life who's ever listened to me.' Whilst this was the most explicit comment of this nature, the same theme of not being listened to, of being 'talked at', or more often 'shouted at', came out in many of the interviews.

Violence was normalised for all these children to such an extent that most of them knew no other means of reacting to life – this was what happened to them and this was the only way they knew to react to others. All the children had suffered from parents or carers who were alcoholics, drug addicts or had mental health problems or any combination of all three. The young people themselves now suffered from the same abuses and problems and would in all likelihood become similar parents unless a successful intervention could take place. For most it was already too late. One of the key findings and recommendations from the report was the importance of early intervention – the recognition by front line workers of when a family needed help and time whilst the child was in the first two years of its life; or intervention as a child begins to show signs of distress or drifting from school – often the last contact a child had before becoming 'detached'.

Railway Children's trustees, Emilie, Andy and Terina, spent some time at the end of the research discussing not just the conclusions, but more importantly, what positive recommendations could be made not only to help such children, but also and perhaps even more importantly, to prevent children falling through the same gaps in society. For that would continue the problems into the next generation, since it was apparent that many of the parents who had abused and rejected these children had themselves been victims of similar neglect and abuse in their own childhood. Many of the problems highlighted would require changes in government policy – more emphasis on home visits to families at risk, more time for health and social workers to interact and the implication on resource numbers to do this; more youth outreach work on the street; more short term refuge facilities for under 16 year olds to help them consider options independently. There was also an overwhelming need to see these young people as children and not stigmatise them, especially in the media. Despite their own violent or self-destructive actions, they were often children crying out for love and acceptance, for being respected, and heard. At a time of recession and concern in some of the media over 'youth crime', this was not going to be an easy message to get across and gain acceptance.

The report 'Off the Radar' was launched in November 2009 before more than 100 invitees at the German Gymnasium centre by St Pancras station. The event was well attended by voluntary sector organisations and Railway Children's corporate and programme partners, but the media and politicians invited were notable by their absence which confirmed for us the difficulty in getting the message across to obtain real change for these children. The Railway Children has since used every opportunity to bring the issue before appropriate bodies who can influence policy – it will be a long haul, requiring sustained interest and action if Britain is not to face an ever increasing number of such children at risk to themselves and others. An opportunity to mount an exhibition in the Houses of Parliament came in November 2010 and this focused particularly on 'Britain's Street Children and the 'Off the Radar' report. There is a big financial penalty in the long-term too if no effective action is taken. A lack of action will cost British Society billions over the next decades. And that's just the financial damage

…

Chapter 13
Fundraising

In our 2001 financial year Railway Children's income was £360,000. In 2002 it was nearly £600,000. We passed the £1million mark in 2004 and the £2million mark in 2009 despite the general recession that was making life difficult for nearly all charities. In fact in the last year our income rose by 21% to £2.6m, with a budgeted £3million annually by 2012. But the issue we are tackling is immense. Even with this increased income we sometimes feel we are only really helping a minority of the children at risk – 25,000 or more every year, yes, but there are so many we could help if we had more resources. Even so, as far as I'm aware, this means that the Railway Children is the largest organisation in the UK working specifically to support street children – a few other members of the Consortium for Street Children are larger, but their portfolio of beneficiaries is much wider including working children, slum-dwelling children, children in conflict with the law and children needing health care and educational interventions. Railway Children's beneficiaries are street children alone and specifically those with little or no parental contact.

As our income has increased we have obviously been able to give support to more children through more projects, but we have had to manage our cash flow carefully to avoid taking on more than we can reliably sustain. You can't dip in and out of a street children programme without potential damage to the children involved as it is psychologically almost worse to give a child hope and then withdraw it than to give no help at all. This means that we have developed a reserves policy that does not just safeguard our legal responsibilities to our staff and debtors should the charity ever fold, but that we have set aside (or 'designated') at least a year's funding for the key projects for which we have ongoing funding agreements, to give them time to find other funding sources should our income be at risk.

From the very beginning the charity has seen the railway industry as its natural funding partner, and almost every year at least half of its income has come in 'unrestricted' form from individuals, companies and events in the privatised industry. The railway industry has widened its scope since privatisation and now includes many equipment and service suppliers as well as train operating companies, infrastructure maintenance and renewal companies, and Network Rail. The former British Rail could never have been such a powerful partner – individuals could have contributed but the nationalised company itself would have found it impossible to provide funding as it was funded by the taxpayer. I had several conversations with the late Gwyneth Dunwoody, my own MP who, until her sudden death, indicated her strong support for the charity. Although totally opposed to the privatisation process, she readily admitted that having a myriad companies involved in the industry – whilst being in her opinion a poor way to run a national railway system – could hardly be bettered for a funding partnership with a charity. There are well over a hundred companies now significantly involved in the industry, all of them potential funders. Some companies match-fund the contributions of their employees. Some make corporate donations for specific programmes or hold fundraising events. Others encourage their employees to take part in major fundraising events such as the annual Railway Ball at the Grosvenor House Hotel or in what has become a traditional annual '3 Peaks by Rail Challenge'.

River Irt' – the narrow gauge engine of the Three Peaks special on the Ravenglass & Eskdale Railway, 2004

This last is not quite what it sounds – although one mountain our teams climb does have a railway running up it (the Snowdon Mountain Railway). Our intrepid climbers eschew that easy option, however, and only use the railway system to deliver them to the foot of the mountains they have to climb. Various railway companies have sponsored provision of the locomotives and rolling stock, train crews, on board catering, track access charges, and road links from station to the start point of the climbs – and the narrow gauge Ravenglass and Eskdale Railway runs a special train for the climbers to Dalegarth where the 50 four person teams hike to Scafell Pike. Finally, Ben Nevis is climbed at dawn after an all-night run to Fort William and the cavalcade of exhausted but fulfilled teams is whisked back to Crewe and London while Railway Children staff estimate the sponsored donations and announce the team which has raised the most. This popular challenge has raised significant sums over the years and brought awareness of the charity to many people at all levels in the different railway associated companies, many of whom match-fund their staff as well as sponsoring elements of the costs so that the profit to the Railway Children is maximised.

We are accompanied by an experienced mountain rescue team but they have never had to deal with any serious injuries - although on the first occasion I managed to become the most embarrassing casualty without even stepping foot on a mountain. I'd travelled in the train to share the experience with the teams and thank them for their efforts and when we got to Fort William I stayed on the train when it was stabled in the carriage sidings to help the train staff clean up the vehicles. I had to walk back to the rear vehicle where the oil-driven generator was located so I could jump down from the train and I skidded in the corridor on spillage from the leaking generator, tearing ligaments as I fell. On the journey back home I became the very first patient of the massage team who were offering free treatment as their donation to the event! A group of even more ambitious climbers tackled the 20,000' Mount Kilimanjaro in 2010 and then visited some of our East African projects with their remaining breath, raising sponsorship funds for us.

Many companies arrange their own fundraising events. Select Service Partners (SSP), the holder of the franchises for the larger station food outlets, won their internal company 'Gold Award' in

2003 for the best charity partnership of any of the global Compass Group companies for their fundraising initiatives with Railway Children. The Railway Children collection boxes are still to be found by every till of each food stall in the SSP franchise at stations throughout the system and between them raise a surprising amount every month for the charity.

The railway heritage industry has also played its part although necessarily on a smaller scale as most heritage railways are charities themselves. Crewe and Doncaster Railway Workshops and the combined Tyseley London Midland and Heritage Works have had Open Days at which a Railway Children presence was invited to raise awareness of the charity as well as raise funds – usually in hundreds or thousands of pounds rather than tens of thousands. The 175th anniversary of the Great Western Railway gave the charity the opportunity to participate in a number of events and Gala Weekends at heritage railways in the former Great Western territory. Vintage Trains at Tyseley invited the charity's volunteers to join some of their advertised railtour excursions to hold raffles – the best being the superb replica 'Bristolian' high speed run from Paddington to Bristol and back behind the splendidly restored 'Castle' locomotive, No.5043 'Earl of Mount Edgcumbe' which arrived back in Paddington 45 minutes early catching out the restaurant car staff who were still serving dinner on arrival. Our raffle volunteer team had been pre-warned that something special was afoot and just managed to complete their fundraising efforts in time. Warm thanks are due to a number of individuals who have given their time and the opportunities to the charity – it is invidious to name individuals although I will mention just one, Bob Meanley of Tyseley, who has been especially generous in his support.

A number of other railway associated clubs have also been donors or have given us the opportunity to meet and exhibit our work to their members. A few large model railway clubs have invited our display and stall to their annual exhibitions – and I have personally been present more than once at the Town Hall in the cathedral city of Wells and at the Solent Model Railway Club in Eastleigh. I mentioned earlier our association with the Darjeeling Himalayan Railway Society and the fact that their Chairman, David Charlesworth, a railway artist, paints a number of water colours for us each year as a basis for our Christmas card brochure.

Every year we provide a selection of railway, religious and secular cards. It is also an excellent way of raising the charity's awareness among those who are not (as yet) on our database. I am a great admirer of David's railway paintings – he has sometimes kindly offered one for auction at the Railway Ball as well – and I have an original that I commissioned of my favourite locomotive, No. 4087 'Cardigan Castle', raising the echoes at the snowy summit at Llanvihangel by the Sugar Loaf mountain near Abergavenny with a North & West express. Although this painting had appeared in the card catalogue as 'Western Express', it featured in 2010 again in recognition of the Great Western Railway 175th Anniversary.

At one time we produced a number of 'bespoke' designs for the corporate Christmas cards of some train companies, but this became difficult when we were obliged to put our card distribution in the hands of a commercial firm. We made this arrangement when we found that our fundraising staff had to drop everything else for about 4-6 weeks in October/November to pack and send out the ever increasing orders received. Even if we employed an army of volunteers, the space required was prohibitive. Now some companies have moved away from sending company cards and announced that they would make a suitable donation to Railway Children instead.

We have also benefited from another aspect of the railway enthusiast world. Several years ago Peter Aldridge, then Managing Director of HSBC Rail, one of the three rolling stock leasing companies, offered a number of electric and diesel locomotive nameplates from life-expired engines for auction. Peter later became a Railway Children trustee. To our surprise and delight, the collection, auctioned for us by Ian Wright of Sheffield Memorabilia Auctions free of any commission, well exceeded our expectations. When our income from Christmas cards, stall sale items and revenue from an internet browser via our Railway Children website homepage looked like exceeding the charity trading limit on a regular basis and not just as a one-off, we formally set up the Railway Children Trading Company with a further gift of nameplates by HSBC Rail forming the initial capital. We also have the Railway Ball Ltd as an associated company whose object is to give all profits from the annual Ball to the charity.

Another of our trustees, Christian Wolmar, is a journalist turned author who has written a number of well researched books on the building and operation of London's Underground Railway, the history of Britain's overland railways, the development of world railways and most recently on railways and war. Each book launch has supported the Railway Children and Christian has given a number of well received illustrated lectures on the books' themes at the Royal Geographical Society and other locations in aid of the charity.

In 2009 Railway Children was one of nineteen charities selected by the UK Girl Guide movement to participate in their centenary year-long celebrations and we were invited to develop a package of information and activities that Brownie and Guide groups could use to increase their knowledge of Britain's homeless and runaway children, lobby parliament for more refuge places to be made available and raise funds for the charity by a number of events including fundraising sleepouts –very popular with many of the groups. The suggestions were taken up by 768 groups involving 17,791 Guides and Brownies and a significant sum was raised during the year with hopefully an ongoing interest among this large number of girls as well as educating them about the dangers of running away themselves.

All this increase in annual revenue had not been achieved, of course, without additional staff. Julia and Katie assisted by Lindsay had worked hard, but they were part time and we had reached the stage when we needed some full time resource. We recruited Jane Simpson as Head of Fundraising and began the task of building a team to support her. This eventually settled down with Dave Ellis joining us as Fundraiser for Corporates and Wendy Brawn, who had served us as a very capable Administrator and Book-keeper, as Fundraiser for Trusts and Grants. With income well over a million pounds a year, we recruited David Brookes as Accountant and Kaye Brindle as Administrator, releasing Wendy to start the trusts fundraising role which involved supervising and reporting on the Comic Relief grant as well as submitting new applications. Ian Watson joined us as our Community Fundraiser and Jane set her mind to devising a fundraising strategy requiring and utilising such resources to the full and looking hard at our brand.

In the early days I had struggled to find an appropriate logo – not my area of expertise – and had tried several drawings even getting my daughter to experiment. Our efforts were rather overcomplicated and involved variations of the child silhouette found in the logos of several children's charities. The printing company of 'Action Stations', our first newspaper, 'Jigsaw' from a local business park, drew a simple sketch of a stylised tunnel mouth (well that was what they said it was) with the strap line, 'Light at the end of the tunnel' and I adopted it without further question; it was simple even if few recognised the tunnel it was meant to represent. Katie and Julia later played around with the idea and devised an ingenious logo based on a set of points that you might find in a child's first model train set, with the ends uplifted as if it were a child waiting to be picked up, with the other part of the points remaining as a grey shadow as if the child's past was being left behind. Coupled with our use of a colour between purple and maroon (cerise?) this logo and house style fulfilled its function for several years but Jane brought fresh focus on the whole issue of image and the need to appear more professional, to support our growing strength and especially enhance our appeal to the corporate world.

She drew up a contract with a small PR company, Stephen Talbot Advertising, also based in Scope House at Crewe next door to our own office. Between them they developed a powerful brand with a very simple logo stressing the word 'children' in the charity's title and forming the 'i' in 'children' as a pawn-like child figure, all in a striking black and luminous police green colour scheme. Our brochures and magazine were revamped and a very professional front was given to the charity, which certainly achieved its objectives of attracting the attention of some of the major corporates. It was not without some controversy, however. Some felt that our image and materials were now too glossy and inappropriate for a charity supporting the poorest of the poor. However, it certainly produced results and at a major conference of International Lions Clubs from Africa and Asia that I addressed in Bombay in 2005 I was complimented on the standard of our materials with the statement that the Lions themselves wished they had brochures and magazines of that quality. The materials being produced locally did not cost as much as they looked, but some –

especially in the rail industry – thought it gave out the wrong message.

The logo was not without its critics either, not so much the logo itself but the strapline 'The Voice for Street Children Worldwide' that had been developed and approved after a lot of debate at the Board. I personally had some misgivings in that it seemed very ambitious and aspirational rather than a true representation of what we were actually doing. I saw duplication with the Consortium for Street Children's stated aims and argued that – as yet - we only focused on children on the street full time with little or no family contact. We did not now work with slum children spending most of the day on the street, which are usually included in the generic term 'street children'. Our key emphasis is still early intervention. Although we have not yet formally changed the strapline, we frequently now use the more accurate 'Getting to Street Children before the Street gets to them' which is slightly overlong for putting on lapel badges and the like, but finding a succinct, accurate but high impact strapline is not easy. (A new strapline 'Fighting for Street Children' was adopted last year after my retirement as Chairman.)

However, the new branding did work and our visibility began to rise. Collecting boxes at the SSP station food outlets were certainly attracting attention and London Underground highlighted our UK messages very publicly under every underground station map showing the road systems and names in the locality. When Jane joined us she initiated a survey test in a number of locations to find out our brand awareness. The result in one sense was dispiriting in that of 730 people questioned in one survey only one person had heard of 'Railway Children' and that turned out by chance to be an acquaintance of mine! In another survey fewer people claimed to have heard of us than claimed to know of a fictitious charity whose name we had invented for the survey! The upside of this information was that financially we were doing well despite this lack of awareness outside the railway industry, so the potential support if we were to become better known was encouraging. The awareness of our charity is certainly much greater now!

Our revamped fundraising organisation set very challenging targets and whilst these were found to be overoptimistic, income increased steadily until 2006 when it levelled off at just under £2million per annum. When Jane was headhunted to be Chief

Executive of a cancer charity, Terina, our Chief Executive, decided to manage the fundraising team directly herself as we were finding gaps opening up between the fundraising and programme teams. This is not an unusual problem in many charities but it was one we wanted to address quickly as we were still a relatively small organisation. Managing such a wide span of control could only be a short term solution and we soon decided to support Terina with a Marketing & Communications Officer to liaise closely with the programmes and ensure the right messages were being used in all our communications, and in a consistent way. The PR firm's Account Executive for the Railway Children's contract work applied for this post as he was most reluctant to lose the work that most highly motivated him, so Rob Capener came on board and immediately set himself the task of upgrading our website to make it more user friendly and lead people more quickly to the point where they could make a donation.

The result of these appointments was evident when the recession struck many charities hard, for Railway Children not only maintained its income but in certain aspects bucked the trend and increased its unrestricted donations in particular. We had become more professional in our fundraising. We were also becoming more professional in other important aspects of our charity's objectives as well.

Chapter 14
Professionalism

Our UK staff had grown to a dozen, augmented by a further ten in India, to support all our activities which by now were being carried out through 40 partner organisations in over seventy locations and reaching more than 20,000 street children each year. Our office at 'Scope House' Crewe, was becoming cramped – fine when some members of staff were out attending meetings or fundraising, or even overseas seeking new partners or reviewing the work of existing ones, but otherwise it felt as though we were playing musical chairs with the last person in having no desk space or computer access. Terina pressed on the Board the need for new accommodation and was authorised to search for more appropriate premises. We might have sought a further office in Scope House, but that building was used by the Borough Council to house growing and developing businesses, part of their plan to diversify away from the traditional reliance on car making and the railways, employment on which Crewe had depended and was declining substantially. We hardly felt like a newly developing company now and it was clear that we should look elsewhere.

We found accommodation with space for further growth in the centre of Sandbach, about five miles north east of Crewe and moved there in 2005. Whilst in many ways better for the staff – it was conveniently near shops and a free car park in the centre of the historic market town – it meant that I no longer had the convenience of leaving my car in the Scope House car park and popping in for a quick word with whoever was in the office before walking to the station for one of my frequent trips to London on Railway Children, Consortium for Street Children or Amnesty business. However, we now had premises with room to grow, a meeting room and ample storage capacity and at a rate that was cheaper than anything available in Crewe itself where new office blocks in the developing business park were more expensive than we felt we could justify. Our new accommodation, with the prestigious address of '1, The Commons, Sandbach', was on the first (top) floor of a fairly modern block that was above a council youth service centre, part of the Crewe area 'Connexions' team, called 'The Hub'.

Just before we left Scope House, however, we had a full day visit from a review team of the Charity Commission to evaluate our charity practices and performance. In the past the Charity Commission carried out investigations into charities where there had been complaints or the Commission had reasons for concern. However, the Commission now had a new policy of reviewing all charities on a regular basis, not just to check on performance but to share good practice and meet their objective of increasing the competence and effectiveness of British charities. They were starting with charities whose annual income was over £500,000 and less than £10million, that is those charities that were in a crucial development stage and needed to adopt more professional practises than were found in small or family-led charities. We were exactly the sort of charity they were targeting and had advised us that they wished to conduct a review. Two members of the Charity Commission spent a day, squashed into the Chief Executive's small office in Scope House, with Terina, Stan Judd as our trustee most concerned with administration and finance, Gordon Pettitt, Vice-Chair, Keith Strickland, Company Secretary, Jane Simpson, Head of Fundraising and myself as Chairman. They were of course interested in checking that we were fully complying with our Articles of Association and Rules and with charity law, but spent more time checking our practices against the Charity Commission's main headings of good practice as outlined in their booklet 'Hallmarks of an Effective Charity'. The review demonstrated that a number of actions we'd taken in the previous two to three years enabled us to pass the Review team's scrutiny with 'flying colours'.

As we had grown and acquired staff, we had been forced to pay more attention to our practices and procedures. Stan had put in place systems that would ensure our financial integrity but with the employment of more staff, we needed to ensure we were meeting all our obligations under employment laws and were, beyond the law, using best practice as employers. Having a 'Human Resource' specialist in trustee Rachel Bennett was extremely helpful and by 2003 we had deemed it beneficial to recruit a Company Secretary with professional qualifications and experience of that work rather than expecting our Chief Executive to fulfil that role among her many other duties. Despite the strides we had made in this area following Terina's appointment, our new recruit, Keith Strickland, drew our attention to a number of gaps in our systems, in particular the need to develop a trustee manual and code of conduct, and the obligation to put new trustees through an induction process that would enable them to understand their responsibilities and learn about the objectives and procedures of the charity itself.

A number of Board Sub-Committees had been put in place, authorised properly through Board Minutes to cover Governance, Fundraising, Programmes and Child Protection, but there were no formal agreed terms of reference for these Committees. It soon became apparent for example that the Programme Committee was taking detailed decisions on each proposal to fund a partner with masses of paper in support. The Board took the sensible decision to delegate certain powers to the Chief Executive, but it needed to be spelt out in proper Job Descriptions for the Chief Executive and other key staff. We had also been developing our Child Protection Policy with the Consortium for Street Children which governed our staff, trustees and volunteers and included anyone from the UK visiting our overseas projects, but such practices did not exist overseas in India or East Africa and we began dialogue with our partners on developing some basic rules, again guided by experience within the CSC.

It was interesting that the charity itself had been founded on the basis of the outcome of a risk assessment that I'd undertaken at the first meeting of the CSC that I'd attended in 1993, but no risk assessment had been undertaken since then of our activities either with our partners and beneficiaries or of our internal systems. In the meantime, the Charity Commission's Statement of Recommended Practice had re-specified how charities were to present their accounts and what matters were to be dealt with by Trustees' annual reports. They called for development of a risk policy and a regular review of identified risks. In 2002, under Terina's guidance we had carried out a comprehensive assessment and had identified a number of risks in five distinct areas of activity for which we identified our policies and actions to control those risks. Even so we recognised that we, along with nearly all NGOs working with children overseas, were vulnerable to potential financial mismanagement or child abuse by individuals in our overseas partner organisations where national rules concerning charity supervision were either more lax or less developed than in the UK. We therefore put the maintenance of supervision of our partners high on the list of priorities to be carried out by our UK and India based Programme Officers, and checked by the Chief Executive.

One area of confusion that Keith quickly discovered and that needed the Board's attention was the conduct of our Annual General Meetings. In the early days we involved our trustees, obviously, a number of other supporters who had been members of the Railway Children Committee before the charity's registration with the Charity Commission, and a few supporters who were prominent in their advocacy on our behalf. However, we were few in number and the charity's rules required a quorum of ten or one third of the membership and I can remember at least three occasions when the start of the AGM was delayed awaiting a tenth member - on one occasion, our supporter from Scotland, Jim Summers, who had come down specially, and on two other occasions we rang someone close at hand in London who was standing by to come if needed. It came to a head one year when we actually had to defer the meeting as we could not get a quorum and Keith helped us define our criteria to be a member. We sent out invitations to a number of key donors and organisations that had supported us on a regular basis. With some 40+ potential members accepting our invitation and being formally acknowledged as members, we have had no further problems in obtaining a quorum at the AGM whilst also having the opportunity to put our activities under the scrutiny of committed people who were a little more objective than those of us in the thick of things. It was also useful to have the opportunity to present our latest developments face to face rather than rely on written or internet communication, however good.

Thus, when the Charity Commission Review Team visited Railway Children, they found not only that we were fully compliant with charity law - apart from one small technical detail on the interpretation and application of one element of the complex charity accounting procedures where they gave us guidance - but also that we were in many areas carrying out what they termed 'good practice' when measured alongside the Commission's 'Hallmarks of an Effective Charity'. The 'Hallmarks' are that a charity should be clear about its purpose and direction; have a strong Board of trustees; be fit for purpose - ie have structures, policies and procedures that enable it to achieve its mission and deliver its services; is constantly learning and improving; is financially sound and prudent; and finally, is accountable and transparent. The practices that we had put in place over the years with the input in particular of Stan, Terina and Keith, together with the Board members of the Governance Committee, enabled us to have a very positive and encouraging dialogue with the members of the Review Team who commented several times that our policies and procedures conformed with 'good practice' and indicated that we might like to publish their report on our website to demonstrate our effectiveness as a charity to our donors and supporters. Apart from the minor issue over the accounting technicality, the only other recommendations they made were about correcting an error in our Articles and Guidelines where there was a small inconsistency and a reminder that although we had carried out a thorough risk assessment in 2002, it was good practice to review this annually, which we have since done.

It was the role of our Governance Committee to take on board these sorts of issues in detail and make recommendations to the full Board. Initially, I chaired it but felt that it might be more appropriate for someone else who was more objective to chair this vital committee. Peter Aldridge with his experience of both general management and finance was ideal and he agreed to take over the role. We would meet in various localities near Euston station - convenient both for London based members and those of us travelling down from Crewe - including the SSP offices in the Euston Road opposite the station, Peter's own office in the block adjacent to the station, and on a couple of occasions on the 26th floor of a tower block on the Euston Road near Great Portland Street tube station, in the offices of a company donor, W.S.Atkins, engineering and safety consultants to the railway. However, we discovered one real drawback to this otherwise spectacular location overlooking Regents Park (and the generous provision by the company of a mouth-watering buffet lunch). Our Company Secretary Keith turned rather pale and asked to sit with his back to the panoramic views over London as he admitted to suffering from vertigo. Michael Holden, another member of the committee, said to him, 'You don't need to worry until you feel the building sway.' I don't think it helped very much and we've since then resumed our meetings, in contrast, in the basement of the SSP office. I haven't received any complaints yet from anyone claiming they suffered from claustrophobia!

Despite the good report of the Charity Commission Review Team, Keith proposed that we should use legal advisers who were versed in charity law to ensure we kept up to date with legal changes in the governance of charities and that we reviewed our practices from time to time with them to keep ahead of the game. Charity law was so specialist that the solicitors we had used via our railway contacts to set up the charity were perhaps not suited to our current needs and Keith recommended we used Stone King Sewell. A number of Board members were hesitant about spending the charity's income on such advice, but over recent years their help in revising our Articles of Association and setting up our Trading Company has been vital and all now value their contribution. Apart from taking advantage of a number of changes allowed by law to make charity administration easier, we needed to extend our charity objective to include young people up to 25 years of age, in addition to children (defined in the UN Convention on the Rights of the Child as being anyone under the age of 18). Several of our partners had expressed concern that children they had supported suddenly found themselves cut off from support once they reached the age of 18, yet still needed help on such things as further education, vocational training, job finding and housing. Whilst it would not be our main focus, we did not want to be prevented from supporting our partners where this might be a key need - as we were finding with the programme of our Kenyan partner, the Undugu Society, whose Association model previously mentioned included young people in their late teens and early twenties as well as younger children.

The Board subsequently met to consider the pilot projects we had established in Central America, Eastern Europe and East Africa, their outcomes and where we should concentrate our resources in the next phase of the charity's development. We had ceased funding the 'Love Russia' shelter projects in the Moscow area and the Siberia Chita scheme, where our input had been primarily of a capital nature, and had concentrated our resources in the NAN partnership in Moscow city itself. This action-research project demonstrated valuable contacts made with children at the Moscow stations and revealed an innate suspicion of the railway and civil police which our NAN and Medecin sans Frontières staff struggled at first to overcome so as to gain the children's trust. However, we were making progress, and the research findings pointed to the value of establishing social workers at these stations to make initial contact with the children and only involve the police if a crime had been committed by the runaway child. Agreement was reached that state funded social workers would be trained by NAN to act as the front line contacts for these children and would establish their reasons for running away and the best options for their future. However, the problems then encountered between the railway ministry responsible for the station environment and the ministry responsible for the police made the progress of the project difficult, so we have held further funding back until the issue is resolved (it hasn't been yet in 2011). Such difficulties of working in the former Soviet Union, with its bureaucratic state culture, made that country a low priority for our further expansion. It was clear that voluntary work in Russia could only be done effectively in partnership with the State - frankly we believed the priority of organisations working there would be to make the creaking state systems operate properly rather than setting up alternative voluntary sector systems.

In Central America we were working with two contrasting NGOs. We had funded Juconi in Mexico for over ten years and had learned much from their intensive child rehabilitation process which we thought we might test in other parts of our programmes. The sheer number of children we were contacting in India made such a staff/child ratio almost prohibitively expensive although we thought that Juconi's methods could be tried wherever the street children problem had not yet reached such endemic proportions. Our programme with Casa Alianza in Guatemala was of interest and badly needed, dealing as it did with children who were at risk of being caught up in the gang culture and often murdered, but we had little experience of working with such children. Our input had been that of providing funds - important, but giving us little opportunity to use our experience and knowledge to add further value to the partners we were funding.

By way of contrast, African NGOs were struggling with little support or input from their governments, and locally based NGOs were often in need of support and advice as well as funds. Since this seemed a situation closely resembling our initial experience in

India we felt we had the knowledge and resources to make a significant impact there. The Board therefore decided to accept the recommendations from Pete Kent and Terina to close or put on hold our partnerships in America and Eastern Europe, by simply completing the agreed funding cycles only, and look to develop our East Africa programmes in Kenya and Tanzania, with a view to increasing from four to six partner projects within a year or so, setting up an African Railway Children office in either Nairobi or Dar-es-Salaam, to mirror the development of the programme in India with the long term intention of supporting an East African programme of similar size and impact.

Having served more than ten years as one of the founding trustees, Stan Judd decided to stand down as a trustee but was keen to remain a volunteer. He continued to come to Sandbach, travelling from Milton Keynes or Rugby via Crewe every couple of weeks to look after our accounting work for the Partnership for Vulnerable Children and to help Terina with the management of the Board and Governance Committee meetings - arranging venues, agendas and taking clear and detailed minutes. Because all operational matters had been delegated to Terina and her team, along with greater powers of financial authority, it was possible to stand down the Fundraising and Programme Committees and instead hold 'ad hoc' forums where appropriate staff and trustees could meet together when a particular issue of significant interest was developing. For instance, we held a couple of Programme Forums around the development of the East African strategy and on the emerging conclusions and analysis from Emilie Smeaton's research on UK street children. A couple of Fundraising Forums were in the main opportunities for trustees to feed in ideas for further fundraising, but the team was in effect handling as much of this work as it could manage and further ideas from trustees were difficult to pick up unless they were very significant or could be led by the trustees themselves. Although Stan stood down as a trustee, he continued his tireless, reliable and so often unsung service, so we were delighted to support and celebrate his award of the OBE for services to charity in the Queen's Birthday Honours list in 2007.

Peter Aldridge acquainted us with the work carried out for his company by the Harvard management consultancy organisation, 'Palladium', in devising and implementing the 'Balanced

Scorecard' performance assessment system. He felt it could prove beneficial to Railway Children to adopt such a system and stated that Palladium had volunteered to help Railway Children trustees and staff to develop it - the first application to a voluntary sector organisation in the UK. The company, who would normally expect heavy fees for such work, adopted Railway Children as their principal pro-bono project for 2007, and without charge exposed the charity to real expertise in strategic thinking. The objective was to identify a dozen or so key objectives the charity needed to fulfil its mission, and put these in a succinct form so that there was clarity and unanimity among staff and trustees on our purpose. These would also help in the communications with potential donors and influencers. Each objective would be backed by Key Performance Indicators (KPIs) - phrased as 'Do Wells' – that is we will achieve our objectives if we do the following things well. Measurements would then be identified against each of the 'Do Wells' to allow performance and effectiveness to be monitored.

At first some trustees were uncertain about the applicability of a top business management technique in the voluntary sector culture, and the staff certainly found the effort to identify the KPIs for their own areas of activity hard and frustrating and the novel language alien to them. However, we persevered, and by January 2008 had developed a balanced scorecard to manage the implementation of our chosen strategic objectives. Terina led the work and although her 'Balanced Scorecard Days' with her key staff were not the most eagerly looked forward to in the calendar, there is no doubt that in hindsight they have been extremely valuable. The method is now an accepted and embedded part of our management process, regularly reviewed by the Board and the Governance Committee. Why should not a charity use the latest techniques to ensure its effectiveness in changing the lives of its beneficiaries for the better? The fear that it would reduce everything to money and hard measurables and ignore quality and care was unfounded - you just have to find the right KPIs to describe the outcomes you desire.

Chapter 15
Networking and advocacy

I seemed to have spent most of my railway career liaising between the different departments and groups in the old British Rail even before privatisation made such fragmentisation official! If I got into trouble it was usually because I said too much, not too little, and passed on information frankly when perhaps someone was trying to keep information restricted in some way, for good or bad reasons. My somewhat esoteric university training in literary stylistic analysis brought out a talent to spot patterns and connections, and although I was rarely an 'inventor' or 'innovator' I was good at spotting opportunities and linkages and building on others' part-expressed ideas and seeing where they might lead if connected with other thoughts or actions that were being discussed or implemented.

I suppose it was that particular gift that helped me recognise the need for a charity like the Railway Children in the first place, seeing that it was through discussions at the newly formed Consortium for Street Children that the concept was born. One of the main purposes of CSC was to encourage its members to exchange information, learn from each other and collaborate on initiatives of mutual interest. It was through Amnesty International that I became a member of CSC as its UK representative - I'd initially joined Amnesty's Working Group for Children. However, I was always uneasy with the characteristic Amnesty reluctance to join with other organisations – born out of their understandable concern to be seen to be unbiased and free of any particular political leaning. So when the opportunity came to act as a representative of Amnesty in another organisation with mutual interests such as CSC, I jumped at it. To be fair to Amnesty, it has become much more open to joint working with other like-minded campaigning organisations and I like to think the Working Group for Children paved the way in 1993 with a conference we organised and held in Stoke-on-Trent. We invited a number of other children's rights organisations in the UK and overseas to join us and, somewhat to our surprise, received the head office's approval. Since then, Amnesty has found that joint campaigning, such as being a member of the Coalition against Child Soldiers, can often be more effective.

CSC started with about a dozen members and I became one of the founding trustees when we registered it with the Charity Commission. The ideas we exchanged in those first few months and the learning we got from speakers returning from overseas and sharing their experiences were stimulating, but we soon found that without any resource to coordinate and document our discussions, little actually happened in consequence. I benefited greatly from the discussions with my colleagues and got encouragement and advice from them about starting the Railway Children, but probably that was the only concrete result so far as we could see in the first couple of years though I'm sure other members must have felt some benefits also and had developed their programmes without telling us the changes they'd made.

We did, however, have access to the Houses of Parliament and made some initial advocacy points to the UK government, particularly about the lack of funding to street children projects through Department for International Development (DFID) grants or other government agencies. After a couple of years the membership had grown and we were able (just) to afford a full time Director, Anita Schrader, who had a particular interest in the situation in Latin America and used her skills as a researcher to get sponsored by DFID and the Foreign & Commonwealth Office (FCO) to undertake research work of benefit to CSC's members – a book was produced on international law and treaties that could be used to protect and defend street children and another on street girls was also published.

The Chair of CSC became vacant in 1998 and as no-one else volunteered to take it on I became the Co-Chair, virtually by default. One of the other founding trustees, Surina Narula, who spent much time in India as well as in the UK, was persuaded to become my Co-Chair. She dealt mainly with funding aspects leaving me to chair meetings and work closely with Anita and successive Directors, Sadia Mahmud-Marshall and Alex Dressler.

Sadia, who had UN connections, developed a series of conferences in different parts of the world to promote the exchange of information and co-operation – networking - between local and national NGOs. Alex made renewed efforts to engage the UK membership in attending workshops and meetings to discuss issues of mutual concern and learn from each other initiatives that were achieving positive results for street children. Alex and I set up five themed groups covering street children and violence; street children and health, especially HIV/AIDS; street children and education; early intervention methodology; and child participation in programmes. In this way I was learning from other NGO Directors and programme staff experiences that were of value to Railway Children, as well as passing on our – at that stage – limited experience. In addition to my own involvement, Pete Kent, by then our Programme Officer covering projects in East Africa and Latin America, attended and contributed to the Working Groups on violence and health, whilst I led the one on early intervention, the area where I felt I had most to contribute.

We soon found that the workload in attending five Working Groups was too heavy for most members whose organisations were comparatively small, so CSC concentrated initially on the violence theme as this tied in with the UN General Assembly report commissioned on children and violence, co-ordinated and written by Professor Paulo Sergio Pinheiro. This Working Group caught the interest of the members and some twenty or so contributed to discussions about the research we had commissioned Sarah Thomas de Benitez to undertake. Sarah, then undertaking a doctorate degree at the London School of Economics, was the founder of Juconi and had been involved closely with the International Children's Trust, a CSC member. Her report was published in booklet form with 33 recommendations which CSC prioritised and formed part of its UK advocacy programme, other recommendations being for members to follow up in their own programmes and activities.

In the autumn of 2007, Alex and I went with Baroness Miller, Joint Chair of the All Party Parliamentary Group on Street Children, to meet senior UNICEF officials in New York to present this report to that organisation and to offer CSC as UNICEF's partner in working and lobbying for street children. This was an issue on which UNICEF had campaigned in the past but had little current activity other than what I would term preventative work in the slums with vulnerable children, programmes they commissioned through local NGO partners. The impact of our meeting in New York was not all we would have wished, partly because so many of the people we met have since moved on or retired. There was one positive outcome, however. CSC was commended to UNICEF offices in various countries as a potential partner for undertaking police training in children's rights, something CSC had been doing with funding from the FCO. This led to a commitment to train the trainers of police in Ethiopia and the resultant ripple effect of the training throughout that police force.

CSC was also keen to build on a UNICEF report on children and HIV/AIDS and at the New York meeting we offered to develop a research report on the subject specific to street children needs, similar to our violence report. We hoped that UNICEF might sponsor our research on this as we had commitment from the CSC Working Group on health and HIV/AIDS, but so far no funding has been made available for us to undertake it. The CSC Working Group, which, as stated earlier, included Pete Kent from Railway Children, was active on this theme and was concerned that street children, although a high-risk group as a result of both sex and drug abuse, were not featuring in major country or large agency priorities for receiving some of the huge sums that have been made available internationally to combat AIDS. Where children were included in education and prevention schemes, these were normally through schools or communities, thus excluding many street children by definition.

A third CSC Working Group that was relatively active was the one I chaired on the theme of 'Early Intervention'. Despite the widespread agreement that early intervention was vital, there were only three or four regular members of this group and I soon realised that most of the input was made by Railway Children with others ready to learn but offering little new. One interesting initiative I did discover was shared by Andy Stockbridge, Director of the NGO, 'Toybox', who had co-ordinated a group of local charities working for street children in Cochabamba in Bolivia. Their aim was to try to use NGOs to identify all access points for new children coming to the streets of that city so that, between them, they covered the city comprehensively. This would improve the chance of all runaway and abandoned children being contacted in the first few days and offered appropriate support, helping to prevent a widespread and continuing problem on the streets. This apparently had been initiated after discussions within the Viva

Network, an evangelical international Christian organisation that linked humanitarian and evangelistic programmes.

I'd been introduced to their International Director, Patrick McDonald, by Railway Children trustee, Henry Clarke. Patrick was so enthusiastic about Railway Children's focus on early intervention that he asked me to set up an 'Early Intervention' e-mail group within the Viva Network, and for Railway Children to consider joining with the Viva Network to develop such initiatives throughout Africa using the considerable volunteer resources of the Christian churches in African countries. A group of our trustees met Patrick in the Viva offices in Oxford and though impressed with Patrick and his vision, were unhappy about the Viva principle of using only Christian outreach resources and were not prepared to sign up to the Viva requirement of commitment to the 'Lausanne Statement' about religious belief. Railway Children was and remains a secular charity and amongst its trustees and staff covers a wide spectrum of religious belief and non-belief - that includes Christians of several denominations, a Jew, a Buddhist, a Hindu Brahmin and at least one avowed Atheist to my certain knowledge! All of them are equally devoted to the cause of helping these children. We are careful to avoid working with partners that use their project work as a prime opportunity to convert children to any particular religious faith and especially so, having experienced a few problems in India (indirectly) with one or two American fundamentalist Christian NGOs. I remember the backlash from one at Howrah station in the 1990s that caused the railway authorities to evict all the NGOs there for a time. The organisation concerned, I'm told, used to offer Mars bars to those children who converted to Christianity. I'm also told that some children converted seven times a week! Street children know how to play the system.

I have made no secret that I am a Methodist and for four years - 1996-2000 - a trustee of the Methodist Relief & Development Fund when it was first separated from the Church itself when it registered as a charity in its own right. We took some criticism from a few church members because we would fund humanitarian work by secular or even Islamic organisations rather than only ever use Christian partners - or even our own overseas Methodist churches - when we believed that the most benefit would result. I felt comfortable with this as I always ask the question, 'What is in the best interest of the beneficiary?' A relevant document, the UN

Convention on the Rights of the Child, Article 3, says that the 'best interests of the child shall be the primary consideration'. That is not far removed from the Christian teaching that is reflected in Judaism and, I understand, also in Confucianism, that you should treat others as you would wish yourself to be treated.

Later, I became a member of the Chester & Stoke District of the Methodist Church's Child Safeguarding Group, tasked with developing robust child protection policies for the 250 or so churches in the District and part of a team of five that was arranging training for all children's and youth workers and others in contact with the churches' children's activities. Having been on the small group developing CSC's child protection policies and having advised Amnesty for years that it should ensure its schools' speakers were checked through the Criminal Records Bureau, and also being a member of Railway Children's Child Protection Committee, I suppose I was in a good position to pass on learning and experience from one organisation to another. This does not stop me requiring a CRB check for each organisation in which I'm involved which I consider an administrative overload, especially when one organisation (Amnesty) does not even require the 'Enhanced' check that the other organisations require, but insists on its own less rigorous 'basic' check. This need of a multiplicity of checks is among those issues being reviewed by government in 2011 in regards to child protection.

A number of the larger London based international NGOs who work for youth and children take part in regular meetings with government departments. The Foreign & Commonwealth Office had a Children's Rights Panel with about a dozen regular NGO advisers on it and for a while I was the representative for three of them - Amnesty, CSC and Railway Children. The FCO varied its priorities - initially it funded police training on children's rights in Latin American countries in conjunction with CSC and after a period of abeyance resumed with some enthusiasm under Ian McCartney MP and Secretary of State for Trade & Industry. Apparently the FCO considered that 'human rights' could be improved through trade agreements and pressure. However, the main debate was whether certain groups of vulnerable children such as child workers, child soldiers and street children should be prioritised for special treatment, or whether the themes of education and health for children generally (including the

Millennium Goals) provided the best way forward. The debate was not concluded before Ian McCartney moved on and subsequent ministers have taken no further obvious interest.

The Department for International Development (DFID) initiated another Advisory Group on Children's rights, promising two meetings a year building on work done by two sub-groups on children and youth in-between times. I joined the Children's Rights Advisory Group (still with my three 'hats' until the CSC appointed an Advocacy Officer) which was chaired by Jennifer Grant, Advocacy Officer of Save the Children UK. This group worked with DFID to develop that organisation's understanding of child rights and approach, and got DFID to agree to an evaluation and mapping exercise on how far children's rights were embedded in its own policies. A number of the larger NGOs in the group put up some funds to undertake the survey and the NGO input was matched by DFID. The Advisory Group selected six priority recommendations from those made and pairs of representatives adopted one each to progress with DFID. I joined with a colleague from 'Everychild' to commend DFID to develop and implement a child protection policy for its own staff and consultants when visiting projects and in evaluating applications made to it through the Civil Society Challenge Fund.

As a result of such interactions, I found myself invited to conferences on children's rights in Europe at Liverpool University and another celebrating 20 years of the UN Convention on the Rights of the Child and evaluating its shortcomings (basically implementation!) at the Institute of Education in London. These led to long briefings back to the Railway Children staff in Sandbach, with contacts to follow up - not always welcome, I'm sure, as resources were always tight.

As a result of these conferences I formed links with two important people in this area – one of which led to an invitation to a one-to-one breakfast meeting with Professor Paulo Pinheiro in Paris, author of the UN study on children and violence, in order for me to appraise him of the CSC Violence report and the work Railway Children was undertaking in India tackling some of the issues highlighted in a comprehensive report on child abuse commissioned by the Indian government and undertaken by UNICEF, Save the Children and an Indian NGO, 'Prayas'. He advised me that he had been pressing for a UN Special

Representative on Children and Violence reporting directly to the UN General Secretary to follow up his work and advised me to maintain contact with Marta Santos Pais, a Portuguese woman who had headed the UNICEF research centre, 'Innocenti', in Florence, and former member of the UN CRC Committee who had just been appointed. It was a recommendation I took up in December 2010 at a conference on children's rights organised by the EU Fundamental Rights Agency in Brussels.

One of the speakers at the conference held at the Institute of Education in London was Nigel Cantwell, who had founded 'Defence for Children International' in Geneva and was one of the main drafters of a document 'Guidelines on Children without Parental Care' which was about to be presented before the UN Human Rights Council and - if approved – would go to the General Assembly for adoption. Nigel told the conference that there were just three countries opposing this intention - China, Canada and the UK, an odd and unexpected mixture. Apparently, the UK's opposition was primarily on technical grounds and Nigel's advocacy persuaded 55 of us in the audience to write a joint letter to David Miliband, then Secretary of State at the Foreign & Commonwealth Office, asking him to withdraw UK's objection. Approval to send the guidelines to the UN General Assembly was duly given, the UK abstaining from the vote. The other countries withdrew their objections when they saw the strength of the overall consensus.

Such opportunities as these not only provide information that strengthens one's own organisation's lobbying, but enhances our profile and gradually increases our ability to gain credibility and be listened to. This is important for a comparatively small organisation such as ours when compared with the standing of large international organisations like UNICEF, Save the Children, Plan International and the like, and Railway Children is beginning to have influence well beyond that which might be expected, both in the UK and India.

I have already written about the helpful contacts I and others have made with the railway authorities and police in India, and Mrinalini Rao and her team in Bombay produced a powerful report in conjunction with our partners there on the situation of children on India's stations. That report, called 'What is and what can be' describes the problems and abuse children face and the ways in which the various stakeholders - station staff, vendors, police and NGOs - could work together to minimise the risks and protect these children. This document has had a wide distribution in India and I discovered just how influential it was during my visits to India in July 2009 and again in February 2011.

Some people see 'networking' as desirable but not essential. Staff and trustees can get on with the job un-distracted by constant meetings, linkages, new and changing ideas, challenges. I find networking indispensable. Without it we would have missed so many opportunities, learned too many things the hard way. There is so much written material – papers and research reports – that have been produced on children's needs and development and so many knowledgeable people with such rich experience exist, but the communication channels that allow one to exploit these and gain full benefit from them are under-utilised. Frankly, without the networking I was involved in through Amnesty and CSC in the early 1990s, it's unlikely that Railway Children would have existed at all.

Chapter 16
Increasing awareness and reputation

Railway Children had been building an enviable reputation among other NGOs, especially fellow colleague members of CSC, some of whom regularly met with, or called, our key staff such as Terina, Pete or Andy for advice and the sharing of experience. Some were envious of our ability to tap the railway industry for nigh on 50% of our income, nearly all of it unrestricted - very different from many charities who found it difficult to raise funds for the general support and research necessary to underpin their grant-funded projects. We had a 'niche' market with our natural link to the railway industry in much the same way that Water Aid has links to the privatised UK water utility companies, and the free phone helpline 'Get Connected' has been partnered by the Carphone Warehouse.

We were therefore tempted in 2008 to enter the annual 'Charity of the Year' competition which announces awards in a number of topic groups, one of which is 'children' and another 'international development'. Terina worked with Mrinalini to identify a particular aspect of our work in India to highlight and we put together a case based on the reintegration of children with their families after early interaction on the railway platforms when this was both practicable and desirable - that is, when the child and family were willing and the situation from which the child had run was not endemically abusive. A lot of the background information about the charity that we had to provide tested the extent of our professionalism and in particular looked at the way in which we conformed to the Charity Commission 'Hallmarks of an Effective Charity' where we knew from our earlier review by the Charity Commission that we were strong. We were therefore delighted to be invited to the prestigious awards reception and ceremony at Battersea Park on learning that we were one of three charities short-listed for an award in the 'International Development' category. The award itself went to a charity called 'Concern Universal' that had helped people in Gambia access the tourist industry. We were named the 'Runner Up' and received a 'Highly Commended' certificate. As a direct result I was asked by the editor of the voluntary sector magazine 'Governance', who was one of the Award judges, to write a piece in the magazine under the regular feature heading, 'My Big Issue'. I chose to highlight the strength of our focus in a complex situation.

A number of events in 2009 really put the charity on the map. Firstly and somewhat unexpectedly, we were contacted by Jade Goody's agent and asked if we would support Jade as she wanted to visit India. Apparently she intended to donate her fee from a recent television programme to a charity working for children in that country. We considered the request and conferred with Mrinalini in India on the possible reaction there if we were to accept. Our own gut instinct was to accept provided our Indian staff did not feel it would cause problems for them as adverse media publicity surrounding Jade at the time was immense.

Mrinalini invited Jade to go to India and meet some street children for whom a donation would be of assistance. Jade accepted the invitation and Mrinalini conducted her around Delhi and visited one of our partners there, 'Anubhav', a small project adjacent to Delhi Cantonment station, pursued by the media of course. However, she did get some privacy with the children and spent a few hours sitting on the primitive floor of their drop-in centre talking with them. She got on splendidly with them - she could empathise with them in many aspects of their lives. Towards the end of her visit she asked the children if they had any questions and one of the boys asked, 'Is it right that you said nasty things to someone on TV?' When Jade admitted that she'd said things which had been criticised, the boy said that he wasn't sure what all the fuss was about because they said nasty things to each other all the time! Jade offered the children the opportunity of asking for a gift and they asked if they could have a computer, which was duly given to them. They also wanted a cricket coach! One of the children then asked, 'When you go on holiday, will you take us with you to Goa?' The media picked up this visit and the Sun gave it a positive two-page spread, which was glorious publicity for us, and among a readership that did not feature heavily on our database.

The children got on famously with Jade and liked her earthy approach, which they understood and felt comfortable with. That contrasted with another visit I heard about, when an Indian professional woman living in the UK, a solicitor I think but I'm not sure, wanted to visit but made the children feel very small with her superior and patronising approach. The children were upset when they heard of Jade's cancer and sent her a message, which was again featured in headlines in the Sun.

We featured in the Sun again that year, this time because of the Danny Boyle film, 'Slumdog Millionaire'. The street children featured in that film which got the media headlines were just the sort of children we were trying to help in the Bombay area - indeed we had - and still have - a project on VT station where substantial parts of 'Slumdog' were filmed. When I saw the film I was amazed at how the film company had managed to clear the station for the final dance sequence until I caught a glance of the station clock, which was showing 00.58. Some of the film was pretty distressing in depicting the abuse suffered by such children and a newspaper got hold of a copy of the film and showed it to a few of our children in the city, asking if it was an accurate reflection of their lives. They agreed on the whole that it was, with one great big exception: they said, 'We're not millionaires at the end!'

The Railway Children staff went to see it 'en bloc' when the film was released and came back into the office to discuss how the film could be used to raise awareness and support for our Indian programme. Two initiatives were followed up and bore fruit. One of our staff managed to contact Danny Boyle through his sister and got him to agree that he and Dev Patel, the star of the film, playing the 'Slumdog', would enter the UK ITV 'Celebrity Millionaire' series on behalf of Railway Children. ITV agreed enthusiastically and the Sun featured this - and the Railway Children - in the publicity following the film's Oscar awards. Unfortunately, the promised programme has not yet been filmed because of the difficulty of getting Danny and Dev in the country at the same time for the scheduled filming. Maybe one day ... Perhaps the programme would like to mirror the film and see that they win the £1 million for us...!

The second break came through an initiative by our Corporate Fundraiser, Dave Ellis. He contacted a Tesco manager he knew from his work in the commercial sector before he joined Railway Children. That was followed up and the upshot was a promise by Tesco to feature Railway Children's literature in the launch of the 'Slumdog Millionaire' DVD in the first two weeks after its release in June 2009 and donate £1 for every DVD sold during its special promotion at every Tesco store that fortnight. The result was fantastic and beyond our expectations and above Tesco's budget for that period - they sold 251,948 copies so we received unrestricted funds of over a quarter of a million pounds towards our Indian street children programme.

This led to a further event and opportunity to raise the awareness of our charity. Channel 4 TV regularly programmes a hard-hitting documentary in their 'Dispatches' series and in January 2010 showed a documentary entitled 'The Real Slumdog Children'. It had been filmed in Bombay by the freelance company 'True Vision' working with Railway Children and featured a former street boy from VT station called Santosh who had been employed in the Railway Children office at one time and now had his own business. The BBC has also been showing a series of documentaries on Indian Railways in the last year or so - 'Monsoon Railway', 'Bombay Railway' and another series about India's Hill Railways - which, although not specifically about street children had several shots and mentions of 'railway children' on the platforms.

Our UK work has also been attracting increasing attention. The launch of the 'Off the Radar' research in November 2009 had been a trifle disappointing in that it was not well attended by the media or politicians although the voluntary sector was well represented. However, rather than making a 'splash' we developed a plan to drip-feed the implications of the report through various communication channels over the following months. There was much for us to say. Andy had been voted back as Chair of the 35-strong NGO coalition of grass root charities working for vulnerable children in the UK, and was still acting as the Secretary of the APPG on English Runaways. Terina had been asked to be Chair of the trustees of an innovative residential rehabilitation centre in Birkenhead, run for some of the most heavily traumatised and damaged children on therapeutic principles – a situation of last resort and chance for the children involved. In addition Andy had become a member of a government/civil service working group on runaway children and Terina was one of two NGO Chief Executives invited to brief parliamentarians at the House of Commons concerning already 'detached' children and children at risk of leaving home. There were a number of breakfast TV appearances mentioning 'Off the Radar' including one by our researcher, Emilie Smeaton, and articles appeared in specialist social services and voluntary sector magazines and in November 2010 'Dispatches' featured another documentary in conjunction with Railway Children - this time on 'Britain's Street Children' highlighting the issues raised by 'Off the Radar' with the stories of four such young people told by themselves.

In the summer of 2009 Aviva, the global financial services company, decided to adopt the street children issue as its five-year corporate social responsibility (CSR) programme, named 'Street to School', and came to the Consortium for Street Children for advice on possible partner organisations working in the countries where the company had a significant presence. Alex Dressler pointed them in the direction of Railway Children for their UK partner and after they had checked us out, the company's CSR personnel started discussions with Terina and Andy. Despite our limited brand awareness, Aviva recognised the focus and passion Railway Children applied to its work and felt we were the right UK partner for them in helping them deliver their global objective of getting 500,000 children off the streets and into education or training.

To introduce Railway Children to their UK staff Aviva ran a series of 'Road Shows' about their global CSR programme and Railway Children staff attended every one. I offered to be at the one in Perth, travelling to Scotland overnight via the sleeping car train from Crewe to Inverness which I took as far as Aviemore (I didn't want to disturb my sleep at Perth at 5.30am for an 11am Road Show start!) so I relaxed and enjoyed the Highland scenery with snow still covering the mountains and took part in three presentations led by David Schofield, Aviva's UK CSR Manager at the time. There was significant interest and many questions about the situation locally in Perth and Dundee as Aviva not only wanted to support some of our programme but to seek volunteering opportunities for their staff as well. Andy went up to see some of the Perth staff later to explore the situation with them in more detail.

After many meetings between Aviva's headquarters staff and Railway Children's Terina, Andy and Claire (a consultant we had contracted to help us develop this relationship five days a month), a programme emerged that was seen to be focusing on two main objectives. We were developing the idea of working closely with schools to identify children – especially those around years 6 and 7 – who were showing signs of distress or disaffection at school and

Aviva agreed to work with us to fund specialists who could support both teachers and the identified vulnerable children and their families, spending time trying to resolve problems before the child dropped out of the system and finished up on the street. Initially this was to be built round our partner, 'Safe@Last' in Sheffield where Aviva also had a large office. With regard to the second objective, Aviva was most concerned at our evidence that only five beds existed in the UK authorised for overnight accommodation for under 16 year olds outside social services emergency accommodation provision. The value of the refuges in Sheffield and Glasgow, both of which we funded, lay in the 'wrap around' services and intensive counselling provided for the child - which other agencies were rarely able to provide - as well as a safe bed for a few nights. Aviva immediately started a campaign on this issue with a petition inviting its staff to sign up and press government to support the development rather than the retraction of such facilities – accommodation in the West Country (Torquay) and London had closed through lack of funding in recent years.

Aviva staff took up the whole 'Street to School' programme with enthusiasm and started fundraising straight away – early on they staged a 'sleep out' at several of their offices hoping to raise a substantial amount which the company would match fund. In fact they doubled their expectation. I attended (the first part only!) at their St Helen's headquarters in the City – they were lucky in having a heatwave for their experience. I spoke to a number of the participants and their enthusiasm was infectious. It quickly became apparent that Aviva was going to be able to raise much more for the Railway Children UK programme than initially expected and we began to discuss with them the possibility of developing a 'REACH' model. This would enable us to roll out many of the services children had requested in Off the Radar, and offer real hope of the first sustainable solution to the issue. To date the 'Reach' model, involving schools, police, social services, family counselling services, and our partner NGO's street workers and refuge staff, is now operating in Sheffield and Glasgow and we opened a 3-Borough London based 'Reach'project (unfortunately without overnight refuge accommodation) in October 2011.

Another major fundraising and publicity opportunity came via a proposal from the Touring Consortium Theatre Company and its Director, Jenny King, to mount a major production of the drama,

'The Railway Children', based on the famous Edith Nesbitt novel, and perform it at the empty Waterloo International Terminal vacated by trains since the opening of the magnificent St Pancras Eurostar station. The drama, directed by Damian Cruden, had been performed for two summer seasons at the National Railway Museum in York by the local theatre company and Jenny King wanted to bring it to London. She got the necessary financial backing and British Rail Residuary Estates Company was willing to provide the venue free as long as the Railway Children charity benefited from both publicity and income. In fact, the previous year the Waterloo premises had been made available for a charity evening with the hedge fund charity foundation ARK and the railway company had obtained thereby a substantial donation for Railway Children, which was repeated in 2010.

We worked closely with Jenny King and her Marketing Director, Matthew Gale, with the result that we were not only promised £1 from every ticket sold, but the publicity through banner posters and exhibition areas for charity displays gave us exposure we'd rarely received before. We were invited to the 'First Night' and the press reviews the following day were such that the longer run seemed now a foregone conclusion. The season was extended from the school summer holidays right through to the New Year. I had invited Sally Thomsett and her husband and daughter to the show – Sally had been Phyllis in the 1970 film version as well as appearing in a number of BBC sitcoms - and she was interested after the show to talk to Louisa Clein, the actress who played the same role in the drama. Afterwards her fame was still evident as it took us over a quarter of an hour to get past the autograph hunters to her taxi!

This sudden burst of activity on all fronts – Slumdog Millionaire and a new £1million grant from Comic Relief for India, the 'Off the Radar' research, the parliamentary activity, the Aviva partnership for the UK work, the opening of an office in Tanzania and the formation of 'Railway Children Africa' - was putting considerable strain on our own staff and the Board authorised Terina urgently to seek additional resources to ensure we did not squander these opportunities. As a result in the late summer of 2010 we appointed two officers to support Andy. The stage was being set for the next major development of the Railway Children.

Chapter 17
Last visit to India?

After fifteen years as Chairman of the Railway Children and nearing my 72nd birthday, I advised the Board in April that I would step down after the AGM in December 2010 and continue in an unofficial voluntary role as long as I could be of help. I therefore expected that a visit to the Indian Railway Children programme from 29th January to 21st February 2011 in company with Haydn Abbott, my successor as Chairman and Henry Clarke, trustee, and his wife, Verena, to be my last in any capacity connected to the charity. Haydn accompanied us on our visits to Bombay, Lucknow and Delhi and then Henry and Verena continued with me to Itarsi.

After that I continued by myself - although accompanied by Railway Children Programme Officers - to Calcutta, and to significant programmes in the State of Andhra Pradesh - Vijayawada, Tirupati and the joint cities of Hyderabad/Secunderabad, to say my farewells to project partners and to understand the situation in India as much as possible, gauging the difference our presence might have had.

Haydn Abbott (centre, back row), Henry Clarke (front left), Indian Trustee Gopal Dutia (extreme right, back), David and staff of Railway Children India and partner Bal Prafulta at VT station, 2011

The most noticeable change since my previous visits was the obvious progress of the Railway Children India strategy of a closer engagement with the government systems, in particular with the Integrated Child Protection System being developed and implemented through the Ministry of Women & Child Development at National and State level and the Ministry of Railways through the RPF and GRP.

In almost every place I visited, Child Welfare Committees (CWCs) and Juvenile Justice Boards (JJBs) had been established and there had been new selections made to CWCs in the last few weeks, replacing many of the former political appointees with social workers and NGO senior personnel who had more appropriate knowledge and experience. There was now general acceptance that children found 'in need of care and protection' should be presented before a CWC and that children would be placed in government-approved homes (that is, a government children's home or an NGO home with a 'fit institution' certificate) or placed in care of an NGO in readiness for home placement or suitable alternative. This had replaced the practice of NGOs taking a child into their own care without presentation to a CWC in spite of the legal requirement to do so (on the statute book since 2000) as the government infrastructure had been weak or non existent.

All the NGOs I visited were now meeting the law in this respect, although there were still some legitimate doubts and worries about the quality of some of the government homes to which children were usually sent and the frequency with which some CWCs were unaware of their powers to allocate children to the care of approved NGOs. Railway Children's policy and that of its partners is to strive to improve the government system, engage with the CWCs and government homes, and monitor the effects. This engagement, after identifying children in need of 'care and protection' and coping with those immediate needs, consisted of accompanying children to CWCs, chaperoning them to hospitals or to their family homes, offering alternative care after CWC presentation, suggesting CWC appointees, training CWC personnel, and involvement at government homes in education, counselling provision and family reintegration.

Close co-operation with government personnel was seen consistently at all the railway stations visited. All NGO, Railway Protection Force (RPF) and Government Railway Police (GRP) staff appeared to work closely together in helping to contact children found on railway stations, especially newly arrived children and were also engaging with station management and other staff, including ticket collectors, coolies and vendors. This was especially evident at Lucknow, Vijayawada and Tirupati where all stakeholders were being involved to make 'Child Friendly' stations - a designation officially embraced at Lucknow station and which should be incorporated within the criteria being established by the Ministry of Railways for the development of 50 nominated 'World Class' stations. One result of this increased effectiveness of early intervention at stations was a marked decrease in the number of children now being found on stations as compared with three to four years ago. This was believed not to be the result of a drop in numbers of children leaving home, but more to the effectiveness of picking up children from stations as soon as they arrived. In any case, the long-term population of street youth and children active on stations was much reduced.

However, a downside of this is the fact that the likelihood of being picked up by police or NGOs at the larger stations is well understood by many street children, some of whom deliberately now frequent smaller stations where NGO or police presence is less marked. This mirrors the UK experience of fifteen to twenty years ago when barrier controls, CCTV and police presence meant that

Coolies at Tirupati station who bring runaway children they find to Railway Children's partner, Grassim, 2011

few children were being seen on UK stations, especially in London, but instead were dispersed to many UK cities and towns and lost in the communities, and therefore much harder to find and help. One implication of this trend was that NGOs including Railway Children now needed to widen their scope of early intervention, to include mapping where children run from; working to contact children whilst still in the main source areas; and helping children when picked up by the CWC and JJB systems.

There are clear signs that government senior personnel are seeking the support of NGOs not only to help contact children in need of 'care and protection' and support the implementation of the child protection policies, but also are encouraging NGOs to monitor the processes and tell the authorities when those systems fail or are absent or inadequate. The NGO role of monitoring the systems was highlighted in several meetings with government personnel.

The State of Andhra Pradesh was one where the senior civil service in both Women & Child Development and Police was actively implementing the National Child Protection Policy and specifically asked Railway Children to work with them and UNICEF in helping them plan the intervention strategies on the State's key railway stations, and co-ordinate the knowledge held by all NGOs working at stations. This presented great opportunities for Railway Children to take a lead nationally at India's railway stations in consultations with other key NGO donors and partners – and underscores a recommendation from a conference of Railway Children partners in CINI Asha's training centre at Monobitan (Calcutta) that Railway Children should be the 'Platform for Platform Children'.

That two-day conference was organised for four local NGO partners (CINI Asha and Don Bosco at Sealdah and Howrah respectively in Calcutta, Conc'rn at New Jalpaiguri and Praajak at a number of stations in West Bengal including Malda and Asansol) to make presentations about their work, and on the second day to review the Railway Children training programmes. At the end of the first day I was asked to summarise the key points that had emerged, which I presented as follows:

1. The need for all NGO partners to facilitate and monitor government schemes under the Juvenile Justice Act and Integrated Child Protection System.

2. The concern about the quality of government homes and the need for Railway Children and partners to get involved to improve these.

3. Because of the falling number of children seen at stations, the need to extend early intervention to source community mapping and child protection.

4. The need to work with older street youth on platforms to convince them to be a positive force for child protection (peer groups, the Kenyan Undugu model).

5. The need for realistic child participation through Youth Groups, Children's Banks, and feedback.

6. The need to share experiences about family reunification and to identify what works best in the longer term. The need to identify NGOs, that can help co-ordinate follow-up for children returning home, in the source areas.

7. The need to gather information about the prevalence of HIV/AIDS among children in the North East of India.

8. Drug addiction – the need for prevention, de-addiction facilities for children and the avoidance of returning to station environment, motivation to abstain from drugs through sport, adventure, music etc.

9. The desperate need for government schemes for physically and mentally challenged children.

10. The need to develop performance indicators to measure our impact and demonstrate our effectiveness in an increasingly competitive culture in India - especially with possible new initiatives forcing large corporates to give 2% of their profits to the voluntary sector.

11. The need to record evidence concerning children affected by violence as input to the UN General Assembly study on children and violence (through Railway Children UK and the UN special representative, Marta Santos Pais).

Some specific recommendations were made to Railway Children by the conference members, namely:

1. To become the agency that is the 'Platform for Platform Children' co-ordinating all NGOs in India that work on railway stations.

2. To use the children mainstreamed back into society to act as advocates for Railway Children.

3. To have school children become aware of street children and talk about the issue to their parents and peers to reduce stigma and pressure government to realise its Child Protection System in a sustainable and sensitive way.

I found enthusiastic partners at all locations I visited and a willingness to engage with the government systems, with existing children in NGO residences being happy and well cared for. I had one overriding impression of the excellence of key people - usually the NGO founder - in each organisation, but conversely, the absence of an obvious deputy or successor in some of them, which is a worry. This seems to be a characteristic of many Indian organisations and may reflect either a paucity of people of substance prepared to work for the voluntary sector when salaries in the burgeoning private sector are several times higher, or - in a few cases - a reluctance to delegate and let go of personal power and influence. One of the rocks on which Railway Children bases its success is the excellence of its people and in the competitive environment in India - a fast-growing economy, with many global corporate organisations established there and a continuing salary escalation in the large international NGOs - it makes it difficult to recruit and hold the very best staff at salaries we can afford. We owe a very great debt to those in our Bombay Office and at the helm of our partners whose motivation has been maintained despite all the obstacles and who have enabled us to make so much progress.

On this last tour I made a number of internal flights (such as Bhopal to Calcutta via Bombay which seems strange geography but was 14 hours faster than a direct train!) and a number of rail journeys including two incredible 15-hour runs by expresses that never left the State they started in - Tirupati to Hyderabad in Andhra Pradesh and Dhamangaon (near Nagpur) to Bombay in Maharastra. I managed to read eight new books on my travels and - on the trains - actually to appreciate some of India's scenery - especially the Western Ghats which for the first time I saw through 'clean' windows in India Railways' air conditioned 2nd class bogies. Indian Railways is changing too. In fact during my visit to Jeevodaya at Itarsi I squeezed in a visit to the A/C Electric locomotive maintenance depot and was astonished to see its scrupulously clean and tidy heavy maintenance area - a situation we had struggled to achieve in the UK when I instigated staff safety initiatives in British Rail's depots back in 1991-2.

At the end of the three week visit I was the guest of Gopal and Asha Dutia in their home near Bombay Victoria Terminus station where together we spent a leisurely three days reflecting on the visit, and I hugely improved my 'street cred' with countless Indian cricket-loving street boys by joining Gopal's dinner party for the guests included Sachin Tendulkar's mother-in-law! In fact, throughout my visit, the one subject that was bound to stir the children into animated questions and response was the imminent Cricket World Cup. I could always get a strong reaction by opining that England would beat India in the final - little was I to know that their first encounter would result in a thrilling and nail-biting tie! The only group I felt really sorry for were the boys at an Observation Home in the small town of Yavatmal in Maharastra for their only TV was broken. I trust it was repaired in time for the cricket for otherwise I sensed a rebellion could ensue.

Finally, I rounded off my Indian experience with a couple of personal visits - meetings which reflected the events that had brought me to India for the first time back in 1989. My family still sponsors a few children through the Theosophical Order of Service in Colaba, in the south of Bombay near the naval dockyard, and I visited the couple, Rusi and Freny Toddywalla, who used to manage the programme under the aegis of Save the Children and who continued the programme for Bombay children when Save the Children discontinued sponsorship (they still manage a sponsorship programme for nearly 500 children from Bombay's slums). Whenever I visit, they arrange for the children we sponsor and their families to join us for a small party. This time, as well as meeting our current families, I was delighted to see Rekha and her young son, for the girl we started sponsoring as a 9 year old is now happily married and came specially to meet me to show off her child, supported by her mother and two of her sisters. Then, on my last day in India, I met up with the girl I visited on that very first trip to India. It was on my way to meet her and her brothers in the Colaba agency that I encountered the young streetgirl on Churchgate station who was the catalyst for the founding of the Railway Children. She is now a 35 year old woman working as the Administrator for a small company. I was delighted that my visit to her aunt's house coincided with her cousin's birthday, so not only was the young woman there, but there was a reunion with her brothers and other family members whom I'd first met over twenty years ago. I'd come full circle.

Chapter 18
Personal reflections on the past and future

In the first chapter of this book I described the event on Churchgate station in Bombay that acted as catalyst and led eventually - five years later - to the founding of the Railway Children charity. Had this experience come 'out of the blue'? The answer may depend on whether you believe in 'guidance', or 'fate' or just luck or coincidence. I had been an orthodox traditional Christian for as long as I can remember. My parents were staunch members of the Methodist Church – as were both sets of grandparents – and much of my early life had been spent in East Molesey Methodist Church in Surrey where my paternal grandparents were Sunday School teachers and my father was Circuit Steward and Treasurer. By the time I was 18, I was a Sunday School teacher myself and Secretary of the Woking Church Youth Club. I was attracted to the radical thinking that Bishop John Robinson of Woolwich expressed in the 1960s in his controversial book 'Honest to God' and had always rejected the literal, or fundamentalist, Christian viewpoint - my own church denomination had never adopted that theology.

In the 1970s and early 80s I found my theologically liberal views often at odds with the increasing number of 'charismatic' Christians in my local church, now in High Wycombe, and felt myself to be drifting from the church, when I read a fascinating and very radical little book called 'Mr God, this is Anna'. That book prompted me strongly to stop engaging in theological argument and get on with life, working to the humanitarian and compassionate demands of the person of Jesus as recorded in the Gospels. Because of a number of positions I held within the church, especially in youth work, I had been afraid to speak out fearing to undermine what I was doing, but I was feeling a bit of a hypocrite. I'd been reading the book just mentioned while on the platform at Maidenhead while waiting for my train one morning and just got to the bit where the six year old precocious Anna talks to her mentor about the importance of 'not being afraid' to take risks in life when my train drew in. It was not the expected diesel multiple unit suburban train, but a long distance commuter train headed by a class '50' diesel electric locomotive, named of all things 'Dreadnought'! Seven years later, still convinced in my mind that I needed to get more involved in something, but not quite sure what, I'm confronted by that small girl on Churchgate station. If challenged for my 'Christian' story, I'll admit to being 'converted' by two six year olds - and a railway engine! And I'm sure it led, in a very roundabout way, to that moment on the concourse at Waterloo station when I'd at last 'stuck my head above the parapet' and taken the risk of failure or of being considered naïve or even eccentric.

Looking back now, I realise how much of my life's experience had prepared me for what I had taken on. During some thirty five years of working within British Rail I'd had considerable direct line management experience, but also, unusually, a very varied career that had included long spells of advisory work - initially on productivity, then later on quality and safety. As well as learning much about management theory and practice, I'd acquired a wide range of contacts throughout the railway industry. In my quality management work I'd worked alongside senior management at the Board and on all five railway regional organisations. Later as part of the task of implementing a proactive safety management system, I'd been directly involved in the training of over 800 top managers in the railway during a 3-day residential course and whilst my memory for names is not that great, as I was one of the main trainers on the course, everyone knew me. When it came later to promoting the fledgling charity, the fact that I was known to so many, when I began to publicise what I was attempting and seek support, gave me a degree of credibility and that helped enormously.

I'd had a grounding in the techniques of 'Total Quality Management' (TQM) and Risk Assessment, both of which I used to identify - and apply to - the scenes I confronted in Bombay in 1989, as I thought about that searing experience over the following years. I'd had the experience of initiating major change back in 1978 when I'd been asked to create an internal consultancy organisation for British Rail on the lines of that I'd developed on the Western Region, then I'd been BR's first Quality & Reliability Manager and had had to create that role from scratch. Again, after the Clapham Junction train accident and judicial inquiry, I'd been required to develop and implement a change in the whole culture of how

British Rail managed safety. Obviously I couldn't have done these things without the support of the Board and many colleagues, but having been so involved in the successful innovations and seen significant changes come about as a result, I had a certain amount of experience and confidence in my ability to innovate something and make it happen. But these things were achieved within a large organisation with colleague relationships and trust that had built up over many years - a safe environment if you like, one where I did not feel threatened or likely to be seriously opposed or ridiculed in what I was attempting.

In conceiving the idea of the Railway Children I felt on less secure ground. I was a newcomer in the area of the voluntary sector and in the issues surrounding street children - among colleagues whose charities had been in existence for many years and among whom I felt very inexperienced and nervous in putting forward my suggestions, finding it inconceivable that they had not already thought of the ideas I was advocating. When I began to realise that perhaps some of my ideas had value, coming as I did from a different culture and seeing things afresh, I found I was being pressured then to act on some of the thoughts I was expressing. I began to feel nervous about talking about these openly among my railway colleagues, as I was now raising an issue that fell outside the normal run of business activity - at least as it was then, although nowadays the development of corporate social responsibility is quite normal in commercial enterprises. I really did feel that people might think I had gone 'soft in the head' and wondered if I was still reacting too emotionally to that incident at Churchgate station that still bothered me after over five years. In the end the words I'd read on Maidenhead station came back to me, and I decided to take the risk and started talking openly to colleagues like Stan Judd and David Rayner. Once I had done that, I had, so to speak, burned my boats and couldn't go back without destroying my own confidence and self-belief. The fact that I was not discouraged, but given help and advice from some of the most senior managers of British Rail was a huge support at this stage.

In the early years of the charity I had to do nearly everything myself, as I had no staff. I did, however, have the support of railway colleagues as advisers and later, as trustees, but certainly as far as identifying projects to fund and values and policies to espouse, I was very much on my own until around the Millennium when I appointed the first two Programme Officers in India, and Terina as Chief Executive in the UK. Once they were established and taking more and more of the weight of the charity on their shoulders, I had to learn what I could delegate and to differentiate between strategic and operational activity - in other words to act as Chair of the Board rather than both that and Chief Executive at the same time – which I found difficult when I had been acting as both for some five years or so. Especially when I was in India I was tempted to take decisions as I met with the various Directors and senior staff of the partner charities - they were used to dealing with me directly and expected to continue to deal with me rather than with new Indian members of staff. I had to learn to let go and discourage our partners from looking to me all the time for decisions. Mrinalini, in particular, was very tolerant but had to remind me gently from time to time that I was encroaching on her operational territory by giving me a gentle tap on the wrist!

I now find in writing this book that many of my most vivid memories and experiences are from the earlier years of the charity as it was then that I was involved in everything and dealing directly with nearly every issue that raised its head. During the last ten years in particular, the charity has taken on a new life as the staff here in the UK and India have initiated so much themselves and now often I find myself surprised to discover developments that they have initiated within the overall policies and strategies we've agreed at the Board. Sometimes as the founder, I felt a little put out or even hurt - no, 'hurt' is too strong a word - but I'm determined that I should let go and allow others develop and take the charity further beyond what I can even imagine. I've seen too many charities or clubs held back by the founder sticking around for too long or not allowing others to take over, so that the organisation collapses when the founder is no longer available for whatever reason. This had happened - because of premature death - to Amnesty UK's 'Working Group for Children' in the late 1980s and the activity had ceased for a couple of years before, luckily, someone inside the Amnesty organisation decided to restart it and got several volunteers - including me - together.

Having reached my 70th birthday a couple of years ago, I decided it was time to hand over the reins of the Consortium for Street Children to another Chair (I'd been Co-Chair since 1998) in the hope that they could find a more stable financial donor-base than I could provide with potentially conflicting fundraising loyalties. I expressed my intention of also retiring from chairing the Board of Railway Children at the end of 2010 and our trustees have selected as my successor, Haydn Abbott, former Managing Director of the Angel Trains rolling stock leasing company and sponsor for many years of elements in the annual Railway Ball. Haydn joined us as a trustee in April 2010 with a view to taking over the Chair after the Annual General Meeting in December 2010. This gave us both time to adapt and me to consider what my role should be after my retirement from the Railway Children Board. I shall remain a volunteer, an Ambassador maybe, continuing as long as I'm able to give talks and take part in events whenever I'm asked and I intend - as long as the new Board is willing - to invite some former trustees and supporters to meet with me, the new Chairman and the Chief Executive quite informally two or three times a year, to be briefed on the latest developments and to see if and how we can best offer support.

This brings me to my vision for the future. The Board has a clear strategy for the development of our work in the three main geographical spheres of operation - India, East Africa and the United Kingdom - and I am wholeheartedly behind these policies. I can do no better than refer you to an edited version of these three strategies on the Railway Children website. They were written by our senior staff - Pete Kent, Country Director East Africa, Mrinalini Rao, Country Director India and her Programme Manager Navin Sellaraju, and Andy McCullough, Head of UK Policy & Public Affairs, all under the direction and supervision of Terina Keene, Chief Executive. My role concerning these has been just the same as for any other Board Member - to receive, test and approve them through discussions on trustee 'Away Days' and at Board Meetings. I'm therefore not directly including these in my reflections in this book as they are the official policies and strategies of the charity for the next three years until 2013. These owe much to the skill and experience of these staff and their colleagues and the Railway Children charity is most fortunate to have been able to recruit such people and retain them. In the next and final chapter I shall attempt to place on record the reasons why I think the Railway Children has been successful and the competence and motivation of our staff will be highlighted as a key factor.

Before I expand on a few thoughts of my own about the future and some of the most interesting potential developments, I'd like take this opportunity to pay tribute to Terina's strategic thinking which has evolved over her time with us. She has developed with the staff our fundamental concept on which the charity is building its future strategies - what she calls the 'three step change agenda'. Fundamentally, our intention is to make positive sustainable change in the lives of children who are alone and at risk and we must do this at three levels:

- We need to create short-term change by meeting the immediate needs of street children through activating and influencing child friendly, safe spaces, people and practices. That is, we are protecting these children from immediate abuse and exploitation and offering them options for development and family reintegration.

- Secondly, at a family and community level, we need to promote a longer term supportive environment so that children can develop to their full potential without stigmatisation and realise their rights as set out in the UN Convention on the Rights of the Child. We need to engage with stakeholders in the cities and rural areas and the poorest communities from which many of these children come.

- Thirdly, at the national level, we need to promote the implementation of child friendly laws and policies and conduct advocacy to ensure governments carry out their responsibilities to the most vulnerable children, especially those who have taken to the streets or are at risk of doing so.

We are therefore seeking to tackle the emergency needs of children and to open up development options for them; prevent them leaving home if possible and reintegrate them into their own communities if they have run away wherever possible; and to influence national policies to ensure the most vulnerable children are given the opportunities that should be available for any child without discrimination. To accomplish the third objective, we need to use the evidence that we've gathered in the work we undertake to fulfil our roles in the first two levels.

Railway Children was founded to promote and implement the concept of early intervention. Because of my experience and the incident that stimulated my action, I saw this initially as linked to railway stations as children arrived in the cities, having run away or been abandoned. Over the years we have widened our understanding of early intervention as this varies in different countries, but have stayed focused on that intervention principle. We are now beginning to explore what I call 'early early' intervention – i.e. prevention, which is the real message of the Total Quality Management (TQM) approach I'd adopted in the latter years of my railway career. In the late 1990s I had identified certain projects for Railway Children support in the slums alongside railway tracks - particularly in Calcutta. We withdrew from these over the years because the children involved, although in great need, still lived with their families and because support for them needed a more holistic approach than we could resource. Railway Children is now looking at re-engaging in some of the areas from which these children come, but rather than being the resource to bring the whole community out of poverty and provide decent facilities - a role for government and the large international aid agencies - we see our role as creating an opportunity to educate children and their communities about the dangers of children running away or being offered 'opportunities' by traffickers. This means also identifying some of the factors which cause children in these situations to feel that they would be better off or safer away from home and therefore educating parents who are in difficulty in the principles of good child care, and seeking support from the whole community in supporting children at risk in their midst.

This is a huge undertaking and Railway Children, along with other NGOs, can only indicate through their experience in a few pilot projects what governments might achieve on a much larger scale by replication. It will require networking with other NGOs, especially the larger ones like Save the Children and UNICEF who are in many cases already working in such communities and other aid agencies such as Water Aid or Christian Aid who may be in the communities undertaking clean water provision or agricultural support. We need to link with them to help the village and urban slum inhabitants they are supporting watch over their children too and thereby create stable communities that protect children and also reduce their risk of running away, and receive and support those children who return to their families after a period on the streets. In some countries like India this means greater interaction with the country's development of the Child Welfare Committees and Juvenile Justice Boards and supporting and educating those appointed in those key roles. In most countries in Africa no such state support exists and a network of NGOs, large and small, will need to work together to provide such coverage whilst also using their advocacy resources to lobby governments to put comprehensive child safeguarding systems in place. As Railway Children's experience of what works increases, it must document the evidence and share it with the larger agencies and governments to replicate good practice on a much larger scale.

All of this applies as much in the UK as elsewhere. The research that Railway Children has undertaken on UK 'detached' children has been made widely available to other British NGOs and it is our hope that many organisations will act on our findings and recommendations. We do not have - at the moment anyway - the resources to implement all our ideas ourselves but through partnership with Aviva and possibly other British firms as well, I would hope that we can demonstrate effective ways forward that can be picked up by the large NGOs like the NSPCC, Barnardo's and Action for Children (the former NCH) and influence the British government despite the problems caused by the current recession, for the costs of ignoring the problem on Britain's streets is in the long run much higher in both financial and societal terms.

I have always been a strong advocate of networking and have deliberately joined many groups set up to coordinate policies and advocacy work – especially the Consortium for Street Children, the FCO Child Rights Panel and DFID Advisory Groups. I have taken every opportunity to attend conferences and make contacts with academics and politicians. Sometimes we tend to test the effectiveness of joining groups by assessing what value we can get out of them. I believe we should also use such groups and contacts as a means of influencing others to take action to help children in ways, which we have found from experience to be effective. We can use our research, our evidence, the skills and experience we have acquired to share with others for the greater benefit of vulnerable children. We should not try to guard such knowledge for our own organisation's benefit and use it just to compete for funds available in the limited voluntary sector pot.

One of the strengths of the CSC is to encourage its members to share their experiences of innovative work so that others may join or replicate it where possible. I would like to see a thorough evaluation of projects like the Toybox one in Cochabamba I mentioned earlier - I think there are lessons about stemming the growing problems of street children in moderately small cities. I initiated a meeting of CSC members working in East Africa recently and I know Pete Kent is working on possible joint projects with some other British partners in Kenya and Tanzania - we already work with others in funding and supporting Mkombozi in Tanzania and are part of the CSC support to the Tanzanian government ministry developing a national plan for street children.

I believe that our attempt to develop coordination between NGOs working on stations in India is one where we must persevere, despite the problems. My vision of voluntary work for street children at a large Indian station is for a network of local NGOs to establish a joint 'child assistance booth' (CAB) - as at Vijayawada - manned by people from the participating NGOs on a rota basis, facilitated by the railway police (RPF and GRP), supported by all the station staff, stall holders and travelling public, and where the long term child residents on the station have been found legitimate work, and have been encouraged to act as outreach workers to contact and bring new arriving children to the child assistance booth. I would envisage the agencies at the booths having contacts with all the NGOs in the area, and knowledge of the programmes of each - their strengths and specialisms, who has medical facilities, who works with girls, who has appropriate vocational training, who has the capacity to undertake therapeutic counselling, drug de-addiction, who is best able to prepare children to return home, and see that they are safe when they do, wherever this is practicable. The volunteer or NGO staff member on duty at the 'CAB' would then meet the immediate needs of the child and refer them, in conjunction with the area CWC, to the NGO that best seems to fit their need, rather than automatically take responsibility for the child in their own NGO. I was delighted to find on my most recent visit, outlined in chapter 17, that this is indeed beginning to happen at certain key stations.

I just mentioned my ideal of harnessing street youth to act as the eyes and ears of NGOs on stations and be the first contact with lone children arriving, in order to bring them support and help rather than - as is often the case now - absorbing them in their gangs, subjecting them to abuse and corrupting them by introducing them to drugs and other nefarious ways of survival. The railway authorities and police are most frustrated by this group of youths and expect NGOs to take them and keep them away from the stations just as much as the newcomers, a forlorn hope. NGOs find having such damaged and often criminalised young people in their shelters frightens other younger children or introduces them quickly to behaviours that are dangerous and injurious. There have been many cases where a former street child has acted as an outreach worker for a station based charity, either informally or employed to do so. One example of this was 'Santosh' who featured in the January 2010 Channel 4 Dispatches documentary entitled 'The Real Slumdog Children'. He had lived for years on Bombay VT station, then had been helped by a Bombay NGO and had worked with Railway Children in some admin and outreach roles. Santosh has his own successful business now but still looks out for the street children to offer help.

Railway Children is currently partnering an African NGO where this type of working is being piloted on a much larger scale. I mentioned the 'association model' being developed by the Undugu Society in Nairobi (see chapter 10) where older street youths are being encouraged to form groups of 25 or so and be trained to become a cooperative and viable unit engaged in law abiding work, using their knowledge and experience to identify newly arriving children and bringing them to the NGO for rehabilitation, counselling and return to their communities before they become absorbed into the street culture. It is too soon to see how successful this is overall, although I have already seen examples where this has operated in a very positive way. The concept has appealed to large numbers of street youth in the Kenyan capital and has spread to the city of Kisumu on Lake Victoria at such a rate that it has become difficult for the NGO to control all the outcomes. However, it appears to be working effectively in enough cases for it to be properly evaluated and provided with the resources to make it effective in a larger number of cases. Many countries have huge problems with the gang culture of street youth and girls and there may be something significant to learn about how to turn such gangs into a positive force. A first step is to pay the young people involved the respect of listening to them and trying to understand their problems, and offering help instead of condemning them and stigmatising them without further thought as so much of the media does and often the police too, and condoned or backed by those in society who have not had their poverty of upbringing.

I have mentioned 'evaluation' several times in this chapter. There is increasing recognition by NGOs that they need to demonstrate the long-term effectiveness of what they are doing. The days when one could satisfy donors and grant-makers, by just providing information on the number of children supported and the number involved in education or vocational training, is passing. We need to know the impact of the education, the ability of children who have had vocational training to get jobs for which they've been trained, to know that children who returned home are still there months, even years, later and free of the problems that caused them to run away. This type of performance monitoring is difficult for most charitable activities but especially so for such a mobile group as street children. We need to know whether the positive changes in a child's life are real and sustainable.

Therefore I foresee that it will be increasingly important to document our work - conduct base line surveys so that the impact throughout a programme can be compared with the start point, document the changes made and follow up to see the long-term results. All major grant-makers now allow costs of independent evaluations to be calculated as part of the grant. I see the role of organisations like the Consortium for Street Children to develop with its partners meaningful indicators and researched statistics that provide the evidence on which to base future policies. Organisations like Railway Children will need to undertake research itself to ensure that their projects and programmes are based on hard evidence and not the first impressions of problems.

So what evidence do we have of the difference Railway Children has made in the lives of children over the last 15 years? We can quote numbers - we are contacting around 25,000 children in 2010 through our Indian, East African and UK partner programmes. I estimate that we have probably had significant contact with more than 200,000 over the lifetime of the charity and many more if one counts the number for whom a casual contact has been made through a phone conversation or advice given by an outreach worker on a railway station or in the street. Some of our partners can tell us how many children were mainstreamed to government schools or passed exams or completed vocational training. We know that in the last three or four years we have reunited about a quarter of the children we've contacted in India with their own families. But we have to do more follow-up to ensure we really do know that the change we've brought about is real and long-lasting. This is a challenge for us and for other NGOs working for vulnerable and street living children.

Soon after I joined Amnesty's Working Group for Children I undertook an analysis of the number of UN CRC articles that were regularly flouted for street children by state authorities, the public and families - it came to around 50% of the convention's 41 'articles' that were approved and ratified by 191 out of the 193 nations who are members of the United Nations. Our aim should be to ensure that street children and children at risk of taking to the street should be protected in just the same way, without discrimination, enjoying all their human rights outlined in the CRC as should all children. Perhaps we should be holding countries accountable under each of these 41 articles, measuring the extent, by country, to which they are firstly, enshrined in law, and secondly robustly implemented.

At the end of the day, however, we can only do what is within our reach, though by combining with others we can extend that reach. The problem is huge. The solutions come one child at a time. I often wonder what the little Bombay girl who inspired the founding of the Railway Children charity would make of it all. She would be about 29 now. Is she still alive? Is she still a beggar – or maybe a prostitute? Does she have a family and live on the street? Or did some organisation rescue her and give her the opportunity that we're trying to provide for the children we contact? Is it even possible that, unknown to me, she benefited from one of our programmes?

Chapter 19
Lessons learned: why has Railway Children been successful?

Looking back over the last fifteen years it is interesting to consider the factors, which have contributed to the growth and success of the charity. I have been a trustee of five other voluntary organisations registered as charities - Consortium for Street Children, Get Connected, the Methodist Relief and Development Fund, my local Methodist Church and the Nantwich Christian Fellowship Trust. All have their strengths, but it is clear to me that the Railway Children has grown the fastest and from many comments made to me, it would seem that its reputation among its peer organisations is high, especially as trustees and staff of other NGOs are often referred to us for advice. In looking through the chapters of this book and from discussions with staff, trustees and other NGOs, particularly members of CSC engaged in helping a similar group of vulnerable children and young people, the following factors would appear to have played a significant part in our success.

1. Clear Focus & Strategy
Clearly identifying the real need for, and noting the lack of focus from other voluntary organisations on early intervention for the increasing number of street children in the world was vital. I used business techniques I was familiar with (risk assessment and 'Total Quality Management') to identify our role and I spent several months researching, testing my idea, and going through a period of contemplation before deciding that the founding of a new charity was justified. During that time I was learning from others in the voluntary sector, making sure that I would not be duplicating the work of any other charity and that it would not be better to become just a member and supporter of another NGO.

As the charity grew, the trustees and staff spent time reviewing our purpose and refining it, not just at Board meetings, but through 'Away Days' where options and strategies could be raised and tested in deeper discussion. Such debates led to decisions that we would be a development organisation and not just a grantmaker, that we would focus on lone children with little or no contact with their families or who were at risk of becoming detached, whilst realising that trying to work in the railway slum communities, as well as on the stations with runaway children, would be spreading the focus too thinly. We spent hours discussing where we should work and eventually narrowed the spread of our activity from ten countries to three geographical areas which we did only after a thorough evaluation of pilot projects in a number of continents. We spent time clarifying our mission and objectives using the discipline of the 'Balanced Scorecard' technique and developed a succession of rolling three-year strategic plans for each of the main strands of our work in India, East Africa and the United Kingdom.

2. High Quality Staff & Trustees

I believe too that the managerial experience we were able to bring to bear on the development of the charity was vital. I felt that many charities had developed expertise in fundraising but often fallen short of professionalism in other aspects of their activities and I wished to avoid doing the same. We identified our vision and stuck to it, staying focused. We put as much effort into refining our objectives, ensuring that what we did was effective, and paying attention to the quality and motivation of our staff.

We harnessed as trustees the contribution of experienced managers from the rail industry - in particular, with general management, financial, public relations, and human resources skills and experience. We augmented this with two senior programme directors with years of experience in a large international children's NGO to give us a full balance of skills and experience in the Board.

We selected a Chief Executive, Terina, who shared our vision and supported her as the charity grew rapidly with top management training at Ashridge – expensive but an invaluable investment. I was fortunate from the start in having the skill of a colleague, Stan Judd, who applied his experience to setting up sound and robust administrative and financial procedures, areas in which I had little time - and even less inclination - to focus upon. This was later further strengthened when we appointed Keith Strickland as our Company Secretary, a man whose professional life was spent in such activity and David Brookes as a full time accountant, supported by dedicated administrators, Wendy and later Kaye. The trustees decided as a priority that we would pay the right level of salary to attract and hold the best staff and spent time and used the human resource skills that we had trying to get this right, with the result that we attracted such people as our key programme staff - Mrinalini, Pete, Andy - a researcher, Emilie, with an established reputation and fundraisers with a range of interests and skills, people who were motivated by the cause as well as by an ambition to succeed in their roles. When we advertised for a specialist in marketing and communications we attracted Rob Capener, who had been handling our account in a commercial firm, and was quick, with our other fundraisers - Dave, Ian, Katie, Lindsay, Wendy and our most recent Head of Fundraising, Karen - to seize the opportunities presented even though at times these caused a workload that stretched them to the limit.

I found key people in India I could trust - especially important in the early days before we had staff there and special thanks are due to Tim Grandage, Edith Wilkins, the late Matthew Norton ('Manihara') and Gopal Dutia, all of whom were invaluable advisers as we developed our India project portfolio. Then Mrinalini was able to build up a respected local team in India that found and maintained real and equal partnerships with strong local Indian NGOs, ably assisted at present by Navin and a team based in Andheri in north Bombay. Again, in the early days I was able to draw on the experience of colleagues in the CSC and use their skills in developing partnerships with overseas NGOs and their monitoring facilities.

Turnover of staff has been remarkably low, especially in the UK. Katie Mason has been with us almost from the beginning and Terina, Mrinalini and Pete joined us in key roles at an early stage and were with us, still highly motivated for the cause ten years or so later, having developed with the charity. Perhaps our location, initially in Crewe and now just five miles away in Sandbach, is a strength. In London where so many charities are based, the competition for good staff is intense and costs are high. We are able to attract high quality staff, who value the lifestyle outside London and have local commitments and interests which perhaps help account for the high staff retention rate. And here I should pay tribute to railway companies, particularly Virgin Trains, who have provided us with free train passes and car parking facilities which we have used innumerable times for the necessary meetings we have in London, and which make the establishment of the base in Cheshire practicable.

3. Motivation

As mentioned above, one of the reasons for attracting and retaining good staff and trustees is motivation for the cause. We try to ensure all staff and trustees wherever possible get a chance to visit our projects overseas and see for themselves the work we are doing with our partners. No-one has yet come back without further fire and determination to work for these vulnerable children. Once again, we have another travel company to thank, this time British Airways for making free flight tickets available to us outside peak periods every year, which we use for both staff and trustee visits and bring our overseas staff here. This not only enhances our motivation but it also enables us to experience the stories of the children at first hand and make all the more effective our talks and contacts with friends and colleagues, and at speaking opportunities at clubs, schools and churches. To be effective in what we do we need the heart as well as the head - not just of the founder but of other staff and trustees too.

4. The Railway Industry Partnership

Having a niche market of donors from the relevant industry – rail – was also crucial, allowing awareness of the charity to build quickly with the support and push from the industry's senior managers several of whom became trustees. Fifty percent of the estimated £15 million raised to date (2011) since the founding of the charity in 1995 has come from individuals, companies and events within the UK railway industry.

The obvious link between that first focus for our intervention, the railway station (and other transport terminal outreach locations), the charity's name and the railway industry made it natural to seek support first from colleagues and people I knew within the privatised railway, while most of the people I'd known from my years in British Rail employment were still around.

Early on I'd had the idea that perhaps I could link interested companies with specific projects that they might adopt, leaving me to act mainly as a coordinator and referral point, but I soon realised I would have to play a more active role as support started coming from individuals within the railway family rather than from organisations, as we were not then mature enough to provide the credibility needed for a company's CSR programme.

One clear advantage of the railway link has been the support I have had from several senior managers with considerable experience between them in the range of skills necessary to manage any organisation, commercial or voluntary. Many of them not only brought their own contribution but, through their contacts, enabled the charity to benefit from pro bono or reduced cost services such as legal help in setting up and registering the charity with the Charity Commission, the auditing of our annual accounts, the provision of free rail tickets to staff when on charity business and the sponsoring of gifts and prizes at our various fundraising events. The latter was particularly valuable for the annual Railway Ball, the first held at the National Railway Museum in 1998, and then at the Grosvenor House Hotel in London from 2000 onwards when annual income from the Ball tickets - augmented by the sponsorship of the costs - realised a profit averaging a quarter of a million pounds, a third of our income in the earlier years. This event also had the effect of raising awareness of the Railway Children throughout the privatised industry and its suppliers, with nearly a thousand guests being present on each occasion. Many companies also sponsored various fundraising events, the most important being the 'Three Peaks Challenge by Rail' which not only benefited from total sponsorship from the rail industry but excited the interest of teams of individuals from the various railway companies, with places for 200 sponsored participants being filled nearly every year.

Stemming from the attendance of their Managing Director at the Railway Ball, we linked with Select Service Partners, benefiting from their continuing partnership and the resultant collection boxes at station food outlets which raised awareness of the charity even further, as did the decision by London Underground to display our name and strap line on posters throughout the system giving the phone number of our partner, the Runaway Helpline, to assist youngsters at risk. Author and transport journalist Christian Wolmar gave book launches and lectures to support us, and various railway magazines and heritage railways joined in the public relations and fundraising programmes.

Finally, because of the historical contacts between British Rail and officers of Indian Railways, I was able to gain access to top managers of the Indian railway and police organisations, and facilitate cooperation and communication between our Indian programme partners and the railway authorities on a regular and official basis.

5. Marketing and Communications

The distinctive and famous name of the charity helped. It was recognisable and quite different from other children's charities many of which have similar titles. Ours appealed to people in the railway industry although it did need frequent explaining outside the industry where people mainly associated it with the children's novel and the 1970 film – but at least that got us noticed. Contact with Dario Mitidieri and his fabulous photos of street children in Bombay and his permission to use them widely in our promotional materials was very valuable and important as was the offer of experienced journalists – Bert Porter from the York railway press office and Christian Wolmar – to edit and produce our early newsletter 'Action Stations'. The professional work of Jane Simpson and Rob Capener in upgrading our 'brand', and Rob's overhaul of our website were further key elements of our success. Lastly I cannot omit the contribution made in raising awareness among a wider audience of our range of Christmas cards, many from original water colour paintings by David Charlesworth, railway artist and Chairman of the Darjeeling Himalayan Railway Society, for these too produced a significant annual income.

6. Fundraising

Many factors, which enabled us to grow our income and – to me – at an astonishing rate, have been mentioned already, especially our relationship with the railway industry. The initial start-up was facilitated enormously by a Railtrack Board Member, Christopher Campbell, who helped us acquire a trust grant to fund our first project. My availability for part-time fee-paying international railway safety consultancy work and my involvement in a panel of retired BR officers to chair UK Rail Accident Inquiries produced an early source of income for the charity as retirement at the privatisation of Railtrack and the resultant 'golden handshake' left me and my family sufficiently provided for. The early decision to work for street and runaway children in the UK as well as overseas was popular with many donors.

We were fortunate in getting a substantial lottery grant at our first ask – although I would emphasise that the focus and hard-headedness of our approach as indicated above in section 1 of this chapter obviously was a factor. This was followed by substantial grants from Comic Relief and the Elton John AIDS Foundation, and the professionalism of our Chief Executive, programme and fundraising staff clearly gave us a great advantage. All these factors have had a wide ripple effect, especially when the Sport Relief BBC telethons showed clips of our partner projects in India, with the name 'Railway Children' very prominent. When the Girl Guide movement chose to support Railway Children (one of their nineteen national charities) as part of its centenary celebrations, the awareness of the charity was raised with a new and younger generation of potential donors.

In the last couple of years Railway Children has also been fortunate in attracting major corporate partners from outside the railway industry, starting with Tesco following the dramatic success and publicity surrounding the 'Slumdog Millionaire' film and then Aviva when that global company decided on street children as the subject of its CSR programme and partnered Railway Children influenced considerably by the evidence in our 'Off the Radar' research.

7. Networking

Networking with other street children charities through the Consortium for Street Children was important too, as it meant we had access to experienced personnel with whom to share ideas and test our concepts, learning fast as we progressed. In fact, I had a network of colleagues far wider than that – through Amnesty International UK's Children's Human Rights Network and the Methodist Relief & Development Fund. Being a trustee of a number of charities and learning from the different styles of operation was valuable experience and I always found colleagues very open and willing to help. Through both Amnesty and CSC, I had the opportunity to be part of the child rights advisory bodies to both the Foreign Office and DFID where I mingled with senior staff of some of the largest UK based national and international NGOs and as a result got notice of, and invitations to, many major conferences on children's rights and welfare, widening my contacts to include a number of eminent academic and international agency experts and specialists.

Because Railway Children always worked through partners both overseas and in the UK, we benefited from the knowledge and experience of people in those organisations and had access therefore to their contacts and sources of knowledge and research. It has always been an important part of Railway Children's principles that we are open and willing to share our knowledge with others, so we find this reciprocated. The work in the UK has undoubtedly grown through our initiative in forming a coalition of NGOs working at the grass roots level here and in consequence acting as the secretariat to the APPG on English Runaways in the 2005-10 Parliament.

8. Governance

Railway Children's trustees were well versed in the routine business practices of setting up robust procedures, financial and management accounting systems, most of which we'd learned during our apprenticeship for management in British Rail. Several were also involved in voluntary sector or local government management and had experience of larger NGOs. After an initial period when first Stan Judd, then Terina, our Chief Executive, acted as Company Secretary, we encountered a professional Company Secretary who volunteered to act for us in that capacity as his contribution to the charity and that also involved him becoming a valued and permanent member of our Governance Committee as well as attending all Board meetings.

The robustness of the systems and procedures we had put in place was well tested and found to be fit for purpose by the Charity Commission in its formal review in 2005. The financial understanding of the Governance Committee, which was chaired by the Managing Director of HSBC Rail and included two very senior line managers (of South East Trains and the Waterloo – Channel Tunnel high speed line) and a former non-executive Board Member of London Transport, was at a very high level of competence and ensured the decisions we took were financially prudent and would hardly ever give us cause for concern.

We were very clear that our decisions at all times were intended to be in the best interests of our children and that called for us to partner the most effective local NGOs irrespective of religion – we were and remain a secular organisation prepared to work through faith groups provided they are effective and rightly motivated.

We were found to be worthy of corporate funding through various due diligence investigations undertaken on behalf of potential CSR partners such as Aviva and major trusts including Comic Relief.

9. Being a Learning Organisation

We said we were a learning organisation and we meant it, prepared to accept that things don't always work, but learning from our own setbacks and from the experiences of others. Through my own networking and that of other trustees we had moved quickly from motivated novices in child protection and development to becoming credible advisors to both Amnesty International UK on children's rights, and trainers on child protection systems within the CSC and the Methodist Church. When the Lottery International Grants team visited one of our Indian projects in 2000 and expressed concern that we were not sharing the experience of some of our more mature partners with others, we quickly learned from this and used the implied criticism to review what value we could add to our partners, thereby becoming true development agents and not just grant-makers.

We learned from our evaluation of the first Comic Relief grant that we had to consider moving closer to the communities from where the children were running. In our second grant programme we obtained the input of the Joint Police Commissioner of Delhi to train our partners in the requirements and obligations under the Indian Juvenile Justice Act 2000 and learned the successful methodology of another partner, Sathi, in reuniting children with their families and used them to train all our Indian partners transforming the number reintegrated successfully from 200-300 a year to around 4,000 – about a quarter of the children we engaged with there. We learned from the struggles we had to set up a formal federation of our Indian partners and although we were under pressure from our grant makers to empower such a body, convinced the funder that in that particular culture, at that time, we were likely to be more successful using local Indian Railway Children resources to share good practice, train NGO staff and conduct advocacy at national government level.

Above all we learned that successful implementation of programmes has to be based on hard evidence of both the issues and the impact of different, tested, solutions and saw the need to institute our own research when the data needed for policy and strategic decision-taking was lacking or weak.

10. Luck
At the end of the day we have to admit that luck always plays a part, although you have to be ready to identify the opportunities that arise and seize the moment. Just two recent examples – the publicity surrounding the 'Oscar' awards to the film 'Slumdog Millionaire' both happened to raise awareness of our work in India and provided over £250,000 of unrestricted income in the middle of the recession through our partnership with Tesco and the release of the DVD – with our brochure enclosed with each - under their special deal with us. It was our pure good fortune that the film came along at the time it did, that it won so many 'Oscars' and therefore so much publicity and that it portrayed so explicitly the lives of children in India whose vulnerability and potential we were trying to address. And it even based a lot of the action around Bombay VT station where we had, and still have, a partner programme. When the Railway Children team in Sandbach realised the potential impact of the film, they went en bloc one afternoon and watched it together and came straight back to the office and had a team meeting to explore just how the charity could benefit from the film and its publicity. From that came a string of suggestions that the team followed up including a link we were able to make with the producer, Danny Boyle and after hard work by Dave Ellis, our 'corporate' fundraiser, the 'Tesco' deal.

And then there was the partnership with the theatre touring company that put on 'The Railway Children' play at Waterloo International station that again raised both cash and awareness. The play had run in the summer holidays to a limited audience at the National Railway Museum in York and contact had been made with the NRM staff, but the opportunities for Railway Children there were slight. Then came the theatre company's idea to stage the play in London by utilising the unused platforms of the former Eurostar terminal and 'out of the blue' an invitation to the charity to be associated with the play. This led to a Board debate on the extent to which the charity could afford to get involved in view of the time and resources involved that might put other fundraising efforts at risk. But we took the decision to seize the opportunity and then go for it wholeheartedly, working closely with the theatre people, developing displays that would engage the theatre-goers with our work as well as raising money, for the company donated £1 for every ticket sold over its run from July 2010 to the end of the Christmas pantomime season in January 2011. The opportunity may have come by chance – the decision to pick it up and exploit that opportunity despite limited resources was a risk we decided to take as the staff and trustees felt that this had potential we could not afford to ignore.

Being in the right place at the right time may be luck. Time and time again over the years Railway Children seems to have been the recipient of good fortune, but as is so often said, you 'make your own luck'. Taking full advantage of opportunities presented – by luck or design - is one of the reasons why Railway Children in 2011 is acknowledged by many of its peers to be a successful and growing organisation.

APPENDICES

1. Railway Children from 2011

The Board asked the Chief Executive to prepare strategy papers for its approval for each of its main areas of activity over the years 2010 to 2013. I can do no better than point you to our website where can be found the strategies prepared by the three Heads of Programmes for East Africa, India and the UK to identify where we believe we are at the time this book is being written (2011) and our intentions for the next three years. The key objectives of the strategies are supported by the intended outcomes or results, which we will publish in our Annual Reports together with our achievements against these, and a three-year budget. All the strategies were approved by the Railway Children Board during 2009 and early 2010.

The Railway Children has also made available its papers and research in a number of areas which can be accessed via the website www.railwaychildren.org.uk or by direct enquiry to the Railway Children office - 1, The Commons, Sandbach CW11 1EG, tel: 01270 757596.

2. Projects funded between 1995 and 2010

The list of projects below includes all those we have funded during Railway Children's existence. Those partnerships, which were still in place at the end of 2010, are indicated. Most other projects were funded for a minimum of three years (through a written partnership agreement with the NGO partner), many for five years or longer. In a few cases, the partnership was for a shorter term to achieve a specific capital need or to help the partner through a short-term funding need.

2.1 Eastern Europe

Romania
ASIS: Bucharest railway station

Russia
ARC: Chita Junction, Siberia (a capital cost grant)

NAN: Kurski, Kazanski, Yaroslavlski, Paveletski, Leningradski mainline railway termini and metro stations Alekseevaskaya, VDNH, Krasnpresnenskaya, Petrovsko-Tazumovskaya and Pushkinskaya, all in Moscow
Love Russia: Two State emergency shelters, Moscow

2.2 Africa

Kenya
KYPT: Kitale street work and shelter (Partnership still operational in 2010)
Pendekezo Letu: Nairobi Matatu stand outreach and rehabilitation farm near Thika for girls.
Undugu Society: Street Associations, Nairobi and Kisumu and rehabilitation centre, Kitengela (Partnership still operational in 2010)

South Africa
IMPACT/Streetwise: Johannesburg, supporting outreach volunteer staff (short-term project)

Tanzania
Adilisha: Mwanza street work (Partnership still operational in 2010)
Mkombozi: Arusha and Moshi street work and advocacy with Tanzanian government (Partnership still operational in 2010)

Zimbabwe
Streets Ahead, Harare through Street Child Africa, outreach and support to street children

2.3 Asia

Bangladesh
CSKS: Dacca, outreach and shelter for boys at Ferry Boat terminal

India
Anubhav: Delhi Cantonment station and shelter
Bal Prafulta: Co-ordination of outreach by NGOs on VT station, Bombay and campaigning for child rights there (Partnership still operational in 2010)

Bal Sakha: Patna, drop-in and rehabilitation centre at the station and outreach work in villages (Partnership still operational in 2010)
Butterflies: Delhi Health Co-operative & Health mobile clinic to key stations and tourist areas
CINI Asha: Rambagan 'red light' area school, Sealdah North and South station drop-in centres and night shelters (Partnership still operational in 2010)
CONC'RN: New Jalpaiguri drop-in centre, shelter and two short-term residential homes (Partnership still operational in 2010)
Cosmos: Seven informal schools on the Calcutta Sealdah - Budge Budge route and informal schools in New Jalpaiguri and Siliguri
Don Bosco: Madras, Katpadi Junction (Vellore) and Villupuram shelters and educational programmes
Don Bosco: Howrah (Calcutta) outreach and shelter for street boys (Partnership still operational in 2010)
EHSAAS: Lucknow, development of a 'child friendly station' in co-operation with the railway police. (Partnership still operational in 2010)
Grassim: Tirupati, in conjunction with Sathi, at Tirupati station and local observation homes. (Partnership still operational in 2010)
Hope Foundation: Calcutta outreach and residential home for boys and girls
Jeevodaya: Itarsi Junction, Madhya Pradesh, boys' and girls' outreach, shelter and residential home and Jabalpur outreach and shelter for boys. (Partnership still operational in 2010)
Khiltee Kalyan: Ajmer and Kota Junction, Rajasthan, outreach and platform work
New Hope: Outreach and emergency shelters at a dozen stations on East Coast including Visakhapatnam, Hyderabad, and Bhubaneswar, AIDS hospice, residential home and vocational training at Kottavalasa, Andhra Pradesh
OFFER: Calcutta Dum Dum Junction, outreach on station and residential home for boys
PBJOK: Calcutta suburban railway slum, drop-in and informal school
Praajak: Asansol, Malda, Bardhman, Kharagpur & Rampurhat stations on the Calcutta - North Bengal route - in close conjunction with the RPF (Partnership still operational in 2010)

Prayas: New Delhi Child Assistance Booth and Boys' Shelter, Samastipur drop-in centre and shelter, post tsunami work in Andaman Islands.
Project Concern International (PCI): Delhi Nizamuddin station, outreach and shelter, street children HIV/AIDS awareness programme
Research Cell on Juvenile Justice (Tata Institute of Social Science) at Yavatmal, Maharashtra, working with local government observation homes and children in conflict with the law (Partnership still operational in 2010)
Saathi: Bombay research on street girls and outreach on Bombay Central, Dadar and Bandra stations
Sabuj Sangha: Calcutta, building of girls' home in red light area beside temple in railway slum
Sathi: Raichur, outreach and camps preparing for family reintegration at a number of stations on the Bombay - Bangalore route and at New Delhi station, outreach Hyderabad (Partnership still operational in 2010)
Sarjan: Ahmedabad, Gujarat, outreach and platform school at Kalapur station and shelter with Childline India
SAVE: Tirupur, Tamil Nadu, outreach to street and working children
SEED: Girls' night shelter at Howrah, boy's drop-in centre and half-way house at Calcutta- Howrah (also some informal schools previously with VSS).
SKCV: Station Child Assistance Booth, Girls' Emergency Shelter, Boys' night shelter and sick bay, at Vijayawada
TNTDS: Jolarpet Junction, Salem and Erode, Tamil Nadu, station outreach and shelter
VSS: Five informal schools in the Sonapur area of the Calcutta Sealdah suburban service and a similar number on the Howrah - Dum Dum - Dhurgapur line (the latter taken over by SEED)
YMCA / Y-Care International: Anantapur, A.P., outreach and residential home for boys, vocational training and platform outreach, also at Gooty Junction and the pilgrim town, Dharmavaram.

Nepal
Child Welfare Scheme: Pokhara, Kaski District, shelter and education for street and working children

2.4 Latin America

Guatemala
Casa Alianza: Guatemala City street work

Mexico
Juconi: Puebla main bus station 'Operation Friendship'

Peru
Aidenica: Lima boys' home (capital grant)

2.5 United Kingdom

United Kingdom
Get Connected: National freephone helpline signposting children's help agencies and other helplines
Railway Children: 'Off the Radar' research (children living on the street in the UK)
Runaway Helpline: National freephone helpline for runaways (night shift workers), part of Missing Persons Helpline

England
ASTRA: Cheltenham, family worker
Centrepoint: London Kings Cross, drop-in & shelter for youth
Safe@Last: Sheffield, 2 bedded refuge and school outreach workers (Partnership still operational in 2010)
Safe in the City: Manchester, drop-in centre and outreach to ethnic youth
Talk Don't Walk: Warrington, drop-in & counselling centre (Partnership still operational in 2010)
The Children's Society: London, research on Roma children

Scotland
Aberlour Trust: 'Running Other Choices' (ROC) 3 bedded refuge (Partnership still operational in 2010)
Street work: Edinburgh outreach work on the street (Partnership still operational in 2010)

3.1 Present Trustees (to December 2010)

Haydn Abbott, Chairman of Railway Children (from January 2011) and former Managing Director of Angel Trains

Peter Aldridge, Chair of the Governance Committee and former Managing Director, HSBC (Rail) and Chairman of Railway Children (Africa)

Rachel Bennett, former Human Resources Director of English, Welsh & Scottish Railways and now HR consultant

Paula Buckton, former Marketing Director of Select Service Partners plc (transport catering franchise holder)

Henry Clarke, Director of the Rail Estate Consultancy Ltd

Rosemary Day, Vice-Chair & Treasurer, former Non Executive Board Member of London Transport

Gopal Dutia, based in Bombay, former field officer for UNICEF

Tim Hartley, Senior Consultant, Harvey Nash (management recruitment)

Michael Holden, former Managing Director of South East Trains and now railway management Consultant

Rebecca Klug, former Director, Customer Services, Virgin Trains (retired as trustee December 2010)

Judy Lister, also trustee of Railway Children (Africa), former Programme Director (Africa) for Save the Children

David Maidment, Chairman (retired December 2010) and Founder, formerly Head of Safety Policy, British Rail

Roger Newton, former Programme Director (SE Asia and East Pacific) for Save the Children

Christian Wolmar, journalist and transport author

Company Secretary: Lucy Allan

3.2 Previous Trustees

Rick Edmondson, former Managing Director of Resco Railways Ltd
Chris Jago, former Chief Executive, Union Railways (South)
Stan Judd, former Marketing Director, Speedlink, British Rail
Steve McColl, former Special Trains Manager, British Rail
Gordon Pettitt, former Vice-Chair, Railway Children, Managing Director, Regional Railways and General Manager, Southern Region, British Rail

Nikhil Roy, formerly Acting Director of the Consortium for Street Children and now Programme Manager for Penal Reform International
Rachel Stephens, former Head of the Methodist Relief & Development Fund
Terry Worrall, formerly Director of Operations, British Rail

Former Company Secretary: Keith Strickland

3.3 Present UK Staff (to December 2010)
Wendy Brawn, Fundraising Officer (Trusts & Grants)
Karen Brayne, Head of Fundraising
Kaye Brindle, Administrator
David Brookes, Head of Finance & Administration
Rob Capener, Head of Marketing & Communications
Dave Ellis, Fundraising Officer (Corporate Partnerships)
Lindsay Gardner, Assistant Fundraising Officer (Events)
Jo Hill, Assistant Adminstrator
Nicole Howard, Information & Learning Officer, UK
Terina Keene, Chief Executive
Pete Kent, East Africa Country Director
Sarah Lanchin, Programme Officer, UK
Katie Mason, Fundraising Officer (Events)
Andy McCullough, Head of UK Policy & Public Affairs

3.4 Volunteers (Sandbach Office)
Frank Gillies
John Walkington

3.5 Present India Staff (to December 2010)
Vinayak Bait, Administrative Assistant
Suhotra Biswas, Head of Development Support
Paramita Chaudhuri, Senior Programme Officer (East)
Deepti Dutt, Research Officer
Aishwarya Iyer, Knowledge Management Officer
Ashutosh Kumar, Programme Officer (North)
Sudhir Rai, Programme Officer (Strategic Alliances)
Mrinalini Rao, India Country Director
Pratima Rao, Accounts & Administration Officer
Debosmita Saha, Training Officer

S Navin Sellaraju, Head of Programmes
Jamuna Shukla, Development Officer
Dr T Thiripurasundari, Programme Officer (South)

3.6 Present East Africa Staff (to December 2010)
Anna Thor, Programme Officer

3.7 Previous Staff (UK)
Helen Collison, Administrator
Jane Simpson, Head of Fundraising
Emilie Smeaton, Researcher
Julia Worthington, Administrator, later Fundraiser
Jo Young, Fundraising Officer (Trusts & Grants)
Ian Watson, Fundraising Officer (Communities)

3.8 Previous Volunteers (UK)
Brian & Coral Carton

3.9 Previous Staff (India)
Rajanikanth Dasi, Programme Officer (South)
Suchira Deengar, Programme Officer (East)
Hazel D'Souza, Programme Officer (Training)
Sapna George, Programme Officer (Training)
Rumpa Gupta, Programme Officer (Advocacy)
Manoj Gurung, Administrative Assistant
Srividya Iyer, Programme Officer (South)
Shama Kamat, Accounts & Administration Officer
Unni Krishnan, Programme Officer (North)
Shivranjani Kulkarni, Associate Programme Manager (Training & Development)
Deepti Mascarenhas, Programme Officer (West & Central)
Sreedhar Mether, Programme Officer (South)
Joanna Pakrasi, Programme Support Officer
Jignasha Pandya
Dhiraj Rankhambe, Programme Officer (East)
Mohan Rao, Programme Officer (South & East)
Sujatha Sadananda, Knowledge Management Officer
Bhavisha Sanadhya
Mahendrasingh Sengar, Programme Officer (West & Central)
Vikramjeet Sinha, Programme Officer (Training)

Anto Thomas (Programme Officer (South))
Sanjay Tiwari, Programme Officer (North)
Neha Trivedi

4. Career of Author/Founder of 'Railway Children, David Maidment

British Rail Manager, 1960 -1994 including:
    Stationmaster, Aberbeeg (Western Valley, Monmouthshire)
    Area Manager, Bridgend
    Train Planning Officer, Cardiff Division
    Management Services Manager, BR Western Region &
        British Railways Board
    Chief Operating Manager, London Midland Region
    Quality & Reliability Manager, British Railways Board
    Head of Safety Policy, British Railways Board
Railtrack, Controller, Safety Policy, 1994 -1996
Associate Principal Consultant, International Risk Management Services, 1996 - 2001
Member of Railway Accident Inquiry Panel of Chairmen, Railtrack & Network Rail, 1996 - 2005
Youth & Children's work leader in Methodist Church at local church level, 1966 - present
Trustee, Methodist Relief & Development Fund, 1996 - 2000
Child Protection & Safeguarding Trainer, Chester & Stoke District, Methodist Church, 2006 - present
Trustee of Nantwich Christian Fellowship Trust from 2004 and Chair from 2010
Chairman of Nantwich Christian Council 2010 (2 year role)
Member of Amnesty International UK Child's Human Rights National Committee from 1990 and Advisor to AIUK on Children's Rights and Chairman of the AIUK Children's HR Network from 2000 - present
Trustee of Consortium for Street Children from 1993 and Co-Chair from 1998 - 2008
Chairman of Railway Children, 1995 - 2010.
Awarded OBE for services to the railway industry 1996
Elwyn Jones Fellow, Lions International, for services to children
Author of the following published works:
    Magazine articles on railway history and nostalgia - 'Steam World', 'Steam Days', 'European Railways', 2001 - 2010.

Chapters on Railway Safety Management in 'New Technologies & Work', academic books on safety science published by the Pergamon Press, 1995 - 2000

Chapter on 'The Worst Forms of Labor: Street Children and Street Trades' in the 'Atlas of Child Labor' published by M.E.Sharpe Inc., USA, 2009

Novel, 'The Child Madonna', published by Melrose Books, 2009

Novel, 'The Missing Madonna', published 2012

5. Donations to Railway Children

All royalties and profits from the sale of this book are being donated to Railway Children. If readers feel inspired to support the work, please send donations via the website, www.railwaychildren.org.uk or directly to the Railway Children, 1, The Commons, Sandbach, Cheshire, CW11 1EG.